The Spells of Frankenstein

BY THE SAME AUTHOR

The Quest of Frankenstein
The Triumph of Frankenstein

Napoleon's Vampire Hunters
The Devil Plague of Naples

Irma Vep and the Great Brain of Mars

The Spells of Frankenstein

by

Frank Schildiner

A Black Coat Press Book

Acknowledgements: Mary Shelley and Jean-Claude Carrière.

Visit our website at www.blackcoatpress.com

ISBN 978-1-61227-892-6. First Printing. September 2019. Published by Black Coat Press, an imprint of Hollywood Comics.com, LLC, P.O. Box 17270, Encino, CA 91416. Printed in the United States of America.

CHAPTER I

"Stern and white as a tomb, older than the memory of the dead, and built by men or devils beyond the recording of myth, is the mansion in which we dwell."

Clark Ashton Smith

Gouroull waited, crouching on the snowy sward as darkness slowly creeped over the steppes. Two humans approached, one carrying a rifle, the other unarmed. They spoke Russian, a language Frankenstein's most terrible creation understood, having learned the odd tongue in recent decades. Human communication was a tool—another weapon in Gouroull's arsenal as he wandered the Earth in search of his destiny.

"...is nearby. This much I can assure you," a gruff, deep, voice said in Siberian accented Russian. "That is all I promise. The rest is in the hands of the Lord and the spirits dark and light."

"Spare me your mumbo-jumbo, my good sir," a second voice replied. "The great Victor Frankenstein proved there is no God save man, and science is his religion. The rest is all fiction."

The accent sounded odd, as if the speaker found Russian pronunciation difficult and unpleasant.

"Is that truly what he and your good self truly believe?" the first asked.

"Of course! Any right-thinking man capable of rejecting superstition would feel exactly as I do. Baron Frankenstein wrote a very telling statement that I never forgot. This is the passage he wrote in his diary during the days of creation. He left the book, as well as his equipment, in a sad little town in Ireland called Kanderley. Can you imagine it? A work of genius disproving all religion abandoned in a misbegotten hamlet filled with bog-trotters and other lesser creatures."

"No," replied the first voice.

The second man stopped walking and exclaimed: "He wrote these telling words: *No one can conceive the variety of feelings which bore me onwards, like a hurricane, in the first enthusiasm of success. Life and death appeared to me ideal bounds, which I should first break through, and pour a torrent of light into our dark world. A new species would bless me as its creator and source; many happy and excellent natures would owe their being to me. No father could claim the gratitude of his child so completely as I should deserve theirs*. There you have it, sir! The truth in its purest form. That is science and the denial of creators and ancient foolish beliefs."

"There is a second explanation you have not considered," the first man said, his voice not hiding his amusement.

"What is that?" the second man asked.

"Simply this—Victor Frankenstein, while a genius in science, was misguided in every other area of life and the universe. He was insane, despite finding new paths in God's creation."

"If you were not my only way of finding my way back to what you Russian call towns, I should shoot you were you stand," the second man shouted. "How dare you? How dare you besmirch the name of the great Victor Frankenstein?"

He stopped a few feet from Gouroull's location.

"I am not Russian, sir. I am Siberian," the first man replied.

His response sounded bored, as if these were words spoken to deaf ears.

"Who cares? All of the countries after Germany are just as bad as the blacks and Jews. None of you are part of the true root races. You are all off-shoot bastardizations of the Atlanteans, the weak fourth race who mated with the unevolved sub-humans of the Earth."

Tired of listening to the ranting, Gouroull stepped from his hiding place and stared at the two men. His yellow phosphorescent eyes pierced the glowing gloom like twin flames—an inhuman, alien, aspect that froze both men mid-step. This provided Frankenstein's monster a moment of quiet, allowing an examination of both humans.

The taller of the two stood several inches above six feet. He possessed broad shoulders, a thick, tangled, black beard, and a wild mane of dark hair that flowed across his shoulders. The face beneath the beard possessed the heavy features of a typical peasant of any region from the Urals to the Mongolian borders. The most striking feature were his eyes, deep-set, dark and possessing a depth that appeared bottomless.

The second man was altogether different, and not in an advantageous way. He was a full head shorter with a narrow, almost emaciated frame, pale, sallow skin, and astonishingly long, bony fingers. This man possessed a weak, almost non-existent chin, a thin nose, small, narrow eyes, and a full mouth twisted in a disapproving moue. In his long, claw-shaped hands was a rifle made from highly polished wood and gleaming metal.

"Oh," the second man said, started by the sight of Gouroull, nearly dropping his gun, "Oh, my!"

"I did warn you," the taller man rumbled.

He stared up at Gouroull with open interest and, surprisingly, little fear.

Gouroull made no move, but watched both humans, his alien orbs gazing upon them with unblinking concentration. He towered over both men and his breadth of shoulders was nearly as large as both standing side by side. Frankenstein's most lethal creation was a titan compared to even the largest humans, a fact that frightened them nearly as much as his inhuman aspect.

"You are as astonishing as all reports have claimed," the smaller man said, his words rushing out in a flow of English.

His accent was alien to Gouroull's ears. He spoke with the long vowels and measured tones of someone hailing from England. Yet his pronunciation was oddly accented, as if he was imitating this style of speech.

Stepping closer to the massive Gouroull, the smaller man smiled broadly, causing his lips to disappear. He possessed large, uneven teeth and bright red gums that appeared too large for his mouth.

"My name is Craig Samuel John Jones, and I have spent a lifetime studying you and your magnificent creator. I first learned of your existence when I was a mere child visiting Switzerland. You killed a relative of the idiots we visited, and they had a poster of you in their library. I stole it and then researched your amazing travels. I bought all the items remaining in the castle at Kanderley and even found the great Victor Frankenstein's notebooks! I went to Cround Island and searched for Doctor Pilljoy's equipment. I have spent all my days and nights searching for you, Gouroull. You are my reason for living! Now, follow me and I shall show you your new home," he added, gripping his gun and practically vibrating with joy as he spoke.

Gouroull made no move, standing so still he appeared to merge with the growing darkness that blanketed the forest. Slowly his black lips peeled back, revealing razor sharp teeth that glinted in the dwindling sunlight.

"I do not believe he is interested, my friend," the larger man said, shaking his heavy head.

"Why would that matter? I am Craig Samuel John Jones of the Mayflower Joneses, and what I want, I get. You there, Gouroull! You need wander no more! I have a small mansion I use to store all my Frankenstein items. I have a room set aside for you as the jewel of my collection. I think the bed shall fit, though I shall order a larger one if it does not. Then, we shall…"

Jones's statement cut off as Gouroull strode forward and now stood mere inches away.

"Now, now!" Jones cried, stepping back. "You must learn manners! Standing so close is not acceptable in modern soc…"

Gouroull's massive mitts closed around Jones's shoulders and lifted the smaller human off the ground without any visible effort. The monster's massive head lunged forward, straightening seconds later. His grotesque dark lips and enormous jaw ran with a viscous crimson fluid that dripped wetly across the ragged tatters that covered his gray-skinned form.

Jones shook in Gouroull's grasp, his mouth opened in a silent scream filled with agony, his every muscle taut and quivering with the agony of the monster's horrific assault. His eyes moved wildly for a moment, then froze and turned glassy as he died seconds later.

Tossing the body aside, Gouroull glanced in the taller man's direction. The other contemplated Frankenstein's monster with frank, unafraid appraisal. The dark eyes locked with Gouroull's amber orbs, staring into the depths, barely blinking for several moments.

"That fool," the dark-eyed man said, "spent the last two weeks regaling me with tales regarding your exploits. You seek a mate? A young of your own?"

Gouroull lowered his chin slightly, the movement easily missed or mistaken as a trick of the lengthening shadows. Craig Jones's blood slowly dribbled down his face, a slight splash of color across the pale, inhuman skin.

"That is natural," the other man replied and smiled.

He possessed large, square teeth that looked grotesque as he grinned.

"Perhaps I can help you," he added. "I shall tell you my thoughts and, if they are acceptable, we can help each other. Is that satisfactory?"

Once again, Gouroull dropped his chin less than an inch and stood waiting for the latter's reaction. His stillness unnerved man and beast, yet this dark-haired Siberian appeared accepting. This factor alone was cause for interest and some concern.

"Excellent," the dark-eyed man said, nodding his shaggy head. "Do you have a name you are called? I discount much said by the dead man you tossed beneath the yew tree.

"Gouroull," Frankenstein's most lethal creation intoned.

His whisper resembled that of rocks clashing rather than the speech of mankind.

The other clapped his hands together and guffawed. "That is what Jones said, I did not believe him. Many madmen and women tell tales to wandering pilgrims such as myself. Very well, Gouroull, my name is Grigori Yefimovich. Most men and women I meet prefer to call me by my surname. It is a good name, so you too may call me, Rasputin."

Without waiting for a response, Rasputin turned away and led Gouroull back down the path. He never looked back to see if the later followed, his long stride carrying him away from the corpse of Craig Jones.

CHAPTER II

Rasputin's dwelling was a simple one-room hut, round with wooden walls and a thatched roof. The hovel's flat, smooth stone floors appeared older than the rest of the house, possessing the worn quality obtained from decades of shod and unshod feet treading across its surfaces. A straw pallet lay in one corner, a short distance from the small fireplace and there were two wooden stools and a three-legged table that appeared sturdier than the thin walls.

Reaching into a small trunk near the straw pallet, Rasputin pulled out a black bottle and two tin cups. Pouring an amber liquid into each cup, he perched on one stool and nodded towards the other.

"Please, sit if you like," he said. "This is *kvass*, a good drink that warms better than vodka."

Gouroull paused and then slowly sat a moment later. He made no move towards the drink but waited with the same patience he had demonstrated earlier in the wilderness.

"Now," Rasputin said, downing his kvass and pouring another, "I must ask you some questions. I only know what that vainglorious fool said—much of which sounded fantastic. However, I now believe some of it after witnessing your actions earlier. Is it true that you were created by a man named Victor Frankenstein? Made from the corpses of the dead and his unusual sciences?"

"Yes," Gouroull rasped, his evil, alien eyes burning with a terrible light.

Rasputin nodded and looked thoughtful.

"Then you are a unique being, a new form of life. That makes some sense. You require another one such as you, a being of your own race. That is what that man with the odd name Pilljoy attempted? The creation of a female of your new species?"

Gouroull did not respond, but the malicious light in his eyes darkened. Rasputin visibly flinched under this terrible gaze, gulping his drink down and coughing as the liquid choked him a moment later.

Clearing his throat, Rasputin raised both hands in a form of surrender.

"I do not mock you, nor intentionally revive unpleasant memories, Gouroull. I seek understanding in all things, especially those where I think I might be of help. I am what is called a *strannik*. Do you know that word? No? It means that I am a holy pilgrim, a wanderer seeking answers from the world. Have you met my like before in your travels?"

Gouroull did not answer, but sat watching the other with the same evil phosphorescent glow in his inhuman eyes. His chest neither rose nor fell, and he demonstrated no other evidence of life.

"I assume not," Rasputin replied, downing another cup of kvass. "I seek truth and I learn from all men and women who possess knowledge of the secrets of the universe. I belong to no order, yet I find the Khlyst philosophy has merit. They believe that, through sin, we learn the truth of the Lord. No matter. I waste time telling you of me and my ways. I learned some tales of you and your quest. I think you are a unique being, and humans are unsuitable mates. You need one such as yourself. Then your line shall continue. I have a method, but the means are perilous. Do you wish to hear more?"

Gouroull nodded again, the movement small, yet unmistakable. His huge, horrific head cocked slightly, causing a slight movement in the animalistic shock of black hair that fell in filthy tangles across his head and shoulders.

"Very well," Rasputin said in a hushed tone. "My dreams told me of a monstrous woman seeking terrible power. She is far worse than the baby-sacrificing magus I met in Rome, or the demon worshipping an order of Templars in the holy city of Jerusalem. This woman is an ancient *charodeyka*...what some call a witch, whose terrible plans could kill millions and would destroy all of Russia. I think this would not disturb you, but I wish to protect my homeland. I would kill the *charodeyka*, or have you perform the deed, if that ended her mad schemes. However, she hides from the world...She is... what is the word? Inaccessible? Yes, that is the word! She is inaccessible from all mankind until the day she begins her ritual. She believes none may reach her and all shall be as she dreamed. But the witch is wrong... She did not count on the visions of Grigori Yefimovich Rasputin. For he dreams, and the hidden world provides him answers... *You* are the answer, friend Gouroull, and Rasputin can solve all if you help him defeat his enemy. Do I go on?"

"Yes," Gouroull said in the same sepulchral tone, his black lips slowly retreating, revealing the dagger points of his terrible teeth.

"There is a way we can prevail. I know the vault where the *charodeyka* is going, and we may enter it at the same time as she. There we shall find the object of her quest—a book filled with terrible spells. There, I shall battle her in a duel of mind and soul. If I lose, all life on this world is imperiled. But if I succeed, the book will grant me the power of creation. As my first act, I shall create your perfect mate. As my second, I shall prevent the future I foresee for my beloved motherland. But I go too far... Planning one's welcome home dinner while one's horse is still in the barn is foolish. I need your help in obtaining three mystic items. With them, I can gain us entry into this hidden vault. Without, Rasputin, his wife and children, shall die, with many millions."

Rasputin turned and reached into his trunk. He removed a small cloth bag and poured a series of flat black stones onto the table. Each rock held a series of odd hieroglyphs that resembled circles, triangles, and odd angles that were difficult on the eyes.

"These are portions of an ancient book known as the *Stanzas of Dzyan*. The language is an inhuman one, used by followers of a lost God who demanded human sacrifices and bizarre orgies from his followers. The writer hated humanity and helped destroy that which the *charodeyka* seeks. Will you help me? I swear by the Almighty that if you bring me the three items, I shall defeat the witch and create your mate as my first act."

Rasputin laid out the stones, jabbing towards each rock with a heavily calloused, sausage shaped digit.

"Yes," Gouroull repeated in the same inhuman voice.

Rasputin sighed and slowly nodded.

"Praise the Good Lord for small mercies. I shall explain all three and where my visions say each lay. The distance is great and the peril greater, yet I believe neither concerns one such as you. You have a short time, exactly ten months. That is the day of the Chinese Ghost Festival. On that day, the worlds of the dead and the living are one. This is the best day for attempting mighty workings of black magic. Return to this very spot and I shall meet you and, together, we shall do as we will. I shall write you a list and tell you of each item."

As the holy pilgrim turned back towards his chest, Gouroull's demoniac smirk widened. His eyes pulsed with a terrible, monstrous light as he concluded his devil's bargain with the monk named Rasputin.

CHAPTER III

Grigori Rasputin stood in the doorway as the monster known as Gouroull vanished from sight. The creature was as terrifying as Jones had indicated—a truly monstrous creation resembling a devil from the tales of ancient man. From the inhuman, horrific amber eyes that pulsed with unnatural energy, to the teeth, more suited for a wolf or bear, Gouroull was a being bathed in the blood and agony of his victims.

"Only his creator, the messiah of science, Baron Victor Frankenstein," Jones had said days earlier, "knew a means of destroying his masterwork. He chased Gouroull, for that was the creature's name for himself, across the globe."

Rasputin had stopped listening to the man's rants at that moment, having heard this speech dozens of times in the last weeks. Jones's presence had been expected by the Siberian mystic, one he had learned of in a vision years ago, even before he undertook the journey of the *Strannik*. None, save a holy elder named Makary, knew that he possessed what his father once referred to as the "witch sight."

Makary, a dark-haired man with the intense dark eyes of a poet and the powerful frame of a blacksmith, was the first to confront Grigori Rasputin upon his pilgrimage to the St. Nicholas Monastery at Verkhoturye. One look from this elder and Grigori Rasputin felt humbled before so great a man.

"You are a sinner, are you not, Grigori Yefimovich?" stated Makary, as Rasputin abased himself before this strong figure in black. "You drink, steal, and show no respect for yourself or others. You cannot read or write the holy word and live as an ignorant reprobate. Do I besmirch your name?"

"No, Father," Rasputin mumbled, his head low.

Makary lifted the larger Rasputin to his feet and said: "Then rise, my son, and I shall teach you reading, writing and the word of the Lord. You shall tell me of the visions that led you here."

Rasputin stared at the church elder in shock. Only his wife, his dear Praskovya Dubrovina, knew that he saw the future in his dreams and, rarely, while awake. His late great uncle, Dmitri Borisovitch, knew and had warned him against ever revealing what he viewed.

"They will call you a witch and you shall die if anyone learns that you have the sight," the old man whispered while crouching behind the barn. "That is how your grandmother's aunt died. The farmers stoned her until she died, and then they threw her body in the Tura. That is the true meaning of our name, Rasputin—between two rivers. This does not mean the Tura and some other water. The rivers are that which lead to Heaven and Hell. We were cursed by the Baba Yaga and must never tell another soul."

Years later, hearing Makary refer to this curse so casually, Grigori Rasputin opened his mouth. He planned on denying it, as he had done since hearing of his great aunt's fate. But the monastery's elder silenced him with a simple look.

"I shall instruct you in the story of Joseph, son of Jacob," Makary explained. "Joseph did not receive visions of the Lord, but was gifted in another manner. He knew who told a true foretelling and its meaning. The Savior of Mankind granted me such a boon, and I have helped others with their burdens. Now, follow me, Brother Grigori. Your lessons begin this day…"

Thus had Malarky transformed Rasputin's life irrevocably.

One such vision that had haunted him since childhood was the inhuman countenance of Gouroull—that twisted, pale-skinned mockery of man, snarling and killing in a brutal, predatory manner. The rest of his dreams were flashes, nightmares almost as haunting as the one that he could not avoid…

Closing the cabin door, Grigori Rasputin once again read the stones, hoping for another method of saving so many lives. He knew this was a fool's hope, but hope was all that he had left.

That and a demoniac being called Gouroull…

CHAPTER IV

Captain Pytor Kryuchkov hated lawlessness. A proud Cossack warrior whose family had served the Tsar since the time of Boris Godunov, he knew that he and his fellows were all that stood between the State and total anarchy. He performed his job with fanatical, almost sadistic, glee, and demanded the same from the men under his command.

A major portion of his work was the railways, the legendary Trans-Siberian Railroad that passed through his area every three days. Many of his fellow Cossacks performed simple cursory checks, usually while pocketing some cash provided by the railroad service. Not Pytor Kryuchkov. He and his men stopped each train, checked each car, each passenger, and even their bags.

Through his zeal, Kryuchkov had caught twelve anarchists wanted by the authorities in Moscow, five escaped prisoners, six smugglers, and seized almost a ton of smuggled goods. The railroad bureaucrats complained regularly, but only the district Cossack Ataman could overrule a local Captain—and Ataman Filimonov loved the success Kryuchkov had brought to his command. The Ataman knew that his underling may one day be considered a problem—overly zealous officers often received such treatment from headquarters—but until that time, Kryuchkov had full license for dealing with any train that passed through his station.

The latest was a large series of boxcars inbound from the Siberian interior. These were often the trains containing escaped prisoners, vagrants hiding in empty cars, and smugglers sending stolen diamonds and gold into Saint-Petersburg. These trains required the most attention and he waited for each with eager anticipation.

A man of medium height with a fringe of dark hair and a long, luxuriant black mustache, Pytor Kryuchkov was a typical Cossack officer for the border between Siberia and Greater Russia. He wore his uniform with aplomb, knowing he looked strong and dangerous as well as upright and heroic. He rode his horses well, used his sword with the flashy skill of a born Cossack, and despised anyone who was not one of their august tribe. This hatred was not limited to bureaucrats and merchants, but also applied to Jews, Poles, Siberians, peasant and noblemen. To Captain Kryuchkov, there were only two sets of useful people on the entire planet: the Tsar and the Cossacks who enforced his will.

"Spread out and search all luggage," Kryuchkov rumbled. "Efficiency and speed prevent the Ataman from listening to the whines of Jew-loving officials and other fools."

This was his standard speech, spoken in a near shout as the train pulled into the station. His eight men stood a step behind him, rifles on their shoulders, faces demonstrating their lack of interest in these actions.

The head conductor appeared before the Cossack officer five minutes later, puffing with the exertion of running from the passengers' cars to the station. He gave Captain Kryuchkov a sketch of a bow and extended his stack of papers.

His name was Gleb Egorov and, at fifty, he had spent the last thirty-five years of his life working on trains. The son of a coal miner, he left home shortly after his father died in a cave-in, and his family had too many mouths and not enough food. His uncle Igor was a fireman, shoveling loads of coal into the engine, working the Saint-Petersburg to Pskov line since he was a boy.

"You want a job, nephew? Good, good! The world needs more train men," Uncle Igor roared. "Forget working the engine. For every ten men who wish the life of the engineer, nine end up firemen or worse. Work with the passengers, make them happy, and spend your life with only foot pain and rudeness as your complaints."

Uncle Igor led a young Gleb towards the rear of the train. That day, he got a job as a kitchen boy on the same train. He left shortly after Uncle Igor died in a boiler explosion, and took an assistant conductor's job on the Saint-Petersburg to Moscow run. Uncle Igor proved prophetic. Geb Egorov did suffer from constant foot pain, though the rudeness of the passengers did not affect him in the slightest. He learned how to smile, ignore, and keep the impatient, wealthy travelers' luggage on their trip. By the time the Trans-Siberian Railroad's operations required personnel, Geb was immediately hired as a head conductor/train's captain.

The one aspect of his job that was uncomfortable was dealing with the Cossack officers throughout the long journey. A fund of small bribes, an unofficial expense accepted as a necessary evil by the unseen rail directors, lay in a safe in Geb's cabin. This was useless when stopping at this small station just outside Omsk. All conductors knew that Captain Kryuchkov considered bribes as an insult, and he was perfectly capable of holding a train for hours if necessary.

"Conductor Egorov, you are looking quite fat," Kryuchkov roared, hearing the guffaws and snickers from his men.

Insulting the supercilious train staff was one of his means of establishing who commanded this area.

"Perhaps I should enlist you. The Cossack life would make you look like a man!"

"I am not worthy of such an honor, Captain, sir," Geb replied, his standard statement when such taunts and teases emerged from men like this officer.

"That much is true," Kryuchkov grunted, while taking the bundle of papers.

He read the list of passengers as well as the manifest of the cargo contained in the boxcars.

"We shall search the passengers first, and then I'll have a quick glance at the cargo. Are there any passengers you suspect, fat man?"

Geb shook his head.

"No, Captain. There are none who appear suspicious to me or my staff. But I will tell you, the animals in the cars are behaving strangely. They are silent and shake with fear day and night. From the cows in the third car to the littlest pussycats in a basket in the passengers' space. In all my years, I've never viewed such behavior."

"Interesting," Kryuchkov said.

He glanced at Sergeant Popov, his bitter, gray-haired second-in-command. Then, shoving the papers back at the heavy-set train official, he added:

"I think we shall start with the cars, then the passengers. Thank you, Egorov."

Pushing past the conductor, Kryuchkov led his men down the row of cars, ignoring the inquiring gazes from the passengers. The odd behavior of animals was a clue that something was wrong—beasts, unlike men, could not lie. Three times had he found escaped convicts hiding in cattle cars. On each occasion, the animals had sent clear signals to observant men such as Captain Pytor Kryuchkov.

Searching a car full of cows and another with horses, Kryuchkov's keen eye recognized that Egorov was correct. The cows mooed, moaned, and rolled their eyes, looking as frightened as animals in a slaughterhouse. The horses whinnied and foamed at the mouth, kicking and biting in terror. The grooms struggled with the animals, protecting themselves and the horses from dire injuries.

"Something is wrong, Sergeant," Kryuchkov said. "This not just some vagrant criminal hiding as they try to escape being sent to a labor camp."

He nodded at the next car. Two men threw open the huge door, revealing rows of crates obscuring the interior. A typical sight in these trains, and a favored hiding spot for many in the Cossack's experience.

"Sergeant," Kryuchkov said, nodding at the interior, "I am less interested in smugglers than men in hiding."

Popov and all but two men climbed aboard, vanishing from sight seconds later. The Captain clasped his hands behind his back, staring left and right for additional suspicious behavior. Nothing stirred; the only sound was the shuffle of Popov and his men from within.

"What? *Boze moi!*" Popov shrieked, followed by screams of pain and sickening wet crashes.

Drawing his saber in one hand and his handgun in the other, Kryuchkov leaped aboard the car, his guards at his side, and charged. His fur hat fell from his head, but he did not look back, his passion rising with each second.

"For the Tsar!" he yelled, vanishing into the darkness.

The interior of the rail car was a tight-fitting series of small rows and deep gloom. It smelled like blood mixed with sawdust and rotted food—a noxious combination.

Kryuchkov gripped his sword tight, crouching low as he stepped deeper into the shadows. He stepped slowly, hearing the harsh, ragged, breathing of the two men at his rear, as well as the heavy, fast thrum of his own racing heartbeat.

A rush of wind across his back almost propelled him forward and he heard a scream of pain a second later. This was followed by a wail of fear from a deeper voice, then by a sickening soft ripping sound.

Kryuchkov whirled around, his mouth dropping in shock. Both bodyguards lay on the wooden floor, their eyes wide in shock, their mouths open, silently screaming, even after death.

However, that was not what froze the Cossack commander in place. It was the being which stood over both dead soldiers that caused Pytor Kryuchkov's scream of terror as he raised his sword over his head. It was the massive, pale monster looming over his men which triggered instinctive horror within the soldier's soul.

He reacted with the atavistic fight-or-flight response, choosing defiance in the face of death. For death was clearly present in the form of this titanic creature shaped in the image of man. Kryuchkov recognized that much in the back of his mind as the fearsome being avoided his sword swing and reached out with a hand the size of his head. This massive mitt grasped the Cossack's arm and tightened, shattering the heavy bones beneath its stony fingers.

Kryuchkov shrieked in agony, dropping the sword and, a moment later, his revolver, as his other arm snapped under an equally vice-like grip.

Lifted as if he were a child, Kryuchkov's last image in life was a set of razor-sharp teeth passing his vision and locking down on his neck. He felt a brief stab of pain across his throat, then a cold numbness settled over his body. He vaguely sensed a wetness across his chin and chest as the demonic creature tossed him aside, then nothingness…

Geb Egorov covered his ears as the screams pierced the silence. He waited a full ten minutes, hoping that the arrogant Cossack Captain was well… while also wishing the man was gone from his life. He stepped outside and spotted no sign of the soldiers. Every door was now shut again. Frowning and hoping he was not making a mistake, he waved a signal to the Engineer and got underway.

Sometimes, Geb thought as he poured himself the remains of a bottle of wine abandoned by a passenger, *blindness is the only way a man survives.*

He also vowed he would never again mention fearful animals if that phenomena arose again in his travels. Best to keep his head down and forget everything…

CHAPTER V

Moscow was a city of shadows. This suited Gouroull well as he alighted from the train, heading towards the distant Bitsa River district. A light snow fell while a harsh biting wind blew across the city, howling like a lost soul, sending residents and visitors racing for the safety of the their homes.

Gouroull moved with a quickness that belied his massive frame, a celerity described by witnesses as unnatural. Even Victor Frankenstein had written as much in his journals, all of which his most lethal creation had read after the death of the mad scientist. He eloquently wrote a very telling passage, occasionally quoted by the late madman's followers:

"*As I said this, I suddenly beheld the figure of a man, at some distance, advancing towards me with superhuman speed. He bounded over the crevices in the ice, among which I had walked with caution; his stature, also, as he approached, seemed to exceed that of man. I was troubled; a mist came over my eyes, and I felt a faintness seize me, but I was quickly restored by the cold gale of the mountains. I perceived, as the shape came nearer (sight tremendous and abhorred!) that it was the wretch whom I had created. I trembled with rage and horror, resolving to wait his approach and then close with him in mortal combat.*"

Telling words, one that explored both the feelings of the infamous creator, and the powers of his creation. The question that had always lingered between Victor and Gouroull was whether the insane genius possessed the method of killing the creature he referred to as "wretch," "fiend," and "demon." Gouroull had received no clues, despite possessing strength greater than even the mightiest human. After over a century's life, he knew he was the apex predator upon this planet, with only the massive monsters of the ocean deep as competition. However, his alien mind did occasionally wonder if Victor had possessed some secret weapon...

This unbidden thought, one that had not occurred to him in decades, propelled him even faster through the dark, desolate streets of Moscow. He had a reason for this celerity, a purpose given to him by the man called Rasputin.

The holy wanderer's face had grown grave as he had leaned closer to Gouroull and whispered his instructions, his voice hushed, his face intense:

"You must head to the Uzkoye, near the Bisa River, in Moscow. The land is that of the Troubetzkoys family, a noble branch of whom I know little, and care less. Their estate, stolen by marriage from a Russian family, is a massive and dense forest, mostly untamed. Enter near the river and seek Old Boris. He sits on a stump every night, smoking his pipe, looking at the sky. Old Boris is a prophet, a teller of the future. This is very different from a soothsayer, or others who seek answers from the future. A prophet is a vessel, a way through which a power speaks to humans and releases portents for the coming days. Speaking to a prophet is an uncomfortable experience. Old Boris will you tell you of what you seek, but you will not like the experience. Will you seek him out?"

Gouroull had agreed, learning something of the lands he sought, and the best approaches. He had even obeyed the holy man's advice and taken the train, a faster method of crossing the enormous distances of Siberia.

Though Gouroull had walked long distances thanks to his inability to suffer from exhaustion, rivers, mountains and towns full of inquisitive peasants had often slowed his progress. Hiding on a train removed such obstacles and he found himself in the city in mere days.

Following Rasputin's directions, Gouroull stepped on a narrow trail full of jutting roots and small stones. The high, ancient trees resembled huge, dreadful skeletons in the darkness, their denuded branches reaching for the sky like spectral fingers. The soft skitter of small animals sliced through the silence, the sounds of their retreating forms briefly breaking the stillness. The snowfall continued, a slow, gentle, pale, curtain that layered the world in frozen purity.

The path wound through the wilderness, the width widening and lessening every dozen or so feet. For hours, Gouroull followed it, his sense of direction being the only reason he did not become hopelessly lost in minutes. The darkness grew, becoming so thick and overwhelming that it appeared as if an inky cloak had fallen across the antediluvian land. The sky, still occasionally visible in small patches, vanished beneath the heavy boughs that hung over the path like a multi-limbed, wooden roof.

Minutes later, Frankenstein's most lethal creation spotted a soft, silver glow in the distance. Heading in that direction, he found himself in a small clearing, a vast array of stars casting a gentle illumination on the circular expanse.

In the center of the path, sitting on a low stump, was an old man. He was a tiny figure, round of head and body. His thick white hair shimmered in the starlight, and a pale downy beard covered his cheeks and chin. He wore a small flat back cap on his head and was bundled in multiple layers of sweaters and jackets. The old man's head pointed upwards, an unblinking gaze upon the heavenly lights dancing in the sky.

"Hello, Gouroull," he said in a deep voice that creaked and crackled with age. "Come closer. I would see the person I speak to this night."

Gouroull stepped in front of the man, his phosphorescent eyes glinting with evil intensity as the elderly figured lowered his gimlet gaze upon the giant figure that was Frankenstein's monster. He waited for the shriek of terror or the look of disgust that invariably emerged from his contacts with humanity. Oddly enough, nothing of the sort came from the tiny, seated man.

"You must have trouble passing through doors," Old Boris said, his bright blue eyes dancing as crinkles and folds appeared across his lined face. "That is not my difficulty. I stopped growing when I was ten, and never reached my old papa's shoulder. A great disappointment for him and my mother. My younger brother gave them some happiness, however. He grew to become a big, strapping young man, who became a miller, like my old papa. They sent me to live with Yedgor the shoemaker in the next town, and forgot that I was alive. I still make shoes… I made a pair for you since we will help each other. You wish the list of three?"

"Yes," Gouroull growled.

Old Boris bobbed his head and smiled wider.

"Good, then you help me, and I help you. The Voice tells me you kill better than most on this planet. The Voice is what I call the one whose words I speak. More, I may not say. As I said, you are a killer. This is true, yes? Ah, this makes my request a simple one. I need you to kill a group, at least a few, of men and women. They are evil, though that will not interest you. I do not care that they play at demon worship either. I wish them dead because, if they live, they shall take my clearing and use it for their foul rites. Will you do me this favor?"

"Yes," Gouroull repeated.

"Thank you, Gouroull. There are four or five of them, and they perform their ceremonies deeper in these woods. Walk down the right path until you come to a fallen tree across the trail. Take the left trail and follow it until the end. There, you will see their clearing, only a short walk away. Kill all of them, or most of them, and I shall tell you the locations of the three."

Old Boris sighed and raised his head to the stars.

Gouroull stepped around the elderly man, spotting the pair of enormous leather boots lying across the right trail. He took them and vanished from sight, his passage as swift and as silent as that of the proverbial Grim Reaper.

CHAPTER VI

The tall, ungainly figured weaved through the market, seemingly oblivious to the stares he earned. A small line of the boldest and hungriest of the criminals followed a few feet at his rear, their knives and clubs held in tight fingers beneath their ragged clothes. They held back, this situation so outlandish that they suspected a trap.

The word *gwailo*, loosely translated to mean "ghost face," hissed back and forth between the denizens of the Kowloon Walled City in Hong Kong. An ancient slum, it was widely considered one of the most dangerous locations in Asia. The residents struggled daily in one of the most crowded regions of the world, largely ignored by the various rulers over the ages.

Recently, the new British rulers had vowed that their forces, coming from overseas, would rid the world of this blight upon lovely Hong Kong. As of now, a few well-armed patrols crossed through the outskirts of Kowloon, but little was accomplished. The British *gwailos* received little respect from the people and were ignored as pests and fools. However, seeing that pale-faced giant of a man with a large sack across his huge shoulders gave the natives pause.

"He does not look like a Britisher," Fung hissed, studying the man up and down as he passed her for the third time. "His skin is not even that of a *gwailo*. It is yellow like a lemon. Have you ever seen anyone the color of a lemon?"

Ho shook his shaggy head, turning his one good eye for a better look at the outsider stooping low as he passed through a tent filled with fish and back onto the street. The sallow-colored man stood several heads taller than the largest men in Kowloon. His thin beard barely disguised a weak chin and made his long, pointed nose look even larger.

Fung, Ho, Li, and the rest of their small group were young predators from the depths of the Kowloon. They were not wolves, like Ki'ing and his gang of thieves and killers who controlled three streets. Nor were they tigers, like the terrifying Master of Kowloon, a hidden man known only as the Golden Scorpion, who ruled through an army of hard-faced warriors. No, they were a lesser breed of criminals. The locals called them *dholes*—a particularly vicious species of wild dog that had rampaged through India and China in ancient days. They were young, small, malnourished creatures with hollow eyes, thin bodies and merciless eyes. They robbed the weak, stole from the poor, and attacked any unwary drunk or opium eater that crossed their path. They fought with rusty knives, makeshift clubs, bricks, and any other object that might serve as a weapon. Their lives were short, brutal, and often easily forgotten in the mass of humanity that made up this terrible slum.

Fung opened her mouth, a plan of attack in mind, when the lemon-colored *gwailo* turned into a small stall with a bright white canopy in front. Both young criminals stared in open horror, glanced at each other, and fled in the opposite direction. Though they were fearless in the face of danger, even the *dholes* knew better than to cross paths with the White Witch and her frightening followers.

The white canvass covering the front of the double-sized market stall appeared unblemished and fresh, as if spun and raised seconds before the odd visitor arrived. A young woman dressed in a too-small cotton shift squatted in the front, her long, fingers scratching symbols in the dirt as her dull eyes slowly glanced up the visitor's nearly seven foot frame. The tangled, filth covered mop of black hair shifted left and right as she stared upward. The motion resembled the furtive movements of a frightened animal, while the stained face remained impassive.

The ungainly figure reached into a deep pants pocket and removed a small coin. He proffered the silver object to the squatting girl, who extended a tiny hand and accepted it without breaking eye contact. The tarnished silver coin lay flat on her palm and she ran a slim finger across its surface for a moment. She then nodded, rose and grasped one of the stranger's fingers in a surprisingly powerful grip.

Leading him inside, she pushed aside a canvas flap and two curtains before stopping in a chamber in the center of the tent. A three-foot multi-color statue of a Tibetan demon lay in the center of the space, the dozens of clawed arms reaching every direction while the fang-filled snout appeared frozen in mid-snarl. Small, low tables were filled with various herbs, clay bowls, bronze knives and wooden wands. The room spelled of jasmine, sulphur, and incense—a small pot lay in an urn by the statue's dancing feet. A series of lanterns hung in a circular pattern about the tent, their yellow glow casting odd, eldritch images across the expanse.

The girl released the visitor's hand and pushed aside a small table, scattering the roots and leaves and sending a brass knife clattering to the stone floor. A pitted black iron ring lay across the floor, attached to a half-circle of similar metal bolted into the floor. The girl grasped the heavy metal and pulled, swinging open a square door downward. Releasing the ring, she snatched a lantern from a hook and extended it to the large, sallow-skinned man.

He took the lantern, the shining brass sparkling as it swung loosely in his grasp. The filthy young girl pointed down at the opening, revealing a set of wide stone steps that led into the bowels of the Earth. Nodding again, the giant stepped down, squeezing through the narrow opening and following the stairs until they stopped in front of a long walkway. The stone passage led off into the distance, vanishing around a sharp corner.

Following the walkway for several miles, the tall man's journey ended at another flight of steps, these leading up to a lit room. The sounds of a piano drifted downward a moment later, the tune a merry, fast one that sounded like the ones he'd heard when visiting big cities like Boston.

"Hezekiah Whateley," a woman's voice said from the unseen room above the man's head, "do come up and sit. We have a great deal to discuss and very little time."

The yellow-faced giant started at hearing his name. Then he shrugged and loped up the stairs, his expression as unchanging as the one across the face of the filth-covered girl he had left behind in Kowloon.

CHAPTER VII

Gouroull heard the voices before the light of a bonfire illuminated the otherwise gloomy woods. They sounded light, their words indistinct though musical in the ears of Frankenstein's Monster. The thrumming of a drum rose above the merry men and women, a steady beat that rose in volume and speed with each passing moment. A light pipe tunelessly joined a moment later and the yells and laughter rose in pitch and volume.

Crossing the snowy sward with the silent step of a born predator, Gouroull halted just outside the bonfire's radiance. A small mass of hooded figures cavorted in the flickering firelight, their semi-naked bodies sweating from their exertions. The majority appeared young, their nubile bodies free of blemish or fat, though there were two exceptions: a tall white bearded man, whose scrawny body and flopping phallus played away on a long wooden pipe, looking quite out-of-place in this young community; and a bald fat man seated on a log, his sweaty, corpulent form wrapped in a heavy red cloak. His eyes gazed out at the dancers—greedy, piggish eyes staring with unbidden lust at the ripened forms of the naked dancers.

"Stop!" an unseen voice said, the sound echoing across the clearing.

A tall man with a thick black beard and a muscular hirsute physique stepped into view. He wore a silver pentagram stitched on his breast and carried a long bronze blade raised in his hairy left hand.

The dancers froze in mid-step, turning as one towards the approaching figure. They bowed their heads and swayed in place, their movements disjointed and difficult on the eyes.

"In the name of our patron, Ferthur, Count of Hell and master of twenty-nine legions of the damned," the newcomer said in an educated tenor, "let us all hail the Lord and Master of the Earth and the Pit. Repeat after me..."

The group recited with their leader, "We hail to you Satan, Master of Two Worlds, Dark Angel, Lucifer, and Unforgiven One. We salute you mighty Ferthur and swear our souls to your eternal service. Let darkness be our guide and encompass the world."

One at a time, each of the followers stepped up to the leader, extending their left hand. The robed leader ran the blade across their palm, evoking a few squeaks and squeals of pain, though none protested. They then ran their bleeding hands across the faces and chests of the two elderly men, streaking face and torso with their crimson *vitae*.

The bloodstained men stepped forward, handing off their instruments to others and dropping to their knees in the densely packed snow. The robed leader waved the dagger over their heads, spattering their shining pates with droplets of scarlet blood.

He intoned in a voice that shook with emotion, "*Nema! livee, morf su revilled tub nushyaitpmet ootni eyth eeb dwohlah nevah ni tra chioo rethoff rewau!* HAIL SATAN! HAIL FERTHUR!"

The two old men screamed and collapsed, their bodies quivering and convulsing. The remainder of the coven swayed on their feet, heads still lowered, mouths emitting odd barking and whimpering sounds.

Then the two men stood, their bodies transformed. Their bodies were rejuvenated, reborn blemish free and as attractive as their fellow cultists appeared. Luxuriant dark hair covered the head of pipe player and the drummer possessed a thin layer of yellow locks. Their faces, formerly filled with deep wrinkles and harsh lines, now looked youthful, taut, and possessing a naked cruelty that appeared almost feral in its intensity.

"Rise, brothers! Rise reborn in the name of darkness!" the cult leader cried, "Once again, our coven defeats the curse of aging!"

The two young men holding the pipe and drum sounded their instruments and the dance commenced again. This time the whirls and twirls of the revelers took on a frenzied, sexual nature. Random partners switched and animal grunts and groans mixed with ecstasy-laden cries of delight and pain.

A pair of women moved closer to Gouroull's location, their eyes only upon each other. Grabbing both by their necks, the Monster twisted once and both fell dead without making a sound. Dropping their bodies to the ground, he stepped into the circle of firelight, silencing the coven in an instant.

"Are you a demon?" a man of medium height with long light hair parted on the left side and a waxed curling mustache asked. "A visitor from the depths of darkness?"

Gouroull lifted the man and shook him twice, resembling a terrier assaulting a rat. A sickening crunch emerged and the man fell to the snow-packed earth, his eyes staring blankly in death.

"Interloper!" the leader shrieked, pointing his blade at the monstrous being in their midst, "Destroy him! Destroy him in Ferthur's name!"

The cultists screamed and pressed towards the titanic Gouroull. He stood above all, a gray-skinned titan assaulted by pale, hairless vermin. None possessed weapons, yet they threw themselves boldly at Frankenstein's most lethal creation, only to crash to the sward, ripped and shattered by the terrible might and razor-sharp teeth of the Monster.

Within moments, only Gouroull and the leader stood in the clearing. The diminishing bonfire cast shadows across the bloodstained Gouroull's twisted countenance. The human *vitae* appeared black in the changing light. He smiled, his massive incisors flashing in the darkness as he stepped closer to the leader.

"No! In the name of Ferthur!" the leader screeched. "In the name of almighty Satan, I demand you stop!"

He pointed his knife towards Gouroull's chest, but Frankenstein's creature sprung forward, slapping the blade aside and clamping his lips down on the magus's throat. With a sound like that of cloth ripping, he tore away his throat, tossing his dying body to the ground near his followers.

Glancing around, Gouroull scanned the scattered corpses, their twisted forms resembling broken toys. Spotting no movement, detecting no breathing, he turned away and vanished into the darkness.

CHAPTER VIII

Hezekiah Whateley's head popped through the trap door, revealing a tiny space barely capable of holding his huge form. He just avoided bumping into a shelf and spotted an open door several inches away from his hand. Realizing he stood in a closet, he stepped out and glanced around.

The hallway surrounding him was long, painted a clean white, and decorated with art that looked elegant and understated. A closed doorway at the far end of the hallway seemed heavy and forbidding, its heavy iron lock and handle adding a dungeon quality to the location. Looking at the other end of the corridor, he spotted a second open doorway, an equal distance away.

Heading to the imposing closed door, Hezekiah pushed the handle and found it opened with some ease. The room thus revealed was a spare, Spartan chamber, possessing the same white walls, a simple round black rug and two chairs. A woman sat in one chair, her face hidden by a thin white gauzy veil. Her body was barely visible, wrapped in voluminous layers of the same light fabric.

"Come in, come in, Hezekiah Whateley," she said. "You are exactly as I pictured. You even passed the last test. Take a seat, we have a great deal to discuss and less time than I would prefer."

Her voice was the one that had greeted him in the tunnels, a light musical tone that sounded like the tinkling of a tiny silver bell.

"What test?" Hezekiah asked.

His voice was a sharp contrast with that of his host. Deep and rumbling in quality, the listener almost felt his words rather than hearing or comprehending their meaning. There was an inhuman quality to his speech, an almost animalistic intonation that resembled that of the roar of a massive bear.

The woman in white tittered for a moment and her head nodded towards the door.

"Had you chosen the open door, my servants were waiting with shotguns. They would have shot you down."

"How was that a test? That was just a choice," Hezekiah Whateley remarked.

His huge hands balled into tight fists, the ivory colored knuckles popped, resembling terrible pale clubs rather than human extremities.

"The best kind! The man I require cannot be one that follows the path of least resistance. He must be one who battles all and destroys barriers imposed upon him by the world. I think you are such a man, Hezekiah Whateley. Paimon, the Great King of Hell, knew that I required a dangerous follower of the truth path who can overcome any human in battle. A creature such as yourself would not walk into an open door, but try the one that I removed from a dungeon. Unconsciously, you sensed the blood, did you not?"

"Who are you calling a creature?" Hezekiah snarled, jumping to his feet.

"I see you, Hezekiah Whateley, the true you. Not the face you show the world, but the one beneath those handmade clothes. I know you, child of Dunwich, and I call you creature and many other names to denote the truth you hide. Do not lie to me, Hezekiah Whateley, I am not one of those fools you placate in your America."

The light tone from the woman now possessed a malicious, gleeful edge. She still spoke with the silken smoothness one might expect from a hungry spider, if such creatures possessed a voice. There was a dreadful sadistic edge to her words, a delight that the man opposite might resist her demands.

"What? I am not one of those Whateleys, witch! I do not serve those unnatural, alien..." Hezekiah spluttered, looming over the seated woman.

"Of course, you do not, Hezekiah Whateley. If you did, you would be of no use to one such as I. Those alien beings possess terrible, overwhelming power, and my masters are their fiercest opponents. You heard the stories from the decayed members of your clan, no doubt. How their masters give power to followers and plan to take back the Earth. Do I besmirch your kin? I can quote your cousin John Whateley if you require more evidence of my knowledge."

Hezekiah Whateley shook his boulder-shaped head and said, "No, you know the truth of it. Since that's a fact, why am I here?"

The woman in the white shroud laughed and a shifting of the layers indicated a rapid headshake.

"Hezekiah," she said, her voice taking on a harsher note, "you follow the old ways, though not the path of your cousin's side of the family. You worship the one called the Dark Angel, the Adversary, Old Nick, Scratch, Satan, Lucifer, the Lightbearer, and about ten thousand other names. You have the blood of many a black cat or stolen baby on your hands, and you are more part of the Pit than the Earth. Now sit down and stop behaving like you are speaking to a town minister accusing you of witchcraft."

Despite himself, Hezekiah lowered himself into the chair, surprised by the power in this hidden woman's voice.

"Why are you wearing a shroud?" he asked.

"You will learn, just not today. I shall continue. Your master and mine sent you here, to my side. They recognize a growing threat and seek to use you as their weapon—if you prove that you are worthy of their trust."

The wall to the left swung inward, revealing a small corridor made of wood. A pair of large men stepped into the room, both holding long sharp knives in their hands. Stepping into the light, they revealed their wide, flat faces, each bisected by multiple gray scars. They wore their hair in long dark braids that they wound around their thick bull necks. They possessed small dark eyes and sneered in Hezekiah's direction.

"What is this?" Hezekiah asked.

He stood up and pushed his chair back.

"These gentlemen," the still unidentified woman said, "are visitors from the island called Australia. They are members of an ancient order of demon worshipers called the Brotherhood of the Ram. Since birth, they train in cruelty and violence, specializing in knife fighting. They are fanatics and some of the deadliest fighters on Earth."

"Why are you telling me this?" Hezekiah demanded, keeping his eyes on both men.

"Simple," the woman in white replied with another musical giggle, "you are the chosen warrior meant to perform the bidding of the Master of Hell. I will test and see if you are capable of facing the forthcoming trials. Therefore, you shall fight the two best killers of the

Brotherhood of the Ram. Either they shall survive, or you shall."

"Die!" the two Children of the Knife screamed, leaping forward, blades flashing.

Hezekiah Whateley snarled and stepped forward, his huge hands outward. A low, subsonic rumble sounded in his chest, though he made no other sound.

The chamber filled with the sounds of ripping flesh and snapping bones, along with. agonized wails that vanished as quickly as they emerged. A pair of human heads rolled across the floor, coming to rest at the feet of the shrouded woman. Hezekiah Whateley appeared seconds later, his hands, chest, and face drenched in blood and other unidentifiable fluids.

"Are you content now, witch? Or should I tear your beating heart from your chest and eat it before your dying eyes?" he growled, raising his crimson-stained hands.

"You may try if you like, Hezekiah Whateley. Please, do as you wish," the shrouded woman said, laughing.

The sound was mocking and malicious, the universal sound made by a bully when viewing the weak.

"Bah!" Hezekiah spat, dropping back into his chair, "what you say of me and some of my kin is true, lady."

"That is why I sent for you," the woman replied, the light tone returning to her voice. "A tool of the Unmentionable Ones is using a terrible creature to assist them in their quest to return to Earth. If they win, not only will the many millennia-old plan of our own masters fail, but this world will find itself swept clean of all life. Then the old gods shall return and start anew..."

CHAPTER IX

Old Boris sat in the same spot, his ancient eyes still gazing upon the few stars visible beneath the gray and black sky. A slight crinkling around his eyes indicated he knew that Gouroull was nearby; yet he did not gaze at Frankenstein's monster. Instead, Old Boris kept his gaze firmly locked upon the sky.

"Many members of humanity," Old Boris said, speaking as if he and Gouroull were in a long conversation, "back since the time when the humans overthrew the Dragon Kings of Lemuria, believed they could see the future in the stars. They cannot—they do not have the gifts necessary for such comprehension. Humans can only receive such talent if they are either related to one of the near-human races, or receive such power as a gift from their patron."

Pausing, Old Boris looked at Gouroull and smiled.

"I am not fully human. I am one fifth a member of a long-forgotten race. I had some gift for seeing the truth in the stars, but only a trace. Then my... patron, for lack of a better term, spoke in my mind. Now, I see the possible futures in many places, though accurate prediction is nearly impossible. Large and small events change the universe's path from moment to moment."

Gouroull moved a little closer, his amber eyes focusing on Old Boris with a malevolent light within their alien depths. He stepped closer, his gargantuan frame dwarfing that of the old man.

"I tell you this for a reason, Gouroull. Every being's possible destiny is available before my ancient eyes. I see the paths and its probable outcome. But not with you, Gouroull. In your case, I find myself staring into a heavy wall, so black it seems to absorb all light, life, and power. I cannot tell you your destiny."

The elderly prophet raised a tiny, chubby hand and added:

This does not mean that I retreat from our bargain. You did me service and I shall give you that which you seek."

Old Boris pulled a small stick from the ground and drew an object in the fallen snow.

"That is the shape of the object you seek. The lesser one is in the country called America. But the greater one shall serve your needs better. You shall find it in the land of Mesopotamia. I shall tell you of a means of getting close to your target. There, within ancient ruins, is a vast maze. You must find your way through that maze and retrieve this object. The dangers are more than any human could bear, but I think it shall be less of a challenge for you, Gouroull. However, I do see other parties intent on destroying any chances you have of receiving a mate. You must follow the route I shall give you, which will take you to Mesopotamia in weeks rather than months. After that, you shall know where you must proceed. The trials of the maze are your primary concern. Your strength, your powers, and unique body might overcome the dangers. If they do not, then all is lost for this world, and you shall be past caring about mates and the future. Now I shall tell you of the other two items…"

Old Boris spoke for another twenty minutes and then sighed.

"The Voice within me has retreated. I have no more for you, Gouroull. Your fate is now your own."

Gouroull studied the images etched in the snow for a moment. Then, he turned away, vanishing into the night.

Old Boris looked back up at the stars, feeling the evil laughter of his patron echoing in his skull. Gouroull had no notion of the cosmic forces arrayed in this battle. In a very real sense, if he succeeded in his quest, the entire world, and all life on Earth, were doomed. But if he failed, the world was still fated for destruction—just in a slower, more sadistic manner.

"At least, my patron and his kind shall end us quickly. Far better than a slow torturous death," Old Boris muttered, still searching the stars for some clue about the creature known as Gouroull.

CHAPTER X

A conclave between the powers was a rarity, one that had happened only three times since the days of the Fourth Crusade. This was not to say there were no issues between the European religious bodies; such a thought was ludicrous. Such conflicts were a facet of life that each accepted and engaged individually. A conclave was not held over such temporal matters. These unheard-of gatherings were held when matters of universal life and death were in the balance.

The site was a ruin called Villa Jovis located on the small island of Capri. The stone buildings once housed the crazed Emperor Tiberius when he believed, rightly, that the Roman people wished him dead. Tales of his bizarre behavior while residing in this villa still passed through word-of-mouth from the residents and various historians who passed through the crumbling walls.

The men arrived within minutes of each other, their arrival lacking fanfare or ceremony. These were powerful men who held the various strings of power throughout their sometimes scattered religious bodies. Each possessed the hard eyes and sleek look of hunters and warriors, and they moved with the dangerous calm one expected from born killers. None resembled the scholars and politicians who commonly represented their religious bodies—such men were unwelcome at the conclave.

"Shall I play host?" a man of medium height with broad shoulders and a scarred face asked.

He spoke Latin, the accepted language of the Conclave, with a harsh Prussian accent and carried himself with the ramrod stiffness of a professional soldier.

"If you wish," replied a dark-skinned bearded man whose sharp nose made him look like a raptor.

He wore a muted dark suit and possessed watchful eyes perpetually scanning every direction.

The first man poured out tea from a large silver urn and waited until the others chose their cups randomly. He took the last, but drank first, nodding and sitting back on the cushioned stone bench.

"I think we all know why such a gathering was required, but let us review the facts in case someone does not know what was foretold. I suggest we move from the right of where I sit around the circle."

"Very well," the man to the German speaker's right replied in an English accent.

He was a tall man with a slender body, pale blond hair, and a languorous manner that was deceptive. He moved with a smoothness that was disquieting for a viewer, belying his almost gentle behavior.

"A certain member of the royal family possesses… gifts. This individual has dreams of terrible occurrences, though, like Cassandra, the visions are often ignored. On this occasion, the dreams returned seven times and we recognized a threat. This brings us to the conclave. What of you, my French friend?"

"A similar situation brought the problem to our notice. A Nazirite who took the vow of Samson received visions of calamity. This often occurs, but two others who made the vow received the exact same prophecy. This happened in the past and we know better than to ignore the possibility of mass destruction."

The speaker was as tall as the Englishman, though with a heavier build and distinct, educated, French accent. This man looked intense and dangerous, someone one should avoid, or at least never anger.

"Our experience is less complex. A soothsayer from our lands predicted the dangers many times in the last months. Her words were always the same, even her intonations. This does not happen, my friends, unless all life is threatened."

The man was of medium height with a round head, a thick head of curly hair and a wide smile. His accent was the harsh Greek tones used by fishermen in the islands, though he switched to the smoother accents of the Athenians with ease. He resembled a man who worked with this hands and body day and night, and earned powerful muscles from his toils. He possessed a merry air and looked quite inoffensive at first glance. This was a deception that fooled his enemies, few of whom survived after facing him in battle.

"For us," said the man with the nose shaped like a falcon's beak in an accent that each recognized as being from Egypt, "the experience was closer to that of my Jewish comrade. A Sufi holy man, one who knew Muhammad Ahmad bin Abd Allah the Mahdi, foretold the end of all. At the same moment that ancient man spoke, a *kahina* in the Topkapi Palace spoke the exact same words. Only a few would ignore such information."

"As to my people," the host said in his rough voice, "a pair of holy pilgrims spoke of the terribly time coming. An abbess remembered the words from her studies and uncovered the exact prediction from a saint back in the time after Attila the Hun rampaged through Europe. We consulted some of you individually and therefore requested the conclave."

"The prophesies are remarkably similar. Can we dispense with the need for analysis of each portion?" the French speaker asked.

"Agreed," the round-faced man replied. "A foretelling overanalyzed always leads to greater disaster. If necessary, I can provide many examples."

"That will not be necessary," the Englishman said, sipping his tea slowly. "We are educated and can acknowledge the truth of your supposition. The reason this conclave exists is because we are not mere scholars."

"Correct," the host said, nodding. "If we are all in agreement of the danger, then we must determine a course of action."

"I suggest," the Englishman said, "a dedicated team with one professional from each of our ranks, made up of soldiers who will not engage in foolish debates over the truth of their beliefs."

"Yes," the Egyptian said, frowning, "but we should also send in a specialist—a lone operator capable of battling evil without assistance. Such professionals are often quite effective when the teams fail."

"The last pair I knew," the Frenchman said, chuckling, "killed each other two years ago in a conflict between my people and our English friends."

The Englishman sighed.

"Yes, a sad loss for both our sides."

"The one in our employ is engaged in work against an anarchist conspiracy in Russia," the Greek said.

He looked at the host, then the Egyptian.

"I know of such a man," the latter said, "though he serves no religious leader, despite his birth. I would need to convince him of the rightness of our cause. May I have copies of each of your reasons for representing your people at conclave?"

The others all nodded, and, after a brief discussion, the meeting ended. The plans were now in place; their execution would follow in the coming days. The fate of the Earth was at stake, and they would not waste time with lesser issues such as the millennia-long battles between their people over religious doctrine.

CHAPTER XI

Gouroull circled the vast burial mound three times, examining the remains of what was once a vast and ancient ziggurat. The massive, crumbling, dusty red-brown stones looked out-of-place in the middle of the desert expanse. A series of shattered stone steps led up to a small platform, while random rows of mud brick walls littered the surroundings near the spiraling platforms.

This was the remains of a city-state, a land whose name was long-lost in the mists of time. According to Old Boris, the great kings of Kish and Uruk rose against the dwellers of this city and put all its inhabitants to death after a terrible battle.

"The great kings, Aga and Lugalbanda, made peace and led their war chariots in battle together, riding out against the monsters of this city," Old Boris had explained to Gouroull back in the Moscow woods. "It was said its inhabitants held the shape of men at first look. But closer examination caused one to see they were really demons and creatures from beyond the void. After defeating its armies, Aga and Lugalbanda killed everyone inside, including the beasts of burden. By the time they left, the city was a ruin."

Following the old man's instructions, Gouroull climbed the ziggurat in a few quick bounds, standing upon the summit mere seconds later. He walked across the small landing to the east end and looked straight down just as the morning light fell upon the shells of ancient buildings. The light revealed, only for a split second, a slight sparkle from one massive fallen stone.

Climbing down, Gouroull approached the circular rock, staring down at the flat surface. Cut into the stone was the image of an off-center, elongated star, as well as an odd object that resembled the branch of a tree. Frankenstein's most lethal creation placed his hands upon these images and pressed downward, feeling a slight vibration in the rock a moment later.

Without warning, the stone slab slid sideways, revealing a gaping void. What little light capable of penetrating this hidden location revealed a vast drop with no visible bottom. The air emerging from the hole was musty and harsh upon the senses, as if a tomb of ancient horrors had just opened onto the Earth.

Taking a step forward, Gouroull dropped into the cavern's mouth, falling twenty or more feet unto a soft sandy floor. His horrific phosphorescent eyes glimmered in the gloom, granting him vision in an underground world where light had not existed since the days of Gilgamesh.

Frankenstein's monster stood in a vast, cavern, one that looked hewn from the rock by the hands of tools rather than water and other elements. The walls were covered with a series of odd runes and etching of strange creatures with tendrils and lamprey-shaped mouths mating with men and women. The ceiling of the tunnel also possessed carvings of stars and planets, as well as massive creatures whose shapes appeared hard to discern even after a long look.

A smaller tunnel on the east side of the cavern led to a corridor cut from the rock. A slight glimmer flickered in the distance, a will-o-the-wisp that vanished as quickly as it had appeared. No sounds drifted from this direction, though the slight light occasionally emerged at random intervals.

Walking into the tunnel, Gouroull spotted similar carvings of the mating rituals of the bizarre creatures with human beings. One aspect stood out among all the etchings: the eyes of the humans involved in these sexual acts—men, women, and sometimes children—all looked upon the protean beasts with wide eyes, filled with obvious adoration. They appeared enthralled by the monstrosities that used them as broodmares or sperm donors, consuming the humans in various grotesque manners in later images.

Unmoved by these horrific images, Gouroull continued forward. The tunnel, as Old Boris had predicted, branched out in three directions, each possessing flickering lights in the distance. Frankenstein's creature sniffed the air, ignored the fusty scents, seeking only further information. A trace of an odor lingered off to the left, one that even the long-lived monster could not identify.

Turning in that direction, he stepped forward. The aroma grew stronger with each step. There was a rotten, viscous smell in the air, as if from the slime that lay beneath the deepest, darkest pools of the Earth.

Turning a corner, Gouroull spotted movement ahead, vanishing a second later. A slight skittering sound filled the air, a rasp like a rodent's, though much larger. The tangle of noise died down as Gouroull approached, disappearing altogether as he stepped around another blind turn.

Gouroull stopped, his luminous eyes tracking a man-sized shape crawling along the ceiling, slowly, silently creeping towards him. The creature's movements resembled that of a massive insect, despite the vaguely human aspect of its arms and legs. A pair of yellow-red eyes studied Gouroull, recognizing within seconds that the inhuman orbs of Frankenstein's Monster tracked every step of his, despite the gloom.

The newcomer released a squawk that resembled the caw of a titanic crow, dropped to the ground, and ran towards Gouroull with a grace and celerity that belied its size. Nearly as tall as Frankenstein's creature, it possessed a long, sinewy body covered in a brown and gray skin that oozed and quivered with each speedy step. Its arms were elongated and hung past a pair of knobby, spike-covered knees. Its seven-fingered hands were oversized and possessed huge hooked talons that oozed a thin, clear fluid. Its legs appeared human in shape, but the supporting feet held three massive reptilian toes containing nails larger and sharper than its talons.

However, all this was secondary compared to its snarling, snapping mouth in a head that looked like a terrifying mixture of human, ape, and wolf. The short snout and slit-shaped nose added to the oddity, and the crooked, red-stained fangs varied in size and shape from tooth to tooth. A pair of deep set yellow-red eyes glimmered with avaricious malice, and a serpentine tongue lashed the air as the demonic being leaped towards Frankenstein's creation.

Gouroull's massive mitts snatched the creature out of the air, locking tightly upon a pair of wrists that squished beneath his iron grasp. But no bones cracked or shattered beneath his lethal grip; the oozing flesh merely compressed and yielded, squirming like that of a slime-covered worm or snail.

The creature's huge feet rose and slashed across Gouroull's chest and stomach, penetrating the gray, unyielding flesh with ease. Slow trickles of a black, viscous ichor oozed from the incisions, dripping across the exposed skin in slow runnels. The *vitae* of Frankenstein's monster were not blood, but a fluid that possessed a thicker, heavier consistency.

The attacking creature's protean head snapped and snarled, slicing through the air, seeking Gouroull's throat. Sliding his enemy closer, Frankenstein's Monster slashed out with his own razor-sharp incisors, tearing away at his enemy's throat. The flesh parted under the terrible teeth, but returned to its original shape seconds later. The skin of this creature was closer to that of mud than the epidermal layer of any sentient being.

Receiving another series of cuts, Gouroull growled and swung his enemy in a hard arc. The demonic creature slammed into a nearby wall with an audible squishing sound. It shrieked, hissing like a massive serpent as rivulets of viscid flesh fell away, dripping across the stone carvings and staining the ancient images.

With a sound that was equal parts evil laughter and bestial snarl, Gouroull swung his enemy against the other wall with the same terrific force. Without pause, he then whipped the body of his enemy against the ceiling and the floor before striking both walls with it once again. A rain of gelatinous epithelium filled the air as pieces of the monstrosity parted from its inhuman body.

Gouroull dropped the limp arms on the stone floor, pausing long enough to grind them and the remains of the skull beneath his heavy, leather boots. Stepping back, he surveyed the wreckage of the corridor as the liquid flesh of the destroyed creature dripped across every surface.

That accomplished, he strode forward, sensing more trials ahead. This was merely the first sentinel protecting the treasure at the center of this maze, beneath a city the name of which had been erased from history by the hands of mankind.

CHAPTER XII

The Cairo Museum was a place of wonderment. One of the largest collections of ancient art and antiques, the sheer volume of its items could keep an archaeologist or art historian busy for several lifetimes. The first floor alone boasted collections from such legendary New Kingdom Pharaohs as Thutmosis III, Thutmosis IV, Amenophis II, and Hatshepsut.

The man who had attended the conclave in Capri strode through the exhibits, looking at a few with some interest, ignoring the vast majority. He thought of the legendary kings of Egypt as relics best forgotten by the world. While some appeared interesting, at least five worshipped the dark deities that he had battled since childhood.

His birth name was lost in time, but now he was known as Masud Asim Gamil, and he was a powerful and dangerous man. Egyptian and Arabian by birth, he was a distant relation of the Ottoman Royal family, as well as of the legendary sheik Mani' ibn Rabi'a al-Muraydi, founder of the House of Saud.

Raised in both his homelands and Europe, Gamil had been chosen at a young age for a special mission, one imbued with more danger than any soldier or secret agent could imagine. Founded almost a thousand years ago in the Sharifate of Mecca, the Children of the Kaaba were a small cadre of men and women whose mission was to protect the world in the name of Islam. The organization, said to have been founded shortly after the death of the prophet Muhammad, protected believers and unbelievers alike from creatures from the darkest depths of Hell or the deepest, coldest, regions of space.

Trained from a young age, the Children of Kaaba were ruthless killers who operated in teams, perpetually seeking true followers of the dark powers. They were all devoted Muslims, trained assassins, and soldiers, and lacked any ambition for temporal power. Gamil's induction to this warrior order had occurred when he was still a callow youth who thought of these duties as an exciting adventure. The swearing-in ceremony had taken place in the holiest site in all of Islam—the Al-Masjid Al-Ḥarām, better known as the Great Mosque of Mecca.

Years later, after losing his foolish pride, he had taken a second oath within the ancient cube-shaped building housing the relic known as the Black Stone. There, he had dedicated himself to the endless battle against evil—one that would not end after his death.

As the leader of the Children of Kaaba since 1897, Gamil still battled the horrors of the dark daily. Purged of pride, he happily worked with Christians and Jews if it protected Earth. Fortunately, the others in the conclave were similar men, though a few might still possess the foolish belief of superiority of their cause or their lands.

"Why are we here?" his assistant Abdul asked.

A well-trained youth just entering adulthood, Abdul would not replace Masud Asim Gamil as leader of the order. He was a follower, though a loyal one. His name meant "Servant of God," and that seemed to fit his personality.

"It is time you met someone outside the order," Gamil explained. "He is respected by our people, but does not serve any master,"

"An infidel?" Abdul asked, sounding astonished.

Gamil guffawed and shook his head, amused by the young man's views. Abdul viewed the world in a very black and white manner. The believers were good, the unbelievers were foolish, but had to be protected the way one does unruly children. And infidels were as dangerous as the cultists who worshipped Iblis, or the Demon Sultan.

"No," Gamil replied, enjoying the way Abdul blushed crimson. "He is a follower of the prophet and even made his Hajj on his own at a young age. Not an unbeliever, Abdul."

Stepping into the chamber devoted to the legendary Pharaoh Hatshepsut, Gamil spotted the man in question. Seated before one of the few statues currently found of the legendary female ruler of Egypt, the first thing one spotted was the man's height. Even seated, he appeared taller than most standing men, and possessed the wide shoulders of an athlete. His face was handsome and almost regal, the countenance one expected from a stage actor playing the part of a romantic desert prince. His hair was a deep black, cut short, and he possessed no beard or mustache, an odd sight among men in this day and age.

"*A salaam alaikum*, my old friend," Gamil said, sitting at the towering man's side.

"*Wa-Alaikum-Salaam*," the other replied in a deep, baritone voice.

He smiled, showing very bright, white teeth.

"Who is your friend?" he inquired.

"This is my assistant, Abdul. Abdul, this is Sheikh Faisal Hashim Haji Sabbah, doctor of medicine, law, religion, and history and the mightiest sword of Islam," Gamil replied, amused by the surprised look on his assistant's face.

"*A salaam alaikum*, young man," Faisal replied.

His eyes returned to the statue.

"Did you know that Pharaoh Hatshepsut led a crusade against the followers of a demon cult ruling a Canaanite tribe?" he added. "Fascinating woman, she purged the priesthood of all followers of the Faceless Pharaoh."

"Is that why we meet here rather than a Cairo hotel or some other spot?" Gamil asked.

Faisal shrugged and continued staring.

"It seemed appropriate. If you require my aid, the situation must be dire indeed. Your men and women are very capable. Is this regarding the tidings told by the Mahdi's favored follower and a certain lady in the court of the Sultan?"

"I would ask how you knew this information, but I learned long ago to expect such revelations from you," Gamil said, rolling his eyes in mock annoyance.

"Yes," Faisal replied. "Tell your team of soldiers that they must not hesitate. The predictions are dire, to say the least."

"Understood. Is there anything you require? Money? Transport? Some to watch your back?" Gamil asked.

"I have enough of the first to last me a lifetime, and my own methods of travel. As to the third…"

Faisal smiled, glancing over Gamil's shoulder.

Gamil and Abdul turned, their mouths dropping in shock. A woman stood mere inches from both, a pair of small revolvers in her hand. She was Gamil's height, with a lithe figure, a stunningly lovely angular face, and long dark hair that flowed like an ebony curtain across her shoulders and back.

"Meet Fatimah," Faisal said, his smile broadening as she flicked her hands and the revolvers vanished.

"She does not like to be known by any other name. She is a daughter of the last remaining Order of Assassins, from the Old Man of the Mountain. One day, those few crazed killers shall kneel at her feet as their living prophet, or so say certain mad soothsayers. She is all the help I require in this battle, or any others."

Fatimah favored Gamil and Abdul with a beaming smile and stepped back a few paces.

"My apologies for the theatrics, gentlemen," she said in a husky voice laced with amusement. "A demonstration tends to prevent the need for long explanations."

"We shall endeavor to prevent what some Christian sects refer to as the End of Days," Faisal concluded, his eyes returning to the statue of the ancient Egyptian ruler.

Gamil stood and gave Faisal and Fatimah a quick bow, leading Abdul on to a room devoted to Thutmose III.

Stopping before a Hedj Club, he said: "Study the weapon, Abdul. We will stand out in the crowd if we do not look interested."

"Yes, sir," Abdul said, his voice numb. "May I ask you why…"

"…Faisal and his charming friend are not members of our cause? He was not known to us until it was far too late to school him in our mysteries. The path he followed was charted by another, who disagreed with some of our choices. As to the woman…"

Gamil hesitated and frowned.

"Yes?" Abdul asked.

"We were unsure if she was real or a fiction invented by gullible fools. We must research the truth of her tale, since our intelligence suggested that the infamous Order of Assassins had died out in the thirteenth century.

Still, I feel better knowing Faisal will fight for our cause…"

Gamil led his younger assistant away.

CHAPTER XIII

Gouroull continued down the hallway, turning at times, occasionally backtracking, until he came to a dead end.

The maze felt endless, but he strode through each passageway only one time. His keen senses prevented him from becoming lost in the twists and turns of the corridors. The strange, unsettling art still covered ever wall and ceiling, though none moved him to feel any emotion. The alien mind of Frankenstein's creation was such that art of this nature held no sway over his spirit. Where normal humans might have reacted with revulsion or anger, Gouroull only felt complete and total disinterest.

Striding into a new tunnel, Gouroull found that its walls appeared wider and its ceiling higher. There was a smoothness different from the other tunnels, and fewer turns. The specks of light grew brighter, casting an ethereal, white glow over the walls, washing out many of the deranged etchings.

Following that tunnel, he eventually arrived into a round room with two more tunnels in the distance, on both the left and right sides. A small rectangular altar made from a smooth green stone lay in the center of the chamber; its floor appeared a particularly repugnant shade of black.

This was the altar of the ancient gods that Old Boris had told Gouroull he had to find. However, that was not all that the old man had said when he had instructed Frankenstein's Monster in the details of the maze located beneath the unknown city in Sumer.

"It is said," Old Boris had revealed, his eyes distant and unfocused, "that the second guardian is one that no sentient being has ever defeated. The creature is capable of destroying armies, and surviving even the worst assaults. If you can somehow defeat it, the object you seek lies within the altar of the lost gods who are still worshipped by the beings of distant Yuggoth."

That was all the elderly man had said, the conscious look returning to his face and eyes a moment later. Gouroull had learned no more and had left, following the secret paths Boris's master had opened for him briefly, allowing the crossing of great distances within days rather than months.

Recognizing the altar, Gouroull stepped forward. A putrescent scent wafted his direction, an odor of rot, filth, and other unnamable aromas. The spoor emerged from every portion of the chamber, an overwhelming sensation capable of nauseating even the strongest stomach.

Yet, Gouroull was unaffected, moving forward without regard for the charnel house smell. The floor squished beneath his feet, oozing and sliding under his heavy boots like muck on the edge of a vast quagmire. With each step, ripples like that of some black pond spread across the floor in ever-widening rings. The viscous secretion shifted and shuddered beneath his heavy tread, thickening as he moved ever closer to the green stone altar.

When he was just six feet away from his goal, the muck held his feet, pulling him back and preventing further steps. Its surface now felt as if it held a hidden adhesive within its depths. The consistency of the exudation deepened, the fluid feeling less like muck and more like some murky protoplasm.

Frankenstein's creation struggled against the glue-like consistency, observing without reaction as the heavy mire slid upward, wrapping around his ankles and knees, holding him like a fly trapped in some vast ebony web. The ripples across the black floor increased in volume and violence, resembling ocean waves from the worst nightmares of the human subconscious.

Then eyes appeared across the surface, randomly popping into existence and blinking with slow, deliberate motions that bore no resemblance to any creature living on the land or under the seas of Earth.

Soon, a profusion of gaping openings, some possessing teeth, others surrounded by oversized lips, emerged, snapping and smacking like mouths designed by a mad mind. Vast cilia and pseudopodia followed, rising and forming a massive barrel shaped trunk with vast globules filled with eyes, and vanishing and appearing tentacles across its Brobdingnagian surface.

Then the many mouths cried out in a chorus of terrible tones the same words repeatedly:

"*Tekeli-li! Tekeli-li!*"

The huge chimeric creature rose up like a gargantuan wave of putrid alluvium and engulfed Gouroull's frozen form. Frankenstein's Monster floated in a vast viscous void, time suddenly frozen, his senses no longer functioning. He could not so much as blink an eye as the rising pressure surrounded him from every direction. The cuts he had received from the previous monster pulsed as the overwhelming ooze mixed with his inhuman *vitae*.

Slowly, the pressure deceased, moving inexorably away from Gouroull in an increasing manner. The dense fluid retreated, weakening and pulling away. Gouroull heard the weak screeches of the monstrosity first, the mad chorus almost moaning bizarre phrases as the liquid entity released his head and flowed away from his still body.

His luminous orbs emerged a moment later, viewing a sickly brown and green streak flowing across the noxious, gooey protoplasm. The creature sloshed away, its howls of "*Tekeli-li! Tekeli-li!*" echoing in the large chamber. A plaintive note entered the sound, growing weaker as the green-brown stain spread with exponential speed.

Gouroull's black lips retreated, revealing his terrible incisors in a demonic smirk. The thick fluid that was his life-blood had poisoned several creatures over the centuries. Vampires burned as they consumed his horrific *vitae*—as had several other predators. The bizarre being that guarded this altar had apparently fallen victim to the same fate. The mad genius of Victor Frankenstein had provided his creation with a defense that overwhelmed even the mightiest monsters.

Striding forward, Gouroull loomed over the green stone altar, observing the same bizarre ritualistic orgies present in stark detail across its surface. Disinterested, he ran his massive hands across the top, feeling for the hidden edges of a lid. Then, with a powerful push, he shoved aside the top, sending it crashing to the floor.

Gazing inside, he spotted the object he sought and pulled it out. The oddity of the item assured him that this was indeed the artifact that Old Boris had stressed was necessary.

"All three pieces are important, though there could be substitutes of the second and third," he had said. "But the first object is essential. Without it, the entire ceremony cannot occur."

"I will take that, mister," a voice suddenly said from the tunnel off to his right. "Hand it to me now and I might let you live."

A huge shadow emerged from the gloom, their step slow and deliberate.

CHAPTER XIV

Gouroull straightened, placing the object in the sack hanging from his ragged pants. His phosphorescent eyes pulsed with malicious fury as he watched the newcomer step into the spare light. He was surprisingly large, nearly the size of Frankenstein Monster, and moved with a fluid grace that was amazing for a being so elephantine.

"My name is Hezekiah Whateley," the newcomer said, flexing his oversized hands into titanic, ivory fists, "and I am taking that thing with me. Now, be a good fellow and hand it to me without a fuss. We don't need to fight."

Gouroull did not reply—he merely smiled again, revealing his terrible teeth. He stopped at the bottom of the steps near the giant interloper and waited. His unblinking gaze locked on Hezekiah Whateley's dark eyes.

"I warn them always and they never listen," grumbled Whateley, shaking his huge, hairy head. "One more chance, Gouroull. Ah, you're surprised that I know you? You are something of a legend, son. The monster made by science wandering in search of a mate. In person, you are both more and less than what they say. Anyway, last warning. Hand it over and we each go our own ways. What you say?"

"No," Gouroull growled, his jaw barely moving as he spoke.

Whateley nodded and smiled, his grin literally spreading from ear to ear. Like a massive, monstrous serpent, he opened his oversized maw, revealing a set of titanic teeth as deadly as Gouroull's. He chuckled, a harsh, grating rasp that sounded like a metal file dragged across a rusty bar.

"You aren't the only one who is more than human, Gouroull," he said. "Last chance, creature. My masters like the chaos and horror you bring to Earth. Back away and find a different route to making babies."

The mild words were belied by the serpentine hiss that accompanied each syllable.

Gouroull stepped forward, his hands raised up. A subsonic rumble emerged from his chest, though whether this was a growl or a laugh was impossible to discern. In the spare light, he resembled a beast more than a man.

Whateley hissed and leaped forward, his massive mitts seeking Gouroull's neck. His oversized jaws clicked and clacked as the enormous teeth snapped. A spattering of foam spittle formed across his lips and his dark eyes grew wider, the pale sclera vanishing leaving only a pair of massive black bottomless pits in its place.

Their hands slapped together, locking in place and halting their mutual progress. Their terrible teeth sliced through the air, never moving close enough to wound the other. The pair strained, their inhuman sinews bunched and thrusting forward against an equally overwhelming force.

Time passed as the standoff continued, neither moving so much as an inch. The only sound echoing through the chamber were the wheezing gasps of Hezekiah Whateley as he gulped air greedily. A thin sheen of sweat slowly streaked his face as he stared into the horrific yellow eyes of Frankenstein's creation.

Then, a slight twitch across his arms and shoulders sent a clear signal that his inhuman muscles approached their limit. A harsh metallic taste entered his mouth and his vision grew cloudy as each passing moment a wave of weariness overwhelmed his massive, mighty, frame. With infinitesimal slowness, his hands and arms bent, and his demonic jaw drooped, appearing incapable of slicing through the space between his and Gouroull's exposed throats.

Feeling pain as his massive fingers slowly splintered, Hezekiah reared up and roared, clamping down on Gouroull's gray-skinned arm. His overwhelming incisors froze in place, penetration of the inhuman flesh occurring so slowly, it almost felt like a test of tensile strength. Which was stronger—the inhuman flesh of the monster birthed from mad science, or the dagger-shaped teeth of the half-human creature, whose origins made him a hidden predator amidst humanity?

Just as Whateley thought he felt the marble-like texture of the epidermis begin yielding, Gouroull attacked. With the speed of a striking adder, Frankenstein's Monster thrust his huge head forward. His massive incisors clamped down of the side of Hezekiah Whateley's exposed neck. The latter gasped in pain as the flesh tore away and his inhuman strength dissipated from his body. He felt his hands and wrists snap under Gouroull's fierce grasp, before dropping to the stone floor with a low moan.

Gouroull spat out the foul flesh of his enemy and turned away. Checking the bizarre stone that lay in his pouch, he retraced his steps. One piece completed, two more left according to the old man and his unseen master.

CHAPTER XV

"Why are we here?" Fatimah asked as she took a dainty bite from her squab.

Her eyes widened at the rich, gentle taste as well as the tender flesh of the game bird.

"You like?" Faisal asked, savoring the same dish. "The Café de la Paix's meat dishes are unsurpassed by any other restaurant in this city. The last time I was here, Oscar Wilde, the English writer, swore the gold figure on the top of the nearby opera house was an angel."

Fatimah smiled slightly and rolled her eyes.

"And people wondered why the prophet warned us against wine!"

Faisal shrugged. "I have a strong belief that Mister Wilde was a victim of a different plant. However, having read the man's wonderful prose, it could well have been his imagination. A remarkable, if overly flamboyant personality."

"You are avoiding my question. Why are we here? The protectors of the faith requested our aid in holding off the djinn from beyond the stars, as well as Iblis and his minions. Yet, instead of action, we've traveled to Paris and ate a leisurely luncheon at this café. Did you surrender to the forces of evil?"

"Never," Faisal replied, placing down his fork, "however, I do know that heading into a battle without knowledge is like trying to grasp two melons in one hand. A foolish impossibility."

"Another quote from your ancestor, the sailor?" Fatimah asked, smiling with good humor.

"Probably," Faisal replied, smiling in return. "He was apparently filled with such aphorisms. However, I shall answer with precise detail rather than making you ask a third time. We are here because we await an Austrian nobleman. His family both embrace and battle evil, having done so for centuries. He is one of the undecayed ones and may hold knowledge we do not hold. Ah, here he is now."

Rising, Faisal towered over the newcomer, a man of medium height with blond hair and olive skin. He possessed deep blue eyes and was handsome in an unconventional manner. His clothes appeared expensive, yet dusty and worn with constant use.

"Good afternoon," the man said in heavily accented Arabic. "Forgive me if I am late. I found myself enraptured by a mistranslated Bridewall passage of *Unaussprechlichen Kulten* in comparison to a recently discovered German edition. I am Maximilian Karnstein and I believe you are Sheikh Faisal Hashim Haji Sabbah. I apologize if I do not know your name, Mademoiselle."

"Fatimah," she replied, favoring the unaffected man with a brief smile.

Usually she found herself ignored by European males—viewed as a servant or some other less savory profession. Finding a man who addressed her directly was a pleasant surprise.

Karnstein clicked his heels, bowed, sat and ordered the squab from a passing waiter.

"I apologize for my poor Arabic. I do find it is preferable to speak in a tongue—even one I am weak in, unfamiliar to others nearby. This will prevent their overhearing something… shall we say, distressing?"

"You speak well enough," Faisal waved a hand. "Your accent is terrible, but understandable. You read the prophesies I included in my wire?"

Karnstein nodded slowly, frowning.

"I did read them, though interpretation of such sibyls is a difficult task. The wrong choice could irrevocably spell the doom of all. However, I do agree with your supposition as to the first part. I believe your enemy seek the horrific artifact some call the Shining Trapezohedron. I thought that this item turned up in an Egyptian expedition fifty or more years past. However, I did find a passage in *Unaussprechlichen Kulten* that suggested there were three such relics hidden throughout the world. Based on that information, I believe your supposition of the lost unnamed city in ancient Sumer is valid."

"A terrible object," Fatimah murmured her eyes distant.

Karnstein nodded and started eating his food without pause.

"Decidedly so, Miss Fatimah. My great-grandmother would spit and hold up the sign against evil if it was mentioned in her presence."

Fatimah smiled and leaned against the table, interested.

"Spitting? I have never heard of a European noblewoman behaving in such a manner. They usually behave with so much decorum it becomes weary spending time in their presence."

Snorting and rolling his eyes, Karnstein replied: "My great-grandmother was a Neapolitan woman who was also one of the few female swordmasters in European history. She never gave a damn about conventions and my great-grandfather cared even less. He was a soldier and warrior, who fought monsters and evil sorcerers his whole life."

Fatimah nodded. "That explains much. In any event, what of the rest of the prophesy?"

Frowning and looking down, Karnstein replied: "I believe, though I cannot be sure, that the second stanza may refer to the relic known as the Skull of Sobek. But I am not sure such an object exists, except as a legend."

"Sobek? The crocodile god of the ancient Egyptians?" Faisal asked, surprised.

"Not quite," Fatimah said. "Sobek was, according to ancient tales, the second greatest priest-king of ancient Stygia. After the terrible Thoth-Amon died battling his greatest foe, Sobek, his closest rival, took control of Stygia. He performed terrible rites and, some say, commanded a legion of demons as his army. After his death, his few remaining followers took his skull and covered the bones in gold and jewels. Followers of the dark gods say that, if you use the skull in a dark summonsing, the ways between worlds open and allow transference. A dangerous device."

"That is," Karnstein said, eyes widening, "a great deal more information than I have on the article. I confess I only know that one of my distant ancestors from the Spanish branch of the family, Baroness Millarca Karnstein, used that artifact as a means of turning herself into a vampire witch. My great-grandfather was unsure if that was true, but he and my great-grandmother did destroy the vampire and her coven of lovers. He never suggested whether the article was real, or a delusion by a mad monster."

"It is quite real," Fatimah said and looked to Faisal, "though I cannot say who possesses the skull today."

Faisal nodded. "I may have a means of tracing this Skull of Sobek. Are there any precautions we should make before handling such a dark artifact?"

Karnstein reached into an inside pocket of his jacket and slid a slip of paper across to the pair.

"This is all the information I have. As to the third stanza, I find twenty-six real and legendary items that may fit the stated oration. Shall I send a wire to the usual location or should I narrow the list down?"

Faisal rose and waved his visitor back to his seat.

"Yes, please, and do finish your meal. The bill is covered and we must be going."

After a brief exchange of farewells, Faisal led Fatimah down the street, their stride fast as they headed towards their waiting carriage.

As they climbed inside, Fatimah paused and asked, "Oh, I forgot, I had a question. What exactly is a squab? A small French game bird of some type?"

Faisal chuckled and said, "After a fashion. A squab is a pigeon."

Fatimah gazed out the coach window at the flocks of dirty birds flapping over the rooftops and monuments.

Her face grew serious as she said, "I will make you pay for this indignity. You shall not know where, and shall learn of it only after it is too late."

"Why? Did you not enjoy the wonderful light flavor?" Faisal said, smiling at her black look.

"Revenge shall be sweet," Fatimah whispered and stared out as a mass of such birds sat on the head and shoulders of a massive statue. "Revenge..."

CHAPTER XVI

Hezekiah Whateley sat up, gasping in pain as the flesh knitted back together across his throat. The bones in his hands and wrists crackled and popped back into position, the pain rising and soon falling as his body self-healed at an extraordinary rate. He had not been this damaged since battling the Dagon followers who had tried establishing one of their evil temples in Seattle.

Closing his eyes, Whateley allowed his body a chance to repair much of the damage. As a being only partially human, he understood his unique body better than anyone else. He required a few hours of rest and calm, then he could decide his next step as protector of the Earth against the monsters from beyond the stars.

Lying back, he closed his eyes and wondered which of his clan could take up the fight, should he fall against the terrifying Gouroull. His cousin Martha's daughter, Sarah Osborn, was shaping up nicely, but she needed time and learning. The creatures in the air and earth lay in wait, only rumbling periodically as they waited for their chance of returning from their long sleep.

Residents of the semi-forgotten Massachusetts town of Dunwich, the Whateleys were among the oldest inhabitants of New England. Their clan was large and disparate, dividing into two distinct factions—decayed and undecayed. The undecayed branch resembled small town farmers and tradesmen, and behaved in a conservative, God-fearing, church-attending, manner. Their children often attended universities such as Harvard, Arkham, and Vassar, and said students rarely returned to the squalid backward village of Dunwich.

The decayed Whateleys were quite different from their nearly cosmopolitan cousins. They resided in crumbling farm houses, the dilapidation of which gave them an air of ancient neglect and poverty-stricken filth. Their farmlands appeared barren and weed-covered, and the few cattle or sheep they owned looked scrawny and sickly. The air about these farms possessed odors reminiscent of dark, ancient molds, of the type often found in early and forgotten burial grounds.

Worse of all were the half-mad residents of these dark, grotesque dwellings. They were a furtive, hunched people, with forbidding, fallen, faces and dark, blank eyes that repelled the few visitors. There was a solitary quality to all residents of Dunwich, and the decayed Whateleys repelled the most bumptious peddlers or inquisitive onlookers.

Hezekiah Whateley's family were members of the decayed branch, though this was secretly by choice. Like many members of their clan, his family possessed much ancient wisdom and lore that they never shared with the outside world. Possessing one of the few copies of the *Black Bible*, an iron-bound tome supposedly dictated by Satan himself to a mad German monk, they had arrived in the American colonies and continued their demonic worship in secret. At the same time, other members of the Whateleys had chosen a different path, a darker one, based in even more antediluvian beliefs.

The members of Hezekiah's immediate family were worshippers of demons, specifically the master of the Fallen, Satan. Whether they called him Satan, Lucifer, Old Nick, Scratch, the Lightbringer, the Dark Angel, the Dragon, or the Adversary, they all dedicated their lives and souls to his service and had done so since before they had arrived on this continent. Their ancient dedication to evil was unknown to the world, and even the greatest witch hunters of Europe and the American colonies had no knowledge of these most fanatical servants of darkness.

The reason for this was simple; they did not behave in the manner expected from devil-worshipers. They attended church weekly, and rarely made sacrifices of animals or humans in the name of their evil master. The reason for this behavior, compared to that of the other followers of the Dark Angel, was that they were charged with a singular mission. According to legend, the first Whateley had discovered a means of summonsing Satan and dedicated his soul to darkness eternal. Not from a desire for power, wealth, or extended life, but out of fear for his life and that of all life upon the Earth.

My brother, Isaac Whateley, read from that terrible book, Giles Whateley had written in his journal.

This was his first entry, one that every member of the family read when they were capable of comprehension.

He changed, speaking of terrible evil, unnatural things. About monsters that once lived upon the Earth before humans or animals. Were they the giants of the Bible? I do not know, but Isaac is not the same any more. He is secretive, and I am going to watch him carefully. God bless.

Many entries followed as Giles shadowed his brother closely, and even read passages from the "terrible book" when possible. Then, the passages in the diary changed abruptly, their handwriting becoming shaky and almost illegible.

Read a segment of the terrible book. The words still haunt me today and I cannot sleep. The beings Isaac worships are monsters that even the Church does not understand. Whom can I tell? He is kin, and you do not turn your back on family, even when they go wrong. But I cannot get those words out of my mind, they ring in my ears. I write them here in hopes that they leave me some peace.

After a small gap, these words appeared in an even shakier hand:

Man rules now where They ruled once; They shall soon rule where man rules now. After summer is winter, after winter summer. They wait, patient and potent, for here shall They reign again.

The next entry was the one which all members of Hezekiah's family had studied with the greatest attention. Giles had written in his least legible hand:

Isaac is lost to me and all of us. He met with the Black Man, the messenger of these beings he calls gods. He signed his name in the book of Azathoth and vanished. He is back, but he is not my brother no more.

The remainder of the story was told only in whispers between family members. Hezekiah's father, Samuel, had explained the story in simple terms, just as they cut their fingers and dropped their blood on the points of the pentagram.

"Giles knew that the Church could not do anything to stop Isaac. So he used old magic and called up Lucifer. He offered his soul and that of his family and their families if he granted him enough power to stop his brother and the rest of the Whateleys that had gone over to the Old Ones. That's why you are bigger and stronger than any of your kin and neighbors, boy. Old Nick has our souls, but he makes us strong enough to keep that what lives in the air and earth from finding their way back."

Samuel then lay his son down and started a chant in a bastardized form of Latin.

Now, Hezekiah felt his body slowly healing as he lay still. Reaching up, he smeared some of his drying blood on his fingers and quickly inscribed a few simple mystic symbols on the smooth stone floor. His eyes remained firmly shut; he could draw these characters from memory. They were a simple charm invoking the name of the Great President of Hell, the demon Barbas.

"Barbas, mighty master of thirty-six legions, heal me faster. I give you my blood as offering and promise you lives as a gift," Hezekiah whispered in that same bizarre, ancient form of Latin.

He heard a sound in his ears that was equal parts laughter and the roaring of a great, enormous lion. A scent of brimstone filled the air and a sharp pain lanced through his enormous body. As the stabbing pains slowly drifted away, so did the weakness and agonies of today's battle. Barbas's gift, which would cost Hezekiah at least one innocent life murdered in the name of the demon, removed all pain and signs of the injuries inflicted by the monster called Gouroull.

Standing up, Hezekiah Whateley then quickly departed the underground chamber. He required aid and advice, and that meant great distances had to be travelled in a very short time...

CHAPTER XVII

Faisal led Fatimah deep beneath the city of Paris, traveling through ancient tunnels and disused sewers which possessed stenches that brought tears to their eyes. The trip took hours and was taxing, even for their well-trained bodies.

Finally, they arrived at a massive tarnished steel door with the English alphabet and a set of numbers from 1-10 engraved upon its surface. A long, thin black metal rod was welded into the right side of the door, about four feet from the floor.

"I will explain momentarily," Faisal said, typing a series of numbers and letters for thirty seconds. "In the name of Allah, the Gracious, the Merciful…"

He then sighed, grasped the handle and pulled. The door swung outward, lightly and silently, and Faisal added:

"Glory to Allah!"

He pulled open a portal over four feet thick and waved Fatimah inside a dark, silent chamber. Another handle lay within and he pulled the door shut a moment later.

A loud clamping sound filled the air and light slowly rose, revealing a square room, about twenty feet-wide with a low ceiling and walls covered in metal. The ceiling and floor looked like someone had chipped them from the very bedrock of the Earth. Set in the floor was a dark metal ring, covered with odd shapes and characters.

"Where are we?" Fatimah asked, examining the walls closely. "Why are we here? And where is the escape tunnel?"

"To answer your last question: the way we came in. There are no secret doors or tunnels. This room is not a refuge, but a location for performing the most dangerous mystic experiments. If they fail in any way, the city above our heads shall remain safe."

Faisal dropped to his knees. He studied the metal circle closely, cleaning the surface gently with a silk handkerchief.

"You built this here? I thought you spent little time in Europe," Fatimah said, running a hand along the ceiling.

"No," Faisal replied, not looking up. "One of my teachers, a genius named Erik, once resided in Paris. He built this for his own work, and granted me permission to use this chamber in case I ever needed it."

"Which brings us to my second question. Why are we here?" she asked, raising a careful sculpted eyebrow.

"We require information and some favors are owed to me by creatures of earth, air, fire, and water. I plan to call a *djinn* and ask for his aid, but one does not summons such spirits without taking precautions."

Faisal stripped off his jacket, tie, and button-down shirt. He dropped each piece of clothing in a small pile by the door, only pausing remove a small thin knife from a pocket.

Naked from the waist down, Faisal was an impressive figure to behold. Possessing carefully sculpted sinews that bunched and rippled with each motion, he resembled an artist's view of human physical achievement. The only marring factor that took away from the display were gray lines of scar tissue across his back, chest and stomach.

"Is there some other path we could take?" Fatimah said, shaking her head. "Confronting the children of Iblis imperils your very soul. When I was young, one of my uncles sought power and a chance to become the Old Man of the Mountain. He made a bargain with a *jinni*, who then killed the man's entire family before fleeing into the desert."

"This is the fastest means of discovering what we seek. Unlike your uncle, I already have bargains in place. This spirit will be grateful to discharge a small piece."

"Did not the Prophet say, 'To overcome evil with good is good, to resist evil by evil is evil'?" Fatimah replied, smiling.

"Yes," Faisal said, smiling back. "However, *djinns* and other spirits do have a chance for redemption. My using them is good in the name of good. Now, we begin. Do not speak to the *djinn*. They live for mischief and silence is the best weapon against their favorite tricks."

He said a few words, waved his blade across the circle and tossed an object in the same area. A large puff of smoke filled the air, and a flame emerged a second later. It grew, danced about, and slowly took on a human shape.

A moment later, a lovely woman with cinnamon-colored skin stepped from the flames. She was tall, at least a few inches over six feet, with long, straight, copper-colored hair that fell to her waist and a buxom figure barely hidden under a few wisps of silk and gauze. Her triangular face was beautiful, yet odd to the eyes, resembling a painting of an attractive woman rather than a living, breathing human.

Her inhumanity became more apparent when viewing her eyes. They held no corneas or irises, but dancing yellow and blue flames that only vanished when she slowly batted her huge eyelashes.

"Faisal Hashim Haji Sabbah and his pet attack dog," the *djinn* said, her voice a musical trilling sound. "Why do you contact me this day? If it is to demand service, you shall owe me, little prince. Not since Suliman the Great has a human held the power required to command me."

Faisal rolled his eyes. "You owe me five favors, Firdaws, you who are also known as the fire-dancer. You shall provide me with information, and thus one service shall be discharged."

Firdaws laughed and clapped her petite hands.

"Only information? Agreed! So let it be written, so let it be done. Ask me, O mortal prince, and as your servant, I shall obey."

"You would lie or give me a tricky answer if I gave you an opportunity, queen of liars," Faisal stated, smiling back. "What I need of you is the exact location of the dreaded Skull of Sobek. This shall include the country and precise map coordinates according to modern sources. You shall also tell me of any guardians of the relic, and all other necessary information for the immediate acquisition of said artifact. And you shall do so only in a tongue that the Lady Fatimah and I understand perfectly."

The *djinn* stared at Faisal for a full minute and then shook her head.

"I dislike dealing with you, Faisal Hashim Haji Sabbah. You are far too clever. Your foolish pet would ask me how to get the skull and I would reply truthfully, 'with your hands,' and vanish laughing. You give me too few options. I shall provide your service without trickery. But just remember, sand flea, one day I shall owe you nothing, and then I shall visit upon you torments so terrible that they shall drive you mad."

“Understood,” Faisal replied, listening careful at the minutiae he had just requested.

At the end, after he had memorized each item of information, he bowed low. By the time he straightened, Firdaws had vanished without a sound.

“You must explain to me one day how you earned such a creature’s favor,” Fatimah said, tossing Faisal his clothing. “Right now, we must retrace our steps and proceed to the air ship. Unless our enemies possess an advanced form of travel, we should reach our intended destination in a very short time.”

“My fear is that the monsters from beyond the stars are utilizing precisely such a method for their own, as yet unknown agent,” Faisal said.

He threw on his shirt and reopened the huge steel door.

CHAPTER XVIII

Gouroull walked day and night through the desert, unmoved by the heat and cold. He never viewed a solitary form of life, not even a high-flying vulture or a skittering rat. The world he traveled through was one of sand, rocks, extreme heat and periods of frighteningly frigid winds under a star-covered sky.

A land devoid of humanity, animals, and vegetation did not torment the mind of Frankenstein's creation. This was the universe he preferred, one in which he and his kind were the only life remaining upon the Earth. Gouroull did not require food, water, or companionship with the living beings that populated the globe. Nor did he desire to emulate their ways, such as the creation of arts and sciences. Once, in the past, he had sought understanding of the beauty mankind created or experienced in life. Victor had written of his own upbringing in such matters, causing great fury in Gouroull's cold, unfeeling chest. The words remained in his mind, more as a reminder of what humanity wished for in their dreary existence.

No human being could have passed a happier childhood than myself, Victor wrote. *My parents were possessed by the very spirit of kindness and indulgence. We felt that they were not the tyrants to rule our lot according to their caprice, but the agents and creators of all the many delights which we enjoyed. When I mingled with other families I distinctly discerned how peculiarly fortunate my lot was, and gratitude assisted the development of filial love.*

Gouroull knew this soppy, sentimental nonsense was a barefaced lie. Victor Frankenstein claimed he resided in a perfect home with a lovely fiancée, devoted parents, and an idyllic existence; yet, the truth was that he hated these surroundings and sought to become something greater than the son of a minor member of the nobility. Victor's madness was such that he sought far more than simply studying the natural world, but bending it to his whims. He sought power over all life, wished to become a tyrannical creator with his scientific progeny sending prayers of thanks and devotion for his benevolent creation.

Unfortunately for him, his creation desired no such relationship. All Gouroull wished was a mate of his own, and distance from his creator and his insane desires. Alas, he received neither and, believing that Victor possessed the secrets to ending his life, had fled in the face of the man's understandable vendetta.

Therefore, a world in which every square inch of its surface was as devoid of life as this desert, was heaven to Gouroull. Victor Frankenstein's only successful experiment survived and thrived in this dead land, and someday, so would his mate.

Stepping over a large rock, Gouroull climbed a tall dune and strode down the other side. He entered a deep bowl, a valley surrounded by high sand mounds on all sides. As he approached the far end of this huge trough, the sand shifted and rose up, forming a small cloud that lingered in the air for a moment.

Gouroull stopped a few feet away, unsurprised that a second, larger, explosion of the fine powder flew into the air.

"Ahhh," said a voice as the sand flew up into the air once again, "a human—yet, not a human. You are something unique, and that is interesting. I would know your name, traveler. The fall removed much of my knowledge and I am diminished. Who are you?"

"Gouroull," the Monster replied.

He sensed something beneath the sands, a massive being hidden deep below and holding immense power within its buried frame. As one neither living, undead, or dead, Gouroull viewed the world differently from others. Sights, such as that of the titanic entity buried deep in the Earth, were clear to his unique eyes.

"Is that a name or a classification? No matter. Gouroull, you trek through these wastes as one on a quest. What is it that you seek? Power? No, you are far greater than the miserable rulers of this tiny planet. Knowledge? If that is your goal, I can tell you secrets that would raise you beyond your sundry existence. You shall never age another day and gain the power to control any living being. That is within my dwindling power. I am Azazel and I was once known as a watcher. I stood above all life and observed in the name of He Who Creates All. All that, and more, could be yours, if you so seek."

Azazel's gentle voice floated from every direction in the bowl.

"No," Gouroull said, though he stood still.

He sensed that this hidden power was not finished sending offers upward.

"Neither knowledge, nor power? Beauty, then? My life force is such that I can remake you, provide you with beauty to such a degree that poets and artists shall consider you the perfect subject. Even in death, you shall remain the embodiment of perfection among humans."

"No," Gouroull repeated, still waiting and watching.

A coughing laugh emerged from the sands.

"Neither power, knowledge, nor beauty? My, you are unique! Then, again, I recognized that when you first stepped on these very sands leagues ago. You were not made by my father, but by the hands of one of the misbegotten bacteria that call themselves rulers of this world. No matter, all that exists hold a price in their heart. As I said, I am Azazel. Have you heard of me?"

"No," Gouroull said a third time.

Azazel laughed lightly, the dust rising and falling for a moment.

"I was what humans call an angel. I spread sin across the globe and spoiled the perfection of Father's creation. As punishment, he sent the Healer, the archangel named Raphael, and his might bound me and cast me into this dark prison. I was once like Raphael, though my powers came from knowledge. Though diminished, I still hold much that could further both your desires and my revenge upon all life. Tell me your wishes and I shall grant them. Your desires; my freedom. For only a mortal can release me from my prison of sand and darkness."

"Not mortal," Gouroull replied, walking past the sand mist.

He started climbing the dunes, each of his steps kicking more sand back into the long trough.

"Wait! Find me a human and I shall reward you both! I am Azazel, Scapegoat of the Desert. I can reward you!" Azazel cried, his inhuman voice plaintive and abject in his plea.

Gouroull looked back and smiled, his grin malicious and terrible as he said a fourth time:

"No."

"Abandon me, monster, and I shall one day rise up and spend an eternity teaching you the meaning of the word pain. The sufferings felt by the inhabitants of Sod-om shall be as a kindness compared to that which you feel by my hands. I, Azazel, so swear by the sands that imprison my body! Obey me!"

A long, heavy stream of sand filled the trough, causing waves of dust to sail through the air.

"You may try," Gouroull replied, moving on, not looking back.

CHAPTER XIX

Hezekiah Whateley hated travel, despising every step of the process. The sheer volume of hassles was terrible, and the time wasted was even worse. He preferred his simple home in Dunwich where his view of Sentinel Hill's standing stones reminded him of his true duty every day. There, back home, he could sit in his chair on his porch, the cattle softly munching their grass, and feel content.

Not so when he left home. Then, he dealt with the odd people around the world, the ones that lived in apartments high in the sky, or spent their days seated behind small desks, scribbling on paper for money. Their ignorance of the world would be contemptible, if it were not so pathetic. Humans, these days, were merely cattle, only concerned with food and sex. They could all be consumed tomorrow, and they would not understand that their foolishness and stupidity had caused their downfall.

Pulling a large hunting knife from his pocket, Hezekiah Whateley sighed. The worst part of travel was the cost. The idiotic people and the odd food were easy enough to ignore, if one tried. But the cost—that was always the troublesome part, requiring more work for him.

Slicing off his right hand, he bit back a yelp of pain and quickly wrapped the stump, staunching the spurting sprays of blood. Picking up the fallen flesh, he whispered a quick plea to his dark master and tossed the cool extremity into the sky. The hand never returned, though the wind grew in speed, emerging from every direction.

Closing his eyes and clutching his right arm, Whateley felt dozens of unseen hands grasp his body. With a jolt, the hands ripped him off the ground, sending him sailing and spiraling through the air. They held him in place, though he felt the winds buffeting his face and body.

He never completely comprehended this form of travel—was he really flying through the sky? Or in-between the worlds? Being tossed through the air by elementals? All he knew was that his master, Satan the Adversary, also held the title of "Prince of the Air." Traveling great distance was possible and quite quick. The cost was a body part each time, though happily they grew back within days. Still, the pain and ever-changing location of the demanded flesh added to Hezekiah's dislike of travel.

The movement slowed, and he willed himself into stillness, knowing that tensing his body made this moment worse. That was when the hands vanished, and he felt his body plummeting down to the Earth.

He landed two second later, crashing onto a heavy snow bank. The landing was relatively soft, far preferable to the time these invisible imps had tossed him onto a cobbled street in Berlin.

Opening his eyes and sitting up, Hezekiah Whateley found himself laying in long field, a small cottage visible in the distance. A light flared in one window of the dwelling, and a shadow crossed the illumination, momentarily plunging the location back into a gloomy stillness.

The shadow moved several seconds later, and a low creak broke the relative silence. A stern voice called out:

"Whoever or whatever you are, you might as well come inside. Your arrival is known to me, and I shall do as you desire. Come on, do not waste time!"

Rising, Whateley crunched through the unbroken snow, arriving at the cottage minutes later. The dwelling was a two-story building, square in shape, and made from brick and wood. The door stood open; a yellow flame flickered and danced in a hearth and an old, grimy chimney fired plumes of white and gray smoke into the air, quickly vanishing in the starless sky.

"Are you going to stand there like a peddler on my threshold? Get inside, or leave. I don't care which, but make a choice," a harsh, Welsh-accented voice spat out from within.

Walking inside, Hezekiah glanced around, unsurprised by the simple, handmade wooden furniture and complete lack of adornments across the plain walls. The dwelling was not unlike his own home in Dunwich, though smaller and older. A wooden door lay at the far end of the cottage, closed, without any source of light or movement visible.

The woman seated near the fire was small, just below five feet tall, with iron gray hair and a face creased with deep, disapproving lines. She wore a simple gray dress made from a thick, unidentifiable cloth, and a heavy, stained brown shawl lay across her thin, bony, shoulders. However, it was her eyes that Whateley found most interesting. They were almost too big for her thin face, enormous lamp-like orbs that pierced the huge man and made him feel small under her powerful gaze.

"Sit down, sit down," she said, waving him towards a heavy, unpadded chair across the room, near the fire. "Warm yourself, young man. The Devil's messengers whispered to me that you needed some help. You do know that it is a very foolish mistake… right? Our master does not like helping his servants overmuch. He chooses us for our abilities and our independence. Dependency is for the weak and the foolish."

"I understand," Whateley replied, settling into the chair.

The wooden frame groaned beneath his huge frame, but did not bend.

"I never requested aid in the past," he added. "But I have no choice, if I am meant to fulfill my mission in the name of Lucifer, master of the Earth."

They both performed the sign of the cross in reverse, and the elderly woman nodded. Her head bobbed like a clucking chicken as she spoke:

"All hail to the master of earth and air. Very well, Hezekiah Whateley of Dunwich. Speak—and if the children of the dark so agree, I shall answer in their name."

Whateley was startled when she spoke his name in such a casual manner, surprised that this witch held such knowledge.

"Before I begin, who are you?"

"My name? It would mean nothing to you and I shall not say it. Names hold power, Hezekiah Whateley. Giving yours away like flinging pennies into a well is foolish behavior. But you may call me Siani Bwt. The locals call me by the fanciful title of the 'Witch of Dolwyn Moor.' Make of that as you will; it shall serve you little. I provide small curses and the likes for the farmers, and ask even less in return. I am a fearful necessity in their minds. If they knew the truth, I would flee for my life, or end up at the end of a hangman's rope. Now, introductions are done, and we should waste more time. What do you want, child of Dunwich? No man requests the aid of the dwellers of the dark without cause."

"I faced a true monster in the name of the Adversary," Whateley explained, his features downcast. "Science created that fiend, who calls himself Gouroull. He's a product of the mind of a madman… neither living, nor dead—not even undead, like some of the Devil's followers. Those, I destroyed when they threw themselves across my path. But this Gouroull, he beat me down, tore out my throat with his teeth—even worse than mine. I survived only because I'm not entirely human, but I can't beat him in a brawl. He is too strong; his skin is too tough for my teeth. I want to do my master's bidding, but I got beat too easily."

"So, you came asking for help from Satan himself? You have courage, boy. Not much sense, but courage. Will you give whatever Scratch demands? Whatever cost he invokes?"

She cackled long and loud.

"Yes," Whateley replied, looking up, his yellow face flushing with growing fury.

The witch nodded once and said:

"So be it, on your head it shall be. The offer is made, follow me, and we shall see how great Lucifer views such a bargain."

With that, she stood up and headed towards the door.

Pausing to take a gnarled, brown wood walking stick, the Witch of Dolwyn Moor glanced back and added:

"Follow me and remember, this was your choice."

Hezekiah Whateley rose and followed the woman who called herself Siani Bwt out the door and into the moonless, starless night. A feeling of trepidation filled his mind and body as they circled around a small hill and into a darkness so deep that it seemed as if a vast black curtain had fallen across the land and sky.

Trust in Lucifer, Whateley thought. *He only lies to those who are not devoted to his demands. Old Nick is true to his real servants, his hands against the creatures beyond the stars and the fools what follow the false prophets from Above.*

Repeating that mantra several times in his mind, Hezekiah Whateley visibly relaxed. He stayed close behind the Witch, knowing one misstep would result in his losing his way… or possibly his life.

CHAPTER XX

Fatimah steered the airship, riding the air currents in a manner that resembled a fish swimming through a fast-moving body of water. She never felt like a bird in this vast tube of metal, cloth, and gas. This was unfortunate since, as a child, she had often dreamed of flying like a hawk above her mountain home. Escape from that microcosm of pain and death was her one desire for many years—the only means of preventing herself from falling into the living dead state that afflicted all members of the Order of Assassins.

Though no longer located in the fortress known as Alamut Castle, the Assassins had not abandoned their tradition of dwelling on the summit of a mighty mountain. After fleeing the vast Mongol hordes, one of their numbers had discovered a series of caves within Mount Ararat. According to legend, the creators of these caves had used them as a means of releasing animals throughout the world after some kind of worldwide disaster.

True or not, the caves of Ararat allowed the Assassins a new chance at imposing their will upon the world. Abandoning the Nizari sect of Islam, they devoted their people to an older, darker worship, one that bore little resemblance to the words written in the Koran. Gone were the lessons of decency and respect, replaced by subservience to an unspeakably terrible power.

"The followers of the Prophet failed our people," the Old Man of the Mountain intoned each night before their small meal. "They speak the words from Allah, but do not understand His ways. Allah was not the God of the Christians or the Hebrews. He came from beyond the stars, from the dark center of ultimate chaos. There, he speaks wisdom as his slaves play lovely pipes day and night. He is the Great One, the Demon Sultan, the true God of All. We serve him, not the foolish Caliphs, Imams and Emirs. He is the true master, Azathoth the Creator, and the Masked Messenger is his prophet. Daily, we spread the word and thousands join us in our crusade. Soon comes the day we shall rule all the Earth in the name of the Demon Sultan."

By day, every member of the Assassins toiled at meaningless tasks meant to break all thoughts of rebellion. One day, one might spend his day bailing out a pool of water with a bucket that possessed no bottom. On another day, the same initiate might have to count every crack in a tunnel that led for miles through the mountain. The masters of the murderous coven assigned thousands of such futile chores, all meant as a means of destruction of one's spirit.

A great granddaughter of the master of the order, Fatimah had learned the hidden paths in the mountain, the secret tunnels and doors unknown to most members. After rest periods, she had explored these labyrinthian twists and turns that lay hidden in their secret base. She, unlike the few freethinkers before her, never disturbed anything she discovered. Nor did she draw any maps, fearful that others might discover her violation of the community's commandments.

Over the course of five years, Fatimah had slowly explored her mountain home, soon knowing all its secrets almost as well as the Old Man himself. This minor rebellion had allowed her to keep the one object lost to all members before they hit puberty—her soul. She toiled besides the others and trained as a killer acquiring all the fearful skills of the assassin. Yet, when freed from duty, she learned more of their world, the infamous Mount Ararat, and the lies told daily by the Old Man of the Mountain and his circle of blood-soaked killers.

The first was that no one called the assassins "beloved warriors of God," except possibly as an ironic taunt. The world considered them either a tale told to frighten children into obedience, or an example of the worst blasphemies. The secret archives, a dusty chamber rarely opened by the leaders of the order, held documents written both before and after their move to this massive mountain. Words such as "infidels," "worshipers of Iblis," and "foul murderers" filled the pages, growing worse as the words of the Masked Messenger began to eclipse the Koran.

That was terrible enough, but the worst was yet to come. Shortly before Fatimah's dedication ceremony, her induction as a full member of the Order of Assassins, she discovered the secret chapel used for such initiations. It was a small round room, roughly cut from the rocks of the mountain, and possessing no adornments, save a small series of tapers placed in niches along the walls.

From her location above the group, peeking through a barely visible vent, Fatimah had viewed in horror as her great grandfather pushed her cousin Ibram onto the cold stone floor and clapped his hands once. The masters and mistress of the order each stepped forward, silently disrobing and surrounding the prone Ibram.

What followed was, for lack of a better term, an orgy. The acts by the various members were violent and worthy of the worst excesses of the Dionysian cults of ancient days. Before Fatimah's disgusted and horrified eyes, she viewed behavior in complete contravention of all the teachings impressed upon her since birth.

Ibram lay face down, uninvolved except as a table by some members. When all, including the bloated, ulcerous Old Man of the Mountain, had finished, they stepped away and supplicated themselves around Ibram's unmoving body. Then they chanted one word, a terrible sound that terrified Fatimah to her very soul.

"Nyarlathotep, Nyarlathotep. Nyarlathotep," they moaned and whispered.

The word echoed through the small chapel, lingering far longer in the air than any normal name.

Then the so-called Masked Messenger had appeared. There was no fanfare, no chariots from Heaven or rays of light. One minute earlier, the space by Ibram's head had stood empty; a moment later, a tall, lean figure in heavy yellow robes occupied that same space.

The Masked Messenger stood slightly taller than anyone present, though this was merely an impression provided upon first glance. He seemed of human height at first, but on second sight, was revealed to be a titanic creature whose true proportions were unimaginable to a mortal mind. Then, in a third look, the Masked Messenger seemed tiny and inoffensive.

His robes were bright yellow, with highly detailed archaic script along the edges. They appeared thick and flowing, but he gave the impression of emaciation to the point of being corpse-like. A long, multicolored mask covered his narrow head, a riot of color that almost pulsed and flowed as it hid all features beneath. A fluttery pair of pale hands peeked out from beneath the robes, their spider-like motions disquieting to the eyes.

"Well, hello to you all. Another initiate joining my master's coterie. How pleasant," a venomous voice had hissed.

"Hail to thee, Masked Messenger," the Old Man of the Mountain had intoned. It is a pleasure to have you among us once again."

He sounded dignified, not as a man covered in blood and seminal fluid, his face pressed against the stone floor.

The Masked Messenger chuckled, a sound that caused Fatimah to both wince and shrink back. If sadism had a sound, it was the laugh of this demonic being from beyond the stars. Never had she heard such evil in a pure form, and she prayed she never would again.

"Yes, I suppose it is," the Masked Messenger replied. "Even I enjoy my own presence since I have such a delightful personality."

"You do, great Dweller in Darkness," the Old Man of the Mountain cried. "We rejoice each time you grace us with your mighty presence. All hail to thee!"

"Hail! Hail! Hail!" the other shouted, their voices muffled by the floor.

"Yes, yes," the Masked Messenger said, sighing and sounding bored. "Let us proceed. Ibram, son of Abdul, do you swear yourself into the service of the Demon Sultan, He Who is Called Chaos, Azathoth?"

"I do so swear," Ibram said, his voice shaky and as muffled as the others.

"What of your other guest?" the Masked Messenger asked, still chuckling.

He pointed a long finger that looked as if it possessed extra knuckles, upwards towards Fatimah.

"What other guest, Black Pharaoh?" the Old Man of the Mountain asked.

"Lift your head, idiotic child," the terrible being asked, cackling as Fatimah quickly slithered backwards.

"Blasphemers!" the Old Man of the Mountain shrieked.

His voice soon chorused with others as some tried climbing the sheer walls, while others ran into the hallway. None bothered to dress; they only paused long enough to grab their knives before chasing the unseen intruder.

Fatimah crawled backwards until she reached a sheer passage upward, one that, based on the dust, had not been used in decades. Halfway up, she dropped down another passage and climbed up another abandoned tunnel. Her strength was rapidly diminishing; the speedy climbs with few handholds taxed her to the limit. Now, as she climbed higher, a growing chill exuded from the stone walls of Mount Ararat. She felt her limbs growing heavier, and her hands bled from the jagged edges of the rocks.

Just as she reached the top, her bloody hands slipped on the stones. She hung over a sheer drop over two hundred feet high by her fingertips alone. Slowly, inexorably, her fingers slid towards the edge, inch by inch as she weakened. Her mind screamed in terror and her feet sought some small hold that could add some stability to her position. All to no avail.

Fatimah closed her eyes, preparing for death, when a pair of powerful hands encircled her wrists. With a quick tug, she found herself lifted and deposited on the ledge, her back to the wall.

"You?" she asked, her mouth dropping.

The Masked Messenger laughed and nodded his huge, hidden head.

"Quite right, little Fatimah, daughter of Hassan. I saved your life. Now, if you follow this tunnel through many spirals downward, you shall find the ancient mechanism that empowers your order's tunnels. If you pull down the red handle, your people shall soon lose all air. You can then escape by the same tunnel. You shall find a bag of gold and diamonds as well as cold weather clothing near the doorway. Take them and go."

"Why? Why would you rescue me?" Fatimah asked.

The terrible being held up on oversized finger.

"Allow me to answer your questions with one statement. I do all you ask because it amuses me. The Order of Assassins no longer interest me, though you do—for now. I set you free on your own path because the results shall make me laugh."

"Even if," Fatimah said, pausing for a breath and continuing, "I oppose you and your followers."

The Masked Messenger leaned closer, his breath rank and smelling of corruption and other unmentionable sickly scents.

"*Especially* if you battle everyone I assist, little girl. My plans are measured by the lives of suns. Your microscopic resistance provides a tiny respite from the dullness that is life upon this planet. Do as you will, Fatimah, soon to be the last of the true line of Assassins. You shall be like a gnat screaming threats at the stars. Despite that, I think I shall find you amusing."

Fatimah backed away, following the terrible creature's instructions to the letter. She felt a tiny moment of trepidation as her hand gripped the red lever. Then she recalled the evil words spoken by the Old Man of the Mountain, his lifetime of lies, and their evil plans for the world. She pulled the lever and left Mount Ararat, only returning five years later to reclaim the records of the evil order.

Today, Fatimah used her skills in the name of good. This modern age possessed few as skilled as her in the art of the Assassin. Guns and bombs had robbed men of their desire for stealth and martial perfection. Faisal was one of the few she respected—but he was far from an average man.

"Two hours until we land if this tailwind continues," she said, reading the barometer.

"I think it shall," Faisal replied, looking up from the scroll he had been studying for hours. "We shall eat after we land and proceed to the target. If necessary, we shall not leave any survivors."

"If the Skull of Sobek is in the hands of someone knowledgeable," Fatimah said, glancing in his direction, "killing all involved is the best choice. That foul item corrupts all who mistakenly try and utilize its foul power."

CHAPTER XXI

The rocky outcroppings preventing visibility extended more than five feet. Gouroull scrambled up the hillocks and cliffs with an ease that even the greatest climbers in the mountains of Nepal would have found uncanny. His powerful fingers and sharp eyes discovered routes that mountain goats might have considered daunting.

A sensation of wrongness overcame him and he knew then that his destination was nearby. A coldness had overtaken the land and air, as if he had left the desert mountain region of the east and suddenly stood in the cold wastes of the north. The scents in the air slowly vanished, replaced by one that was unidentifiable, thanks to its uniqueness. It was at once sweetly cloying and overwhelming, filled with a decaying corruption that reminded one of an abattoir. There was a sense of an oily stickiness, an almost viscous quality that felt quite at odds with the desert breeze.

Climbing higher, Frankenstein's creation spotted the gate a short distance ahead. A rounded arch made from a dark stone lay within a deep gully, a rift cut through the rocks by some ancient stream or spring, long dried up, leaving behind a runnel within the hills that served no true purpose any longer.

The arch was approximately nine feet high and made from a stone so dark it was hard to examine its surface. Barely visible runes and etchings were traced across its surface, though none grew in visibility when a slight glimmer of sunlight chased across the stone.

As Gouroull approached, a rune flashed briefly, an odd symbol he had viewed in the past. The inscription resembled a denuded leaf, a simple line with five smaller branches, three on one side, and two on the other. For some reason, this pulsing symbol exuded a sense of wrongness as powerful as that of the stone monolith.

Gouroull stepped through the portal and into an abyssal darkness, a true and absolute void lacking even a trace of light. Moving forward, his feet sunk into an unstable ground that shifted and changed shape with each stride. One moment, he felt as if he strode through some vast marsh, the next a gentle grassy sward. The reality in which he travelled appeared ever shifting, altering from moment to moment, without any apparent reason. Yet, always taking place in this deep, unending void.

After a period, for time was impossible to quantify in this dark fissure in the universe, voices rose. At first, the words were mere traces of sounds, whispers of jangling letters and odd, inhuman pronunciations that emerged from various directions.

"*Y'AI'NG'NGAH THRODOG IA IA IA...*" the voices moaned and shrieked ceaselessly.

Other sounds, equally odd and inhuman, drifted in Gouroull's direction.

Then, a period of silence followed, a hush as deep as the surrounding blackness. A normal human would have gone mad in this realm where the only noise was the beating of one's heart, the rushing of one's blood, and the gasping of one's lungs as they gulped down the spare, frigid air.

Not so with Gouroull. His alien mind rejected this world, viewing this brief prison as merely another step in his long journey. Since the day of his rising, for "birth" was an incorrect term for a creature created from corpses and raised by science, he had always walked through a universe of darkness. This was both a reality and a metaphor, one that even Victor Frankenstein could never comprehend. The twisted scientist possessed a slight inkling of the horror he had unleashed, though he attributed it to his own black soul.

Who shall conceive the horrors of my secret toil as I dabbled among the unhallowed damps of the grave or tortured the living animal to animate the lifeless clay? Victor had written in the same diary that still lingered in Gouroull's mind.

What the madman never conceived was that his creation, an Adam to Victor's Heavenly Father, had been conceived in evil and horror. Upon rising from his stony bed, the Monster had spoken his name, the one word that forever told his tale.

"Gouroull…" he had whispered to the horror-struck Frankenstein.

The mad scientist had fled, possibly understanding the demonic plague he had just unleashed upon an unsuspecting Earth.

"Gouroull," suddenly crooned a soft voice, the sound emerging from every direction and none, "Gouroull, destroyer of dreams, alive and dead, human in shape, yet not human. You were such a terrible disappointment to poor Victor Frankenstein..."

Each time after the silence, the gentle, soothing, malicious voice emerged. Its words possessed the poisonous beauty of a brightly-colored, venomous reptile. There was no warmth in the mocking tones, just an overwhelming pleasure in the infliction of pain.

"Victor imagined himself as a scientific God, the designer of a new and perfect race, a race of angelic beings that would one day raise humanity to the heights of the Divine. Instead, the poor man created a new fallen angel, a Luciferian horror who wishes the destruction of the living in favor of his new, infernal breed. Poor man, poor sad man…"

Laughter lurked beneath the surface of each vile statement. But Gouroull continued onward, unmoved by the insults. He had heard worse from his crazed creator and accepted all the words with amusement and relish.

"Would you like to be beautiful, Gouroull? I know you received such an offer from the wild ass of the desert, and rejected it in a manner unseen since the time of the Philistine kings. But I, I would ask nothing in return, not a single thing. Say yes, and I shall remake your outer appearance only. I shall ignore your mind, for that is what makes you so interesting. Say yes, and you shall resemble Adonis, the human version of perfection. Women shall battle for your attention, men shall fall at your feet and beg for your guidance. Not since the days when humans worshipped their gods would there be such desire and allegiance to a single being. Humanity would raise temples in your name, since you would be their living god. All you must do is say yes to me, Gouroull. Say yes…"

The voice practically pled as Gouroull strode forward through this endless tunnel of nothingness.

"No," Gouroull said, his response stated without any pause between the speaker and his reply.

A long, sad sigh emerged from the void, the despair nearly a physical force assailing him.

"How very sad," the voice whispered. "I had such hopes for you. The malice within your mind is simply delightful. Gazing into what the humans call your soul is like staring into a mirror. You delight in your malicious assaults upon the inhabitants of Earth. Your treatment of

Ingrid Schleger was delightful. She still resides in a madhouse, shrieking and moaning, her insanity the result of your actions. Truly a work of art, a masterpiece few upon your tiny world are capable of creating. One last chance, ugly one. Say yes, and you shall have all you desire."

This time, Gouroull did not even speak. He merely continued onward. Though a malicious glint appeared in his eyes upon learning that Ingrid Schleger still lived. Perhaps, she was the exception and might have borne him a child?

Gouroull decided he might look for her in the future.

CHAPTER XXII

The path the Witch of Dolwyn Moor had chosen was a rough one, full of briars, brambles and hidden tree roots that sent Hezekiah Whateley stumbling in her wake. By the time they emerged from the forest, he was a bloody mess. His clothes were in tatters, small cuts covered his arms, legs and torso, and he felt thorns stuck in his hair. A slow trickle of blood dribbled down the side of his head, just behind his right ear.

"The woods do not like your scent, child of Dunwich," she remarked, not looking behind her as she led him through a wider, gentler path. "You are in opposition to the very nature of the wild."

"I would burn it all down and lay down pastures for cows and chickens," Whateley spat back.

He shot a venomous look behind him, wishing he possessed the power of controlling fires. The woods at his rear seemed to shift before his eyes, an untamed malevolence emanating from the trees and the hidden inhabitants.

"Ridiculous," the Witch spat back. "Evil for evil's sake is like screaming into the wind—a waste of time. Did you secretly devote your time to breaking the Christians' Seven deadly sins?"

"Yes, of course."

The Witch barked a quick laugh and shook her wooly head.

"You sell your soul to Satan, the Dark Prince, and ensure your eternal damnation. However, you waste your time on this planet in proving you are evil by behaving badly. Think, child! Your place in the Pit is assured. Not even the Creator of all life can change that destiny, unless you yourself make a concerted effort. Why act like a naughty child, demanding attention?"

Whateley felt heat run up his face and neck. "It is the duty for all followers of the Great Dragon to reject all that the Creator holds as good and wonderful. We soldiers of Satan are at war with the light! Kindness and decency are the actions of the weak!"

The Witch of Dolwyn Moor stopped, turned around and favored him with a yellow-toothed smile. She looked the very picture of the evil witch of legend, the subject of dozens of folk tales around the world.

"Is that how you see yourself, Hezekiah Whateley? A warrior fighting for darkness in the name of the Adversary?" she asked, studying him.

Straightening to his full, impressive height, he cried: "Of course!"

"Ha!" the Witch chortled. "Ha! The greatest lies are that we tell ourselves, young man. Ha!"

Flushing again, Whateley narrowed his dark eyes. "Explain yourself, witch," he said.

Still snorting with laughter, the Witch of Dolwyn Moor did not reply for a minute or two. She then looked grave and stopped smiling.

"Very well, child of Dunwich, you did ask and I shall tell. You are not a soldier or a warrior fighting in Lucifer's unholy name. You are naught but a prison guard."

"That is not true!" Whateley snarled back, baring his terrible fangs.

"Spare me your displays of temper. I shall not die by your hands, nor shall you even touch my body. Mine are the words from the darkest pit, the truth you never allowed yourself to admit. You and your ancestors sold your souls to Satan as a means of protecting the Earth from the alien beings your incestuous kin worship. The Whateleys that gaze into the angles of the planes and see the secret city beneath the poles are your assignment. You stop them from opening the gates and killing the ones from the air and earth. That is not being a warrior, Hezekiah Whateley, that is being a prison guard."

Her voice was almost gentle as she laid out the details of his life.

"If that is so," Whateley asked slowly after a period of silent reflection, "then why am I here? Why did I get told to go to Kowloon, and then to a lost city in the middle of a desert?"

"Because," she replied with a fluttering hand, "you are the best tool the master had at hand. In a way, you may consider this a promotion, a raise in rank. If you succeed in stopping the many-angled ones and their servant, the science monster called Gouroull, you shall become a true agent of the circles of Hell. But if you fail… Well, there shall be no life left on this world in any event. Should the Sleeping One beneath the waves rise up, or the Black Goat unleash her young upon the world, humanity is doomed. Should the way be opened for the Lurker at the Threshold, Earth shall become barren, and our master's war upon them at the dawn of time would have been for nothing."

Whateley frowned, but then he nodded his head and replied: "Very well."

The Witch cackled again. "You accept the truth? Good, good, I feared you would waste time wailing like a spoiled child. We shall continue on our path—a short walk now. Stay close. Lose me and you shall find yourself in the wild. The Great One known as the Wind Walker would hunt you down like a wolf after a rabbit."

Hezekiah Whateley shuddered, having heard the legend of the ethereal being called the Wind Walker by some people. According to his family records, the native tribes referred to this evil deity as the Wendigo, and their legends had frightened him as a child. One of the first members of the family in the New World was said to have violated the monster's lands and been torn apart by its massive claws and fangs.

"Fear of the Wild Walker is natural and normal," The Witch said, her voice gentler than before. "That one, like the Haunter of the Dark, possess characteristics closer to that of humanity. That makes them all the more terrible than the Black Goat or the Lurker. Those gods are impossible for a human mind to comprehend. Their scale is cosmic, and we are like dust mites before them. We fear them the same way we do the sun and the stars, but we never fully understand them."

"Yes, I can see that," Whateley said. "Some members of my kin, the ones that follow those… things… believe Satan and the Dark Man are the same being."

Nodding, the Witch continued forward on her path.

"That has been bandied about since the days of Ivar the Boneless. They play the same game, tempting and leading mortals into evil. Who can say which came first?"

She paused a moment and continued:

"The difference is, our master, the Lightbringer, adheres to his agreements precisely. In a sense, he was the first lawyer. He writes his pacts so that he always gets the better part of the deal, and uses that against anyone who chooses his patronage."

"What of the Dark Man?" Hezekiah asked, interested in this topic despite his trepidations. "He has as many names as Lucifer; some are even the same as the ones used by the Fallen One."

"I should think the similarity and the many names are on purpose, don't you, young man? From what I have read of the God of a Thousand Names—for that is the best name for such a being—he is more capricious than our master. Some days, like the Devil, he seeks souls and respects his agreements. Other days, he leads the foolish to their own ends and laughs, as they die feeling betrayed. Few do well after entering a deal with either. No matter, we are here."

They stepped into a second clearing, this one wider and precisely circular in shape. A same ring of four standing stones, each about four feet high, lay in the center. None of the stones possessed so much as a flake of snow across their gray, granite surface. No symbols appeared etched onto their surfaces, nor was there any evidence or recent use. There was a powerful stillness about the circle, as if all sound ceased within an invisible barrier erected just before the standing stones.

The Witch of Dolwyn Moor walked into the circle, standing next to one stone. She rummaged in a pouch under her shawl. She looked up at Hezekiah Whateley, her eyes softening slightly as she examined him from toe to crown.

"This is your last chance," she stated as her hand removed a dark object from the pouch. "You may walk away now and use what resources you possess fighting the enemy's avatar. If you agree and remain here, your fate is forever out of your hands."

Whateley shook his head quickly. He remembered the cold lips and needle sharp fangs that had ripped his throat… the agonizing snap of his hands, fingers, and wrists under the terrible power of the monster called

Gouroull. Allowing such a creature the freedom to roam the world was as horrific as the antediluvian nightmares his cousin Joseph worshipped in secret. He made his choice; he would not back away from this decision.

"You must say the words out loud," the Witch said, her voice hardening. "Do you, Hezekiah Whateley, child of Dunwich, servant of the Devil, beg your master for power enough to destroy Gouroull?"

"Yes," Whateley breathed the word, more an exhalation than a response.

The Witch raised an object in her tiny, withered hand; it was a black triangle that radiated an air of ancient evil.

A few seconds later, Whateley's eyes adjusted and he viewed the item clearly. The Witch of Dolwyn Moor held a small knife, a blade created from a chipped piece of flint. It resembled one of the Stone Age tools often seen in museums, created by the early humans known as cave dwellers. But unlike those tools, this device exuded an ethereal coldness that felt almost demonic. Whateley could almost imagine the spirit of a hungry demon residing within the tiny, ancient knife, eagerly slicing through human flesh and consuming the precious, crimson *vitae*.

"The pact," the Witch stated, "is sealed. Extend your hand."

Whateley offered his one remaining hand and was unsurprised as the elderly evil woman sliced his palm open to the bone in one swift stroke. The area turned numb instantly, a coldness spreading over his limb as the blood bubbled to the surface of the incision. The Witch, still holding his hand in a tight grip, led him over to each stone. Dipping her finger in his blood, she drew a reverse crucifix on the northern stone, a pentagram with a five pointed star on the east, an odd symbol known as a leviathan cross on the south, and a trident on the west.

"Stand in the center," she ordered.

When he stood where she indicated, hands at her side, she crooned:

"*Ô toi, le plus savant et le plus beau des Anges, Dieu trahi par le sort et privé de louanges, Ô Satan, prends pitié de ma longue misère…*"

Lights slowly rose from each of the stone, blinding Hezekiah Whateley. He shaded his eyes as the fires leaped up just outside the circle, and the scent of Sulphur and brimstone filled the air. The gates between Earth and Hell opened, and he knew that the master of the Pit was on his way…

CHAPTER XXIII

Gouroull emerged from the plutonian tunnel into a land of sunshine, flowers and merrily tweeting birds. The air felt crisp and sweet, and the cobblestone walk beneath his feet clean of weeds or debris. Tall, lovely trees rose up the sky, their branches full of brightly-colored leaves and tiny, fluffy squirrels and chipmunks. Low, well-coiffed bushes lined the walk and all seemed at peace throughout this small corner of the world.

After a second glance, an oddity that crept in the mind caused a disquieting sensation. The shrubs appeared precisely the same size, the trees almost geometrically placed in a pattern, the animals well-fed, young, healthy and lacking visible predators.

Striding forward, Gouroull sensed the past presence of humans, a large group. The spoor was at least two hours-old and a tart tang of sweat lingered in the air. Frankenstein's creation released a low rumble from his chest, amused by these details and his own knowledge of humanity and the wild.

This location, for all its impressive beauty, was completely artificial. The uniformity of the vegetation, the gentle tweeting of the birds, all looked lovely. Lacking were the harsh caws of less attractive avian species, the buzzing of annoying insects-like flies, and the roughness of the cobblestone walk.

Gouroull deduced that a team of men toiled daily for the sole purpose of maintaining this false Eden. Frankenstein's monster felt a slight trace of amusement, but little else. He could destroy all he surveyed with ease, but there was no need for such labors. The humans that endured the hard work of maintaining this imitation of the natural world were setting themselves up for failure. Something would eventually spoil the beauty and lay waste to this lovely land and its joyful inhabitants. It would not take much—nature possessed millions of tools in the forms of weather, insects, predatory animals, and more. One or more would intrude upon this tiny universe and the transformation would commence.

That was enough for Gouroull—a fate amusing enough to prevent his sadistic inclinations from assaulting this artificial Eden. His only sorrow was that he would not be present when the creator of this paradise viewed its destruction by the metaphorical hands of Nature. Their reaction to the rejection of their plans would, no doubt, be volatile and amusing. There were times when events were a greater sadist than anything in the universe.

Emerging from the trees, Gouroull stepped into a long, manicured garden. The grass appeared precisely cut, with circular hedges too exactly round for natural surroundings. A huge marble fountain lay in the center, with a massive statue of Triton surrounded by frolic nymphs and leaping fishes. From the mouths of the fish emerged streams of sparkling, clear water, bubbling across the clean surface of the fountain.

The roof of a long, high mansion lay in the distance. Frankenstein's creation crossed the lawn and headed in that direction though a gap in the verges. A second garden lay beyond the hedges, Japanese in style. A Zen rock garden stood in its precise center, each pebble seemingly the same size, shape and color. The circular pattern of the stones appeared perfect, the result of planning rather than inner tranquility. A gentle brook bubbled near the rock garden with four circular posts bridging the sides, each also the same size, color and shape.

As before, Gouroull did not bother with acts of petty destruction; the obvious obsessive nature of the owner of these gardens did not require his malice. They would not, and could not, be satisfied with the labor that created such perfection. Something would be incorrect, a minute flaw that would render all the toil for naught. Humanity was, in many ways, far more destructive to themselves than any monster on Earth. Their inability to feel satisfaction led them to foolish wars, horrific crimes, terrible sadism, wanton destruction, and, most amusingly to Gouroull, his own creation.

For that was the true reason for his existence. Mad Victor had found the natural order of existence unsatisfactory; therefore he had chosen a path of denial and scientific insanity. He had ignored that even the very stars possessed limited lifespans, though that time was much greater than that of all living creatures on Earth. Unlike many, Victor had been successful in his ambition, though not in the manner he had expected. This was one of the few things about his creator that Gouroull found rather amusing.

Exiting the over-manicured Japanese Garden, Gouroull found himself into what appeared to be a Roman, or Greek, garden. The flat lawns came complete with statues of naked men wrestling and performing athletic activities, and lovely goddesses posing either seductively or in chaste manners, despite their nudity. This was followed by a long lawn and a falsely ancient stone wall and the ruin of a water wheel across a small brook. Fortunately, the house lay close now, though Gouroull did spot a hedge maze in the distance.

A set of heavy glass doors lay open and a short man with a round head full of wooly white hair, a bulbous nose, and a soft, fleshy face that looked wrinkle-free, stood there. He smiled broadly, his wide face shining in the bright sunlight as the massive monster approached in a cautious walk.

"I know you!" the man said in a deep, well-modulated voice. "You are Gouroull, Victor Frankenstein's creation. I am so very delighted to make your acquaintance. Do come in! I have much to show you, so much. I am absolutely fascinated by your story. Such a delight!"

The little man popped back inside, pushing the doors open wide for Gouroull. The Monster stepped inside, discovering himself in a long, wide room, lined with statues covered with worn, though well-cared-for, suits of armor. The one closest to the door was made from polished steel, a little over six feet in height, with veins of gold chasing along the chest, arms and legs. The armor was shaped like a barrel and made from a very light, thin metal that probably could not protect the wearer from any object heavier than a small stone.

"That is the armor of none other than King Henry the Eighth, towards the end of his life," the little man explained. "He was so very fat, and gout-ridden, the armor could not be made as true protection. Next to that is his armor from his younger days, when he was young, vigorous, and strong. The thickness and craftsmanship of his original armor made him resemble an ancient knight of legend. I placed this pair here because they are so perfect, just like this samurai armor once worn by the Regent of that country, Toyotomi Hideyoshi. Such exquisite workmanship is it not?"

The man led Gouroull deeper into the house, through a room filled with swords. He threw open another set of doors, stopped, turned, and smiled again.

"Oh, do forgive me, I am quite remiss in my excitement. My dear, departed mama always said my enthusiasms caused me to forget my manners. My name is Percy Queely, and I am one of the most renowned collectors of unusual objects. I only seek the best and most perfect specimens in every area I find interesting. I possess mansions full of wonderful items, and I sell those which exhibit any flaws. Is that not what all men seek? Now, I must show you my special, unique wing of this house…"

Leading Gouroull through a room full of statues, followed by one filled exclusively from floor to ceiling with books of various age and sizes, he stopped before a heavy steel door. Pulling a key from around his neck, Percy unlocked the massive lock, revealing a set of steps made from white marble. Leading Frankenstein's Monster down, he paused and locked the door behind him with the same massive metal key.

The steps proved well-lit, with crafted gas lights softly glowing every few paces. The unadorned walls appeared free of dust or grime. At the bottom lay a second door held in place by a heavy wooden bolt. Percy struggled to slide the bar aside. This revealed a corridor with multiple doorways, each possessing metal doors like the one at the top of the stairs.

A second look revealed these doors held slides built into the top and bottom; the bottom slide was square in shape and about eighteen inches high and wide; the top slide was only a few inches in length and width, allowing a view within the individual room. No sounds emerged from the corridor, or any of the rooms, with only Percy's excited breathing breaking the silence.

Percy slid aside the top slide in the first door and waved Gouroull closer.

"This was my first collectible from the occult universe. I discovered her in the Antilles, a slave of a weird little man who called himself a witch doctor. Pierre was his name and he took this lady from an evil sorcerer that had raised her from the dead."

Gouroull glanced through the slide, seeing a small chamber about eight feet long and four wide. A tall woman stood in the center of the room, her long blond hair falling across her shoulders and back like tangled wheat-colored tendrils. Her triangular face held a harsh beauty, with thin pale lips and large bright eyes. Even though they appeared lovely at first glance, they held no light of reasoning. They were unfeeling agate chips, the inhuman orbs of a puppet or a waxwork figure instead of a human female.

"In the Antilles, they call these men and women, zombies. They are bewitched and have no will or life left in them. This one was named Antoinette, and she was the daughter of a wealthy man. She made the mistake of stealing the fiancé of a very vindictive lady, who paid a magician to make little Antoinette into a zombie. Since she cannot be cured, I bought her and keep her here as my perfect living dead lady."

Percy walked to the next door, sliding it open.

"This one was rather harder for me to collect," he explained, grinning up at Gouroull.

The room within was longer and wider, with a circular pool filled with murky black water filling its center. A green scaly head with large black eyes peeked out of the water, vanishing silently a moment later.

"Some say my fish-man is a member of a lost race," Percy explained as he snapped the slide shut. "One both ancient and possessing very advanced science in their undersea homes. I am not sure, but I found this one in South America. I see intelligence in his terrible eyes. I am not sure if he qualifies as an occult exhibit, but I think he might."

Turning and facing Gouroull, his smile grew wider.

"Perhaps *occult* is the incorrect term. I think of my collections as the truly unusual. I have a soul clone of the legendary Count Dracula in the next cell. This version moved to China in hopes of starting a cult of vampire worshippers and feeding on the inhabitants of a village. A very sad excuse for a vampire, though not the worst. There is an elderly soul clone who hopes to one day retire and reside in a city, performing stage illusions..."

He paused briefly and considered for a moment.

"Let us leave the vampires alone, even a little light might upset their delicate skin. I think I shall also forego showing you my two werewolves. One is dependent on the moon and is merely a man who complains a great deal. The other transforms into a creature more wolf than man when hungry or enraged. The former will try and talk endlessly, and the latter would fly into a rage and create a terrible mess. I am lacking a living-dead Egyptian mummy, though I possess the case of an Aztec one that is still unrevived in a locked store room. I also lack a Serbian cat-woman. They are not extinct, but are often circumspect, since they are just as vulnerable to an injury as a large feline. No, I think I shall show you why I was so delighted seeing you this day..."

Percy strode to the end of the hall and pulled open another door, waving Gouroull closer. Frankenstein's creation stepped into the doorway and stared inside, his luminous yellow eyes absorbing every detail.

The room was about forty feet long and equally wide, and appeared dimly lit. A long gray stone slab lay on the left side of the chamber, at least ten feet long, and gave the impression of great age and weight. Along the other walls were a series of metal machines, all dusty and possessing the carefully tooled details of handmade objects.

Gouroull turned and looked down at the little man, his lower lip drooping and revealing a pair of serrated fangs. The harsh gleam in his amber orbs grew darker and his massive hands opened and closed slowly.

"Ahhh," Percy said, almost moaning the sound, "I see you recognize the accoutrements I purchased them from Kanderley—the place you where slept for years. It's the remaining equipment from Victor Frankenstein's laboratory. Aren't they exquisite? Every device designed and built by the infamous Frankenstein himself, the maddest genius who ever walked the Earth. I discovered the truth of your existence and determined I had to collect everything about you, Gouroull. I must find more of your master's notes for my book collections. However, that can wait until later. Today, I add you to my menagerie, Gouroull, a monster built from the pieces of the dead and given the spark of life by the hands of a madman!"

Just behind Percy and Gouroull, a door opened and tall, stiff-backed man in a black suit, white shirt and tie stepped into view. He raised a long bronze colored gun with an extended barrel and a long, wide canister by the handle. Without wasting a motion, he squeezed the oversized trigger, sending a dart deep into Gouroull's chest.

He fired a second time, sending another dart into Frankenstein's monster's massive shoulder.

Gouroull pulled out the darts, dropping the metal shards to the stone floor. He silently snarled at the little man and his companion, his eyes narrowing with a menacing light.

Percy stepped back and clapped his hands with obvious delight.

"Well done, Frederick! The drug should take hold shortly. How long did it take to knock the fish-man unconscious?"

"Ten seconds, sir," Frederick intoned. "No more than five for the others in your collection."

Percy smiled up at Gouroull.

"That sensation you are feeling is from a rare drug synthesized by a tribe of hairless pygmies from the Anderman Islands," he explained. "They are expert hunters who cook the most delicious *bak bon dzhow*. This drug is their favorite method of trapping their prey. As a gift, after your first year as part of my collection, I shall provide you with some *bak bon dzhow*. In any event, I thank you for joining my collection and ask that you do not damage yourself when you fall unconscious."

Gouroull's eyes drooped as the little man spoke...

CHAPTER XXIV

"A hedge maze? Why are westerners continually obsessed with such ridiculous puzzles?" Fatimah asked as she walked along the top of the verges, leading Faisal through the huge puzzle.

"There are many studies on the subject, since mazes have been a means of secrecy since the dawn of time," Faisal replied, turning the direction she indicated. "King Minos of Crete possessed a legendary one that supposedly contained the monstrous Minotaur."

"Mythical sophistry," Fatimah snorted, shaking her head.

She wore a silk scarlet hijab and a tight matching pair of khaki pants and blouse. A long dagger lay sheathed in her belt, which also held many small pouches.

"Not at all," Faisal replied, shaking his head. "Minos was a true man, and he did hide a cannibalistic creature in his maze. I doubt the monster was anything so simplistic as a half-man, half-bull, as the Greeks suggested. More likely it was a being so horrific that it was easier for them to spin the tale of the minotaur. However, the study of mazes is not as odd as you may believe. An entire segment of higher mathematics, called topology, was invented by Leonhard Euler with respect to mazes and other unique objects."

"More nonsense. Name another use for these wealthy people's amusement," Fatimah challenged, leaping over Faisal's head and landing on the hedge.

"I have three. First, several European kings, such as Francis the First of France and Louis the Fourteenth of the same country, used them as a means of conducting secret meetings. Less chances of being overheard in the center of one of these structures," Faisal said, changing direction as Fatimah found the proper route out of the maze.

"That sounds somewhat wise," Fatimah conceded, "Two more?"

"Yes," Faisal said, "Second, the ancient people used them as a means of hiding inheritances or important papers before they died. In ancient China, this was a practice for the wealthy when they possessed pernicious relatives. One of the legendary statesmen, a magistrate named Dee, famously solved such a puzzle. As to the third, the ancient Egyptians built several mazes, most notably one in the city now known as Faiyum. I believe it both protected the tombs and possessed holy symbolism related to the crocodile."

"Very well," Fatimah said, pointing to the left. "There is the exit. But I still fail to see why we must traverse this ridiculous structure."

"The methods of entry were two-fold," explained Faisal. "First, a large lake possessing only one row boat. There is a terrible vulnerability in crossing unfamiliar water, especially in daylight. A well-trained rifle man could kill a full boat in seconds. A maze, while irritating, is less dangerous when you walk on the borders. Any thought the owner may have of surprising you is rendered quite difficult when you can see past the corners."

"How true, sire," Fatimah said, giving him a quick look.

Faisal slowed his pace, keeping the corner of his eye on Fatimah. Her calling him by some ridiculous royal title was their clue that danger was ahead.

"I do hope the owner of this dwelling is a reasonable man," he replied.

At the same time, he made a quick series of motions, a form of sign language only known to the lost Order of the Assassins. He had learned it from her shortly after they had met, having discovered it was an effective means of communicating secretly.

"We changed the language every twenty years," Fatimah had said as she taught him the various styles of unspoken speech she knew. "We did not wish complacency to overtake the Order's self-protection. The Old Man of the Mountain would randomly declare a month of silence, in which this was the only method of communication, other than writing in some obscure language."

"What do you see?" Faisal asked.

"Little," Fatimah sent back as she chattered away inconsequentially about wealthy people. "I see the bushes moving and I heard a clink of metal. Something awaits us."

"Then we shall pretend we do not know of their presence and head forward. I think you shall be their first target since you are exposed. Be careful."

Seconds later, Fatimah threw herself flat of the hedge top as a series of small objects buzzed past where she stood. The sound was like that of angry hornets intent on assaulting their enemy.

Quickly rolling aside and landing in a low crouch, Faisal also heard the buzzing sound as well as a light rattling of the bushes. A thin sliver of wood landed by his feet, and he examined the item without picking it up. He tilted his head left and right, and even leaned closer, waving a hand in front of the sliver and sniffing slowly.

"We may have stumbled into a trap," he finally signed. "This is a dart from a blowpipe. The poison on it is from the Andaman Islands. They are weapons used by the dreaded Tcho-Tcho tribe. They are worshippers of the many-angled ones and are as frightening a group of people as one is likely to ever experience."

"You did mention them in the past," Fatimah signed back. "Clever and completely evil. Perhaps we can use that against them this time."

"Agreed. Here is my plan," Faisal signed, adding, "Be careful of their swords. They are small, only slightly larger than a dagger; yet, they cut through even the strongest substance. Once, I observed one cut a bronze statue as easily as if it had been made of paper."

"Noted," Fatimah replied

She vanished from sight. Faisal waited, sitting on his haunches for a full ten minutes. He wore khaki jodhpurs, a soft white shirt, and a belt with even more pouches than Fatimah. Strapped to his waist was a curved sword, an ancient *kilij* once used by his ancestors in battle. The weapon, known as Aleadalat Aldamawia, or Bloody Justice, was said to have executed an evil wizard who summonsed demons as servants of an evil sultan.

Straightening, Faisal pulled a round ball from a pouch and moved a few feet forward. With an ululating cry, he leaped up and threw the ball in the direction of the darts. He then dropped to the soft ground and crawled forward, his movements swift, his passage nearly silent. He stopped a few feet later, about ten feet from the location he had just tossed the ball.

A soft sound like an exhalation occurred two seconds later and a stream of red smoke appeared in the air. Cries of fear and fury filled the air, followed by a stream of darts flooding the spot where Faisal had once stood.

Counting to five, he smiled as the wheezing hacks of coughs replaced the whistle of darts. That was the signal Faisal had hoped to hear, causing him to smile as he rose. Charging forward, he ran around a corner spotting five tiny men with livid red skin and absolutely no hair across their muscular bodies. Their eyes were an odd shade of orange, and each held a long blowpipe in their oversized hands. Across their proportionally broad backs rested silver swords, the blades sparkling brightly in the sunlight.

These were the Tcho-Tcho, a tribe reviled throughout Asia for their abominable actions towards outsiders. No story could exaggerate the evils done by these men. It was known that they resided in a series of ruined cities and worshipped ancient gods through bloody, frightening rites. Their favored diet was *bak bon dzhow*, which was a paste, made from human organs. Consequently, they viewed everyone as a possible meal.

Statements such as these were common through history. Similar claims had emerged regarding opposing tribes or countries—often mere propaganda used to justify wars and other ignominious actions. The tales of the Tcho-Tcho were received with amused disregard by outsiders when whispered by the natives. Civilized men and women sent ambassadors, and later scientists and anthropologists, for the purpose of dismissing the stories as political and racist fiction. Missions of high-minded people, starting with the Eastern Zhou of ancient China all the way through a party of anthropologists and medical doctors from Paris, London, and Boston two years prior, had trekked into the depths of the unplumbed forests of Asia.

The few that returned alive told tales that made the legends look gentle and mild. They spoke of terrible, frightening men whose bloody religious rituals rivaled the maddest tales of Gothic horror. The Tcho-Tcho seemed to possess a love of sadistic actions and a total disregard for the basic rules most societies use to survive and thrive.

Though Faisal preferred avoiding bloodshed, he had no such deference for the Tcho-Tcho. He believed, as he had learned from one of his teachers, that these men were not quite human, but a race separate and alien to mankind. This was not prejudice on his part, but empirical evidence based on a careful study of their biology and psychology. Under a microscope, all human blood looks essentially the same, despite the outward differences of the humans. Tcho-Tcho blood, on the other hand, resembled an odd chimerical compound of human and reptile *vitae*. The fluid was so odd, so clearly alien. That several famous medical journals had dismissed the discovery as a ludicrous hoax.

Faisal drew his blade in a smooth motion and sliced through the hand and neck of the closest tribesman. The others whirled his direction, reaching for the swords across their back, as *Aleadalat Aldamawia* slew a second Tcho-Tcho. The remaining three stepped forward, their tearing eyes narrowing when Fatimah dropped to their rear and killed two with a pair of swift swings from her dagger.

As the final one whirled, hearing the moan of his fellows, Faisal slashed him, removing his snarling, hairless head in one movement. The body dropped to the ground as a fountain of scarlet and black blood spilled out over the hedge. The plants touched by the blood crumpled and died from the foul Tcho-Tcho blood and a terrible scent filled the air.

"Do not touch the blood," Faisal said, disgusted by the inhuman, corrupt odor that wafted his direction. "The blood of a Tcho-Tcho is poison to the living."

Leaping over the tiny, bloody bodies, he pulled a cloth from his belt and cleaned his sword. Fatimah performed the same act, tossing the bloody fabric onto the bodies. Her eyes moved about the area, though nothing stirred despite their battle cries.

"They were not particular formidable, despite their reputation," she stated. "We killed five in less than ten seconds."

"That was the advance party," Faisal said.

He nodded towards the house and the hedge maze, and added: "I think they shall now take us far more seriously."

"Who are you discussing?" Fatimah asked, looking at the house and the maze, but not seeing anyone in either location.

That was when the doors of the house opened, and a flood of tiny, hairless men poured out of the glass doors. The verges shook as the tiny men popped out, each one bearing a small silver sword. Their sharp teeth snarled and gnashed, and they all screamed the same words in a dreadful demonic chant:

"*Zhar, Lloigor, Zhar, Lloigor, Zhar, Lloigor, Zhar, Lloigor*," they howled, their voices becoming one as they approached.

"No need for an answer," Fatimah said. "I see what you mean." She stood back to back with Faisal. "What is your plan?" she inquired.

"I am open to ideas," Faisal replied as the Tcho-Tcho moved closer, their tiny terrible knives in hand.

CHAPTER XXXV

The pain overwhelmed Hezekiah Whateley, his body feeling both aflame as well as shivering from a wind so icy that it froze the very air. He opened his mouth, intent on shrieking, but the agony rose and all that emerged from his cracked, swollen lips was a soft, wheezing whine. He fell to the frozen ground, his back sinking into the soft snow.

The Witch hovered above him, her face tinged with undisguised amusement.

"You looked surprised," she noted. "Did you truly believe you would gain power from the Dark One without sacrifice? Our master does not give gifts without recompense. Your suffering is His way of reminding you of your place."

That was when his muscles all cramped at the same time, sending fresh stabs of agony throughout his entire massive frame. Whateley moaned and shook as every tendon tightened and ripped. He tasted blood in his mouth and his vision swam as the pain heightened with slow regularity.

"Our Master, Lucifer," the Witch intoned, "First of the Fallen, Brightest Star in the Heavens, Prince of Lies, and Lord of Darkness, agrees to assist you in your mission. You are not sufficiently strong to face the one known as Gouroull. But you shall become his equal. Raising you above that is not possible. To do so would upset His plans for this world. You must succeed in the name of the Master of the Nine Circles of Hell, or else you shall receive an eternity of torments."

Hezekiah Whateley opened his mouth, wishing to both accept the bargain and beg for a release from the agony. But again, nothing emerged from his raw throat, not even the soft, pathetic creaking sound from earlier.

"No," the Witch of Dolwyn Moor said, placing her small hand over his mouth, "do not bother. You already made the offer, and I cannot end your suffering. Nor would I, were that in my power. If a servant asks his master for power, he should feel the torments of the damned as recompense. Charity is for the weak. The Devil's servants must never follow the path of that ilk."

Feeling a wave of fury fill his body, Whateley threw off part of the pain that still sought his to break his mind and body.

"Not…weak…" he whispered.

The Witch patted his face and cackled. "Of course, you are not, child of Dunwich. Had you been so, your death would have come on swift wings. The Angel of Death is brother to our master, and he collects the souls of His failures. Do you fully understand the trust the Dark Angel has placed in you?"

"No," Whateley groaned, fighting against the torture once again.

"He wishes your understanding," the Witch of Dolwyn Moor said. "I am but his vessel, so listen well. I cannot repeat any of the mysteries you will learn this night. If you try to write these words, He shall remove your eyes. If you try to speak these words, He shall remove your tongue. Do you comprehend? These are not human threats, like that of your brethren in Cornwall Coombe. Violate these mysteries, and the suffering you experience now shall be magnified and occur over a lifetime. He once kept a transgressor alive far beyond the lifespan of humanity, just so that she may suffer longer. Do you agree?"

"Yes," Whateley spat out, tired of the constant threats and tales of misery.

His agreement with the Devil, the true protector of the Earth, was inviolate.

"Do not grow angry at my warnings," the Witch spat back. "I state the words because men endlessly choose the foolish paths in life. By telling you the rules, our master prevents an eternity of insisting that you did not know your limitations. An English monarch once offered his soul to the Devil. The king sought a continuation of his bloodline on the throne for as long as there is an England. He was quite unhappy that this did not protect his royal neck from a headman's axe."

"I… under… stand…" Whateley mumbled, his vision cloudy.

His mouth filled with blood, and he spat it on the ground by his side.

"Very well," the Witch of Dolwyn Moor said. "Millions of years ago, before humanity was even a concept, the Outer Gods held sway over this world. Their children, known as the Elder Things, the Mi-Go and the Silurians, built great cities for their kind. Then, a great conflagration struck the Earth and those races weakened, many falling. The Mi-Go returned to their cities on Pluto and Yuggoth. The Elder Things fought a war with their own servants, and retreated to their caves. Some Silurians retreated into vaults to sleep through the ages; others stayed behind and degenerated into serpent-men or a reptile race known as the dragon-kings."

"This, I know," Whateley said, feeling his *vitae* leak from his nose and eyes.

Yet, he refused to scream in pain, rejecting the torturous agonies even as his vision grew weaker.

"Good," the Witch said. "Then, you save me time. A battle—in truth, a great war—occurred between the Outer Gods and the Host of angels. Great Lucifer stood by the side of His brother, Michael. The alien deities retreated, locking themselves away from our universe. The great betrayer in the Heavens raised our kind, humanity, as his greatest creation, above even the angels. A second war over this violation occurred, and our master's followers fell into perdition, and He took the name, Satan. Did you know that portion of the tale?"

"No," Whateley breathed, no longer seeing the elderly speaker.

The Witch cackled. "I thought not. Few know the truth of the Great War in Heaven. Even the ancient peoples that possessed some knowledge did not know of the Outer Gods. Even I, a vessel speaking for the Adversary, cannot comprehend its true meaning. However, our master shall grant you the merest glimmer of understanding. I shall not lie—this shall hurt you far more than the suffering you underwent this day..."

Her dry finger brushed across Hezekiah Whateley's head, a simple gentle gesture quite common among intimate friends. He heard her sigh, the sound full of regret, then she stepped away.

A metaphorical third eye opened on the spot the Witch had touched—an ethereal vessel Whateley felt. A bright light flooded through this unseen orb and he viewed the past, a time millions of years ago and unseen by the eyes of man. The Earth was still young, unspoiled, and vastly different from the world of his birth. A massive landmass existed, the unbroken Pangea, drifting in an ocean so great and mighty it dwarfed the land.

Then they came, the alien beings, the legendary Outer Gods, written about in such detail by the mad Arab Abdul Alhazred. Yet, seeing these deities, these primeval horrors whose shapes were beyond comprehension, Whateley's mind shattered, incapable of grasping the vast terrible magnitude of these… He could find no word that made sense for classification of that which he witnessed.

This memory of days so distant the human mind could not grasp the sheer amount of time passed destroyed a part of Hezekiah Whateley. This part of him was the human portion left in his mind and spirit, the essential part, untouched by the demoniac hand of Lucifer, the Fallen Angel and Master of the Nine Circles of Hell. In showing the truth of the universe, secrets not meant for humanity or any sentient being across our plane of existence, the Evil One had extinguished this spark remaining in His servant. What remained was a being less than human, yet more than a beast.

The shrieks, moans, and wails of Hezekiah Whateley slowly died away, as did the physical torments of the demonical transfiguration of his body. The huge man opened his eyes and rose, towering above the Witch of Dolwyn Moor.

"It is complete," Whateley said slowly, his voice lower and harsher than before. "We shall meet again, witch."

The Witch of Dolwyn Moor did not reply, but watched as the massive form vanished into the trees. Once the remade Hezekiah Whateley had vanished from view, she shuddered in disgust and horror. The memory of the yellow eyes and dead gray skin of the transformed man filled her with a loathing she had not thought possible in decades.

CHAPTER XXVI

Gouroull's massive head lolled for a moment and then he straightened. His huge hand plucked the darts from his body and he dropped them to the floor with a light clatter. He then smiled and snatched the shocked and frozen Percy up from the ground, holding the tiny man without effort. Then he smiled, his frightening fangs causing the wealthy collector to blanch with terror.

"Oh, dear Lord!" Percy whimpered as the blood drained from his face.

"Sir, sir! Get away!" Frederick screamed, firing the gun three more times and striking Gouroull's back with all three shots.

Frankenstein's lethal creation dropped Percy to the hard floor, the man's elaborate shirt tearing away with an audible ripping sound. He turned towards the charging butler and, with three quick strides, stood before him.

Frederick was a tall man, well over six feet in height, with broad shoulders, a narrow waist and a ramrod stiff bearing. His partially bald head gleamed in the gaslight and his stern, Puritanical face stared at the massive Gouroull with calm defiance.

Gouroull tore the gun from Frederick's powerful grasp, bending the weapon in half. He then dropped the metal device to the floor just as the huge servant removed a large knife from his inside jacket pocket. Without pausing, Frederick thrust upward, aiming the blow for beneath the ribs and towards his enemy's heart.

The huge palm of Frankenstein Monster caught Frederick's hand, the powerful grip encompassing from the fingers to the wrist. The bones beneath the skin's surface splintered into shards, reducing the extremity to little more than a sack of skin and blood. The long steel blade fell from Frederick's destroyed fist, and his mouth drooped open from shock.

The butler tried to scream, but Gouroull bit down on his exposed neck. A bubbling, liquid sigh fell from Frederick's bloody lips and he collapsed, dead before he hit the ground. A slowly growing puddle of scarlet *vitae* formed around his head, spreading across the clean floor.

""Frederick!" Percy shrieked as he pressed his hand over his mouth. "Why would you do such a thing? He was a good man, who helped me so much over the years. Why would you do such a thing, you monster? Why? Why, Why, Why?"

Gouroull gnashed his teeth and whispered back:

"Why not?'

Percy straightened himself to his full height, raising himself approximately to Gouroull's lower chest.

"You cannot escape, you horrible, ugly, creature! There is only one way out of my menagerie, and I am the sole holder!"

Gouroull raised his monstrously huge hand, the sausage-shaped figures, the expensive shirt still held loosely in his grip. He released the fabric allowing the cloth a gentle, silent drop to the floor. Gouroull then raised a small object up, a tiny piece of metal that glimmered in the light.

"My key! Give that back to me, you, you, you, freak!" Percy screeched, taking a step towards the massive monster.

He then stopped, his face falling upon a second look at Gouroull's enormous frame.

"Please," Percy said, his voice low. "I apologize for my insults… I am not a well man. I will not try to keep you in my collection. I will even give you anything you want. Would you like a Gutenberg Bible? I have three, including one that is complete. No? How about the remaining jewels from the treasure of Captain Kidd? Oh, I know! I have four of the silver denarii coins given to Judas Iscariot after he betrayed Jesus Christ!"

"The Skull of Sobek," Gouroull replied, his yellow eyes sparking with alien malice.

"That old thing? You can have it! It is in the next room," Percy said, his voice dropping conspiratorially. "I keep all my esoterica on one floor. I will show you."

Frankenstein's creation smiled wider, the sight of his horrific incisors frightening Percy anew. The tiny man took a step back, keeping far away from his foe.

Gouroull turned and reached out, placing the key in the nearest lock. With a gentle twist, the bolt slid free and the door opened several inches. With a quick step, he repeated the procedure at the next steel door, all the while staring Percy's direction. His amber eyes glinted with malicious glee as the realization of his actions reached the wealthy collector.

"No! No, stop! Stop!" Percy said, his voice rising in panic. "You don't know what you are doing! Stop! Help! Help!"

The doors all unlocked, Gouroull returned to the exit, leaving the menagerie. He glanced back, spotting a hairy snout nosing open one door, while a huge, green webbed hand pushed open one close to the exit.

Percy's screams cut off as Gouroull turned the corner and entered a huge chamber with a low ceiling and plain brick walls. A series of small platforms dotted the chamber, rectangular altars with glass coverings. Though as spotless as the rest of the mansion, a musty scent filled the air. The room resembled a museum exhibit that had fallen to disuse over time.

Each item possessed a carefully typed label, adding to the feeling that one had entered a private museum. Words like: *The Lesser Eye of Agamotto, Cohuleen druith, Ibisstick, Kusanagi-no-tsurugi* and *Darkhold* adorned the displays, with careful details of providence and location discovered. For all his disinterest in this area of study, Percy had treated each piece with apparent respect.

Gouroull spotted the skull a moment later, not far from the door, placed in an area one might reserve for some odd item of no real interest. The Skull of Sobek was a slightly oversized human cranium, covered in a thin layer of gold. Within the eye sockets lay a pair of matching rubies, their facets twinkling and sending crimson rainbows across the case. Instead of teeth, carefully sculpted jewels lay in pace. The ancient artist had carved these green, white, blue, and black stones into jagged, ragged, fangs. The effect was that of a demonical being, a monster lost in time, but remaining as a terrifying hobgoblin hidden in humanity's collective nightmares.

Striding before the case, Gouroull tossed the glass aside and picked up the skull. A pulse of cold energy ran up his titanic arm, seeking his mind. The power of the skull sought control of his inhuman body. Sobek, the master of dark magic from a time before recorded history, aroused from his ancient slumber. His powers, though weakened, were still greater than any who now resided on this world.

Sobek launched himself at Gouroull, his terrible eldritch energies flooding into the body of the monster…

and he screamed. Not in triumph, but in agony, as the horror that was Frankenstein's Monster burned the ancient wizard's black soul. With a howl of terror, Sobek returned to his skull, forcing himself into another period of oblivion.

A loud alarm bell suddenly shattered the silence and red lights flashed, strobing the long room and adding an odd visual to the array of strange articles.

Disinterested in the clamor, Gouroull tucked the skull into his pouch and walked away. Two items captured, one remaining.

CHAPTER XXVII

The Tcho-Tcho waved their silver swords in slow arcs over their inhuman heads as they chanted and approached Fatimah and Faisal. They appeared almost hypnotized by their call, their fervor growing as they surrounded the pair, their movements precisely in time with the terrible words they recited in the same guttural tongue.

"*Zhar, Lloigor, Zhar, Lloigor, Zhar, Lloigor, Zhar, Lloigor*," they called, moving ever closer.

"What are they saying? And what shall we do?" Fatimah asked, as she raised her blades in her strong hand.

"Those are the names of their gods, also called the Twin Obscenities," Faisal replied. "I only have one thought, but I doubt…"

His words were drowned out by a loud jangling from the nearby house. An alarm shook the windows and doors, and a pulsing red light flared through the building.

The Tcho-Tcho released a loud cry, a sound of horror and dismay, upon hearing the alarm. As one, they turned towards the house, the tiny men racing past Faisal and Fatimah without regard for their presence. The pair barely kept their balance as the inhuman tribesmen jostled past, all thoughts of killing the pair lost for the moment.

"That was…" Faisal said and paused.

"Lucky," Fatimah finished, sighing. "Praise Allah we received deliverance. A second or two more and they should have overwhelmed us with ease."

"Luck is what happens when preparation meets opportunity," Faisal replied.

He frowned as he stared at the house. Fatimah cocked her head and asked:

"Where is that from? It does not sound like the Koran."

"Seneca," Faisal replied absently. "A Roman statesmen, playwright and philosopher, early Empire... I think we must follow the Tcho-Tcho."

"Are you mad?" Fatimah asked, whirling his direction. "We only survived by the merest chance. I do not wish a second encounter with those creatures. You were not wrong, they are not human."

"Fatimah, we have no choice. We must find the Skull of Sobek and stop the return of the Outer Gods and their servants. Otherwise, nothing shall exist. Humans, animals, insects… those aliens… I do not even have words that can describe the inhuman, mind-shatter horror of those monsters… even the smallest blade of grass shall be reduced to dust if they break into our world…"

Fatimah studied him for a few seconds.

"I have never seen you so fearful," she said in a hushed voice. "Is that truly who the Masked Messenger served?"

"Yes," Faisal replied, nodding his head, "I shall tell you more soon. First, let us follow those horrible creatures and seek the Skull of Sobek."

"Agreed," Fatimah replied. "However, we shall revisit this discussion."

Without any further word, they ran inside the mansion, spotting the last members of the Tcho-Tcho a short distance away. Faisal took the lead, a defensive arrangement since he, as the larger target, was often the first attacked.

Keeping their distance, they followed the tribesmen down a long flight of stairs. That was when the screams of agony, roars, and indistinguishable sounds mixed and mingled with the tumult.

Slowing, Fatimah stepped in front, moving with a silent step that would have been impressive at any other moment. Now, with the sounds of an inhuman riot drifting up from the hidden basement, she could have been striding on hobnail boots and still not be heard over the din.

Stopping in the middle of the stairs, they caught sight of a pair of Tcho-Tcho falling onto the bottom. What they viewed were two halves of the terrible tribesmen plummeting, reddish black blood spraying in every direction. A crouching figure with a fur-covered face and hands and long black claws loped past, growling as he slashed the backs of two other Tcho-Tcho. A scaled green figure threw another tribesman with one hand, while his other sliced the faces of the other charging Tcho-Tcho.

"We must retreat," Faisal said, stepping back. "I recognize two forms of werewolves and a vampire that may be one who is a true plague on mankind. Any of them alone could tax our skills."

Fatimah, who was already two steps above him now, glanced back.

"Faisal, my dearest one, you need to shut up and find us a different method of entry," she said. "Moving through that tide of monsters and malevolent savages shall mean our instant death."

He followed her through the mansion and into the area near the maze. The already decomposing corpses of the five Tcho-Tcho exuded an odor that smelled of week-old rotting meat. The tiny, twisted men's bodies appeared shrunken and their blood was already changing from virulent crimson to an odd shade of brown.

"Interesting," Faisal stated, squatting near one of the corpses. "Their deterioration is far greater than any human or animal I have ever witnessed. A clear mark of their inhumanity."

"You do find the least opportune moments in which to become fascinated by science," Fatimah snapped. "You can examine them later. The Skull of Sobek is of greater import."

"Yes, of course," said Faisal, straightening. "However, this information may be useful in the future. I will take a sample for examination later. Follow me."

Turning to the left, he led Fatimah around the side of the building, halting near a large attached carriage house. A small door set in the side of the house swung listlessly on broken hinges and the sounds of diminishing discord drifted their direction.

Before Faisal or Fatimah could enter, a large bat flew from the house, vanishing seconds later in the nearby trees. A tall man dressed in a tattered dark shirt, light colored pants and no shoes stepped out a moment later, shielding his eyes from the sun's glare.

"Don't go in there, friends. There is blood everywhere and nothing is alive," he said.

The newcomer pushed his unruly dark hair back from his forehead and sighed. He had a wide, jowly face and sad, watery eyes.

"Thank you," Faisal said.

He removed a small revolver and shot the man in the chest.

The man in the tattered shirt stared at the gun, smiled.

"A silver bullet?"

"Yes," Faisal replied, shooting again as the other dropped to his knees.

"Thank you, thank you so much," the man whispered, before falling forward, unmoving.

"That was unexpected," Fatimah said. "He was the werewolf?"

"Correct," Faisal said as he stepped past the corpse and through the door. "Though a silver bullet is only a temporary solution. Once someone removes it, this sad man will live again and periodically kill like a mad animal. A true curse."

"What is the solution, the cure to that disease?" Fatimah asked, smelling the rusty tang of blood along with the rotting odors of the dead Tcho-Tcho.

"When I find one, I shall tell you," Faisal replied.

He stepped into a long corridor with a series of doors set on the right side of the hallway, clearly visible even at a great distance. The modern-looking gas lamps every few feet, as well as the unadorned walls and plain floors, exuded a sterile, almost medical air.

A pair of Tcho-Tcho limped into sight, traveling slowly down the hallway and opened a door a dozen or so yards away from Fatimah and Faisal. They did not look in their direction, but vanished from view a few seconds later. Fatimah took the lead now and they walked closer, her step soundless, his hushed by a very slow, gentle tread.

The ajar door revealed a large room filled with small cases with glass coverings. A pair of dead Tcho-Tcho offset the museum style of the room. The pair's bloody trail led them over to one case, empty, its glass covering tossed aside.

Fatimah walked past the dead creatures and read the card.

"*The Skull of Sobek.* We were too late."

Faisal stepped over to another case with a highly carved conch shell in the center. He walked around it three times, his eyes scanning the dais and the edges near the glass. He then walked over to another case, this one containing a black diamond. He ignored the item, spending his time examining the container.

After five minutes, Fatimah found her patience tested. Finally, as Faisal looked at a fourth case, she asked:

"Did you not hear me? The skull is gone!"

"I heard you," Faisal said, completing another circuit before he looked up. "The skull was removed when the alarm sounded. I doubt the thief, probably the dreaded Gouroull, spent much time in this area after the bells and lights resounded. He broke through the door and was a mile or more away by the time we climbed down the steps and witnessed the battle."

"I know this is a mistake," Fatimah said, shaking her head, "however, I shall ask: how do you know this?"

"Observation," Faisal replied, pulling a notebook out and scribbling down the name of each item. "The cases are connected to the alarms. The Tcho-Tcho charged downstairs. I would hazard to guess Gouroull first released the werewolf and the other monsters this man held as part of his collection."

"Then why are we not out chasing him? He cannot have gotten far!" Fatimah snarled.

Faisal did not look up from his writing.

"We are less than two miles from the ocean. Frankenstein's Monster once walked beneath a frigid sea as a means of getting to a small Scottish island. He is long gone, but we have several choices of directions. Until then, we have another duty. Many of these items are infernal and must not return into the hands of mankind.

Over there is a device once dubbed the Hand of Nergal; in the case opposite is the Black Blade of Baghdad; and across the room is a Philetas edition of the *Necronomicon*. Shall I go on?"

"No," Fatimah said and turned towards the door. "I shall radio for assistance."

"Thank you," Faisal replied.

They could guard the occult treasures in case of more Tcho-Tcho or other monsters returning. With the aid forthcoming, they would have time to exorcise any possessed item and weaken others.

"A Bison Cult coup stick? Hmm, that we can return to the proper people, along with this Tsuut'ina medicine bag," Faisal mused, as he stepped over and read some of the other descriptions. "The Amulet of Osiris and the LeMarchand box are other matters. I am not sure there is a vault deep enough for those… This collector was insane. Even being in the same building as these items can corrupt your soul after a time…"

CHAPTER XXVIII

Gouroull stepped out of the sea, the salt water streaming over the rags covering his massive body. Only his boots, Old Boris' gift, resembled anything like the clothing of a human. That was unimportant to Frankenstein's creature, a by-product of his creation. Perhaps someday he would abandon such silly human constructs, but not this day. Until his mate was present and the world populated by their young, Gouroull would use the barely adequate semblance of humanity as his basis for behavior.

He strode up a rocky shore with some traces of sand below the boulders, the sharp tang of sea air and rotting fish blowing across his damp face. Then, a second scent struck his keen senses, one that he had learned to recognize after many years traversing the world—old, dried blood, dust, and rotting soil, a combination only seen in one type of creature: vampires, the so-called masters of the night.

As a being that traveled and lived mostly by night, Gouroull had encountered many of these undead humans as they held court over others of their kind, or human slaves. He found them ridiculous and somewhat amusing at times, though mostly useless to his wants and needs.

Therefore, when confronted by one of these so-called kings and queens of darkness, he often treated them with the same violent disinterest as he did humans that sought to use him for their own selfish desires. His last encounter had occurred on the border of Austria and Hungary, a wild region full of mountains, thick forests and ruined castles. Gouroull had chosen one of these moldering wrecks as shelter, until he moved on towards Poland.

That was when she had appeared, her entrance both theatrical and completely ridiculous to Frankenstein's Monster. First, the roofless room slowly had filled with a layer of mist. This fog had risen only about two feet from the ground and drifted in lazy patterns, obscuring the fading carvings along the walls.

Second, the horrific scent that permeated through the cold, undead flesh of every vampire had wafted in his direction. Had humans, who so easily fell prey to these creatures, experienced the revolting, graveyard decay that surrounded these creatures, they would have fled in disgust. The only beings that exuded a more disgusting smell than vampires were the walking dead that some called Revenants, and a few in the New World zombies.

As the mist thickened, the vampire had glided into view. Her gait was supernaturally smooth, motions beyond the scope of even the best dancers and ballerinas who graced the stages of the world. She possessed long, blonde hair that fell in a golden shower across her pale shoulders, large, artless, seemingly innocent blue eyes, and an impressive figure that her diaphanous white gown enhanced. Her plump red lips spread into a wide smile as she approached, perfect pearly teeth peeking out and adding to her luster.

"My," she had said, her voice filled with an undertone of silvery laughter. "You are a big one. What are you doing in my home?"

Gouroull had looked down at the vampire, his face expressionless, his body as still as one dead. His amber eyes stared at her with unblinking intensity, seeing her true self. Humans, a species to which he did not belong, were easily fooled by the outward visuals the undead projected. They appeared as lovely, unchanging, epitomes of physical perfection to human eyes.

To Gouroull, they appeared as waxen corpses who only held back the deterioration of their bodies through the theft of blood or energy from the living. Take their impressive strength away, and they reverted to a bizarre mixture of corpse and leech.

"Not a talker?" she had whispered as she had come closer. "Hmm, you are most definitely more interesting than most who come and visit me. My name is Millarca and I can make all your dreams come true. Do you think I am beautiful?"

"No," Gouroull had answered, knowing this was the worst insult one could use when addressing a vampire.

He had once witnessed a male vampire snap his potential victim's neck and hurl her into a river in fury when she had said he smelled bad.

"What?" Millarca had replied, her eyes widening. "How dare you? Who do you think you are, you troll?"

She had then stared into his eyes, her sapphire colored orbs widening and boring into him with overwhelming intensity. Long pointed fangs had peeked from her wide mouth and she had smiled in triumph.

An expression that had slipped a moment later. Her eyes suddenly blinked twice, a slow movement that had not appeared natural. A tint pink tongue had slipped to the edge of her mouth and Millarca had pushed her face forward and stared into Gouroull's yellow eyes.

Gouroull had felt her mental thrusts towards his mind, tiny tendrils of invisible force seeking a means of enveloping him and his thoughts. But the threads had fallen away upon contact with his alien intelligence, vanishing like wisps of fog in strong sunlight.

Millarca had stepped backwards, her lovely countenance dropping away as her features melted away. Her hair had become pale tendrils, her face a skeletal ruin, her mouth overwide and filled with jagged, brown teeth. Raising a pair of overlong, bony hands, she had extended pointed black nails from each finger and hissed.

"What are you?" Millarca had asked, snarling.

Gouroull had smiled, his razor-sharp teeth further revealing his inhumanity. He had not spoken out, but his eyes had danced with the evil light of a predator staring at a tiny, feisty, pathetic prey.

Millarca had hissed again and leaped forward. Her explosive celerity might have overwhelmed any unwary human, but she was but slow and ungainly compared to Gouroull. He had waited until she was inches away and then slapped her from the air with a heavy, stony hand. She had crashed to the stone floor, the mist parting as she fell.

Stepping forward, Gouroull had placed a massive foot on the vampire's head. With slow, sadistic deliberation, he had pressed downward, the flabby flesh and hard bone parting beneath his inhuman force. He had ignored the screams of pain and her wiggling, flapping body as he had slowly ground Millarca's skull into paste.

Gouroull had then left her, moving to another part of the room as the shattered body had feebly struggled upon the floor.

When he had left, three days later, the vampire still twitched and quivered, her undead life still present, but her body incapable of regeneration. A wonderful torment that might last decades. Gouroull had felt a slight sense of satisfaction from such an act.

Back to the present, Gouroull turned his head towards the scent, spotting the vampire standing near a copse of trees. He was a little over six feet tall, with a cadaverous body and a long oblong face with a thin, well-groomed, mustache. He wore a formal black suit, white tie, and a black cape that lay across his narrow shoulders. A top hat sat atop his head, making him look regal in an Old World manner.

"You took long enough, Gouroull," he said, his voice silken smooth. "I have waited hours."

"Vampire," Gouroull said, the words more of a growl from his throat.

"Correct," the vampire said, doffing his hat and bowing slightly. "I am Dracula and you have my thanks."

Gouroull stared at the vampire who called himself Dracula. Finally, he said:

"No."

Dracula smiled, though only through a movement of his lips. His teeth never became visible and his dark eyes glinted with amusement.

"Ah," he said. "You doubt that I am Count Dracula? You met the one who used that name?"

"Yes," Gouroull rasped back.

Dracula chuckled and nodded.

"I have no doubt. In the world of the undead, Dracula is the protean king of the night. He appears everywhere, his face rarely the same, his powers inconsistent, his demands and intentions ever changing."

Gouroull waited but did listen to the vampire's words. The man who called himself Dracula appeared almost benevolent towards Frankenstein's lethal creation. This was odd, since every vampire he had met prior to this moment had sought power over Gouroull's mind and body.

"Dracula is many men, and many faces. You met one, you shall confront others. Who is the true Dracula? I cannot say. Perhaps I, perhaps a slow-moving Transylvanian. Possibly a tall, elegant vampire with an imperious means of address and a lust for all lovely women. The list is rather long and occasionally sordid. Some say Dracula is one man. Others that he possesses the bodies of many and sits like a bloated spider in some rotting castle, lost in the mountains of Wallachia. I speak only for myself. I am Dracula, and I thank you for freeing me from imprisonment. Dracula does not forget those who provide him aid. Shall we do you a service now?" he asked, his manner intense.

Gouroull nodded once, the movement slow and almost imperceptible. Even as he performed this slight motion, the Monster's inhumanity heightened. There was nothing natural about his manner and even small attempts at human actions appeared outlandish and incorrect.

"First, a piece of advice. Dracula always seeks his mate for his eternity of night. The quest of centuries encompasses many of his failures. This is the path you take, for I know something of your history. Dracula's advice, one earned through more lives than any realize, is simple: Beware! A mate for those who exist through centuries is a rarity. A being who called himself Satan offered Dracula the perfect match once. It was what Americans call, fool's gold. Bright and perfect outwardly, worthless beneath the surface. That is Dracula's advice: Beware! Do you understand?"

Dracula waited for several moments, spotting no response from Gouroull. Like the supposed vampire king, Frankenstein's Monster stood with a stillness that was unsettling for an outsider's view. Their mutual state appeared on a knife's edge between living and dead, though their conditions were quite different. Dracula was undead, a creature who remained mobile and thinking through the theft of blood and power from the living. Gouroull was something altogether different, a being unseen before, or since, his birth.

"Very well," Dracula said, breaking the silence. "The second is the aid I promised. The entities who requested your help will offer you everything. However, they rarely fulfill their promises. This is their greatest power over the living. The living call them gods, though some say they are an ancient race from the stars. Their powers are impossible to comprehend with our limited minds. Yet, Dracula always considered one question when they offered him power and wealth. If these entities are gods, why are they trapped? And why do they require the assistance of humanity to free them from their prison?"

Stepping back, Dracula lifted his cape, resembling a massive bat for a moment.

"That is my advice and aid, Gouroull, creation of Victor Frankenstein. I shall not hinder your quest. I cannot speak for others who use the name Dracula. If we are many controlled by one mind, perhaps the others shall walk softly in your presence. If we are many with no controls, then I speak only for myself. No matter. Remember the words of Count Dracula, for he does not lie to those who perform fair service for him, even inadvertently."

With that final word, he faded away, his body turning pale and vanishing into the growing darkness. His scent vanished a moment later, disappearing as quickly as the loquacious vampire himself.

Gouroull turned away and trekked west, having over one hundred miles to walk before reaching the next gate. One final piece of this puzzle remained, and Frankenstein's creation would not fail. The stakes were as high as any he had experienced since his unprecedented birth from the stolen corpses of Europe.

CHAPTER XXIX

Faisal watched as the final carriage vanished into the distance, the final box of forbidden artifacts placed into custody by his people. *His* people, not that of his fellow Muslims, or even their occasional allies, the Conclave. The people of Sheikh Faisal Hashim Haji Sabbah were not merely the tribesmen of his birth, but also men and women from other parts of the world, as well as other faiths. His people were an organization devoted to the protection of all life upon this planet, not merely one national identity or religious faith.

"I spoke to Nilar," his loyal and faithful Fatimah said as she appeared at his side.

Her stealth was like that of a leopard; one simply blinked, and she vanished or returned without any apparent sound.

"She said you are sending these items to a special vault. Why have I never heard of this treasure trove? Who guards it?"

Faisal smiled, amused by her annoyance. She took her self-appointed duty as his guardian quite seriously. Secrets, of which he had many, always irritated her when they emerged in their exciting lives.

"I created several holding facilities throughout the world," he answered. "Each is inaccessible, even by me."

He divided the occult items between those that required more study, and those that were too dangerous for humanity to handle. A few still disturbed him, but he chose caution over his natural curiosity.

"Explain, if you please," Fatimah asked, placing a slim, calloused hand over his. "How can one access a vault one cannot reach?"

Faisal looked up and replied:

"By making a difficult means of entry in a location beyond the reach of mankind. Have you ever heard of the Marianas Trench?"

"No," Fatimah replied, raising an eyebrow.

Faisal knew this was her signal for him to continue without unnecessary details.

"It is the deepest natural location upon the Earth. It is approximately seven miles below the surface, and the pressure of the water is overwhelming. Do you remember Mount Everest? Yes, I thought as much, that mountain is rather memorable..."

"Quite so," she agreed, "though the dog-faced Erlik assassins chasing us into those misbegotten ice peaks made it even a location I shall dread forever."

"A tale we can never tell the world, though the climb was impressive. No matter. I have long recognized the need for vaults beyond mankind's reach, so I adapted the plans being worked on by an American for an expedition beneath the crust of the Earth. I then enlisted elementals as pilots and created vaults throughout the globe that no man may access. The ones scattered through that terrible trench are deep beneath both water and earth. They open only once and sink deep below the silt at the bottom. You could drop the Everest in it, and over a mile of ocean would still remain above."

"What if another uses witchcraft or whatever term you wish and drags the vault from the bottom? Did you consider that much?"

"Yes, I did," Faisal replied. "Any form of tampering, even a shift in the ocean floor, will tip the vault into an undersea volcano. These are my secret methods for protecting the world from such terrible dangers. The living beings of the Earth need not fear the horrors of the Rhinegold, or the Smoking Mirror of Tezcatlipoca again."

"What of the books and other pieces you sent to your various homes? Are you delving into the *Al Azif*? That Iblis-damned tome brought about the fall of my people."

"I have read it before," Faisal said, raising an eyebrow at her shocked expression. "I had no choice. Without reading the words these cults follow, I could not fight them with full knowledge. I read every infernal tome on this world that exists—save one."

Fatimah pulled her hand away narrowed her eyes.

"You never told me this," she said.

"You never asked," Faisal replied, shrugging. "Your gratitude for my help prevented your willingness in discovering more of my history. Now, when confronted with horrors almost inconceivable, you wisely do not accept my word without questioning."

"And now you shall dispense with me?" she asked, placing hands on her daggers.

Faisal laughed and shook his head.

"Quite the opposite! Now, you are even more indispensable. Did you not realize you have been my second in-command for two years now? Do you think Nilar would tell anyone my orders? She spent her life battling the followers of a demon god whose temple is located close to her village. Nobody keeps a secret so well as one under perpetual threat on their own life."

Fatimah's hands did not drop, but she cocked her head to the left in thought.

"Therefore, I may fight your choices of actions and issue orders of my own to the organization?"

"Yes, you may," Faisal confirmed, "and you already do, quite often. You are apparently unaware of your full latitude."

"Acceptable," Fatimah said. "Then, you shall tell me how you know so much of those horrific Tcho-Tcho creatures, as well as why I should trust a man who openly admits to having read the accursed *Al Azif*."

"I will do so as we travel. We have a long journey ahead of us, and hopefully a means of defeating the monster known as Gouroull."

Faisal led her out of the mansion of the wealthy, dead collector. He showed no interest in any of the dozens expensive paintings, old manuscripts, and other toys that had entranced its owner. He was not a collector of anything, other than information and tools in his battle against the eldritch forces that existed beyond sight and reason. Men like the former owner of this mansion only elicited a vague sense of sadness in him. Men and women like this Percy were sad, lonely creatures, who only valued the acquisition of items—not the actual art or devices on their own merit. These people possessed a hole in their soul, an emptiness in their spirit, that they filled briefly through the purchase of whatever caught their momentary fancy. The brief thrill of obtaining something gave them a short-lived delight, an artificial happiness, that fell away quickly. Then the search resumed, its thrill only enhanced by the idea that they bought or stole an object desired by another.

Having a very different upbringing, Faisal found such amusements a waste of time. Strength from within and without, learning new skills, new languages, new information, made ownership of anything unimportant in his opinion. Especially in a world where men and women sought the return of demons or alien gods of nearly infinite power.

Two quotes lived within his mind on this subject, the first from the legendary Eastern sage, Lao Tzu when he wrote, "*When wealth and honors lead to arrogance, this brings its evil on itself.*"

The second was a quote from the Koran that his mother had always repeated when they had struggled finding food, while others enjoyed sumptuous meals.

She always said, "*Do not be impressed by their money or their children. Allah causes these to be sources of misery for them in this world, and their souls depart as disbelievers.*"

Wise words—ones that had caused a young Faisal Hashim Haji Sabbah, even after his rise to the title of Sheikh, to never become complacent with wealth or luxury. People were far more important.

Stepping into his airship, he felt Fatimah's eyes on him. She would have many questions in the coming days and he knew he must exercise patience. Still, this would not be a restful trip…

CHAPTER XXX

Gouroull strode through the hills and dales of this region, alone, except for the small animals inhabiting the trees and bushes. The only predators in this area were small foxes and tame dogs and cats owned by the local inhabitants. Those creatures steered far away from Frankenstein's monster, recognizing a creature far beyond their capabilities. Animals were wise in that manner, a reason Gouroull all but ignored them wherever he travelled. They acted in an instinctive manner that humanity failed to comprehend—his disinclination for their company.

Though he used men and women in various manners, Frankenstein's creation held them in scant regard. They were greedy, short-sighted, lustful animals who filled the Earth, destroying everything in their path. That last characteristic was amusing and useful at least, the only aspect of humans that was worthy of his respect.

The rest, however, that was where they failed and incurred his disgust-filled wrath. Take Vrollo, for instance, the tramp who had brought about Gouroull's revival. The fool had viewed Frankenstein's monster as a tool he could use to punish the villagers who treated him with understandable disgust. For a time, Gouroull had assisted the silly plans Vrollo had whispered to him in that dark castle in Ireland. But the reason for this acceptance was simple—the lust-filled derelict had told him of a local beauty…

"Perfect hair… alabaster skin… intelligent… hips made for bearing children… teach her to show respect to me…" were among the statements Vrollo had made about the woman named Helen Coostle, a visiting beauty.

His words about child-bearing had sparked Gouroull's interest, reigniting an old wound unhealed by time. He wished for another of his kind, a female capable of bearing his children. Would a human suffice? He did not know, but decided to attempt it. Following Vrollo's plans, he had eventually kidnapped the lovely Helen and destroyed the evil, lustful tramp.

Unfortunately, Gouroull never had an opportunity to experiment with the possibly conflict of biology between his new species and that of his weaker cousins, humanity. Helen's admirers had rescued her, and Frankenstein's monster had been forced to flee the scene, unprepared as he was in face of possible destruction by the natives.

Close to morning, Gouroull spotted an abandoned house, a ruined shell of a home whose only inhabitants were, according to the scents, rats, mice, and small insects. There were not even any lingering smells of humanity, a spoor that lasted a surprisingly long time. This was a good place he could use, until it was time to continue his journey.

The front door was a chipped, deteriorating, formerly elaborate wooden portal painted white. The brass handle turned easily, and the door swung inward with a soft creak. The unlit chamber within was a small front hallway that lead to a large room with a heavy layer of dust and cobwebs. A low table lay along the far wall with a portrait of a severe-looking man in dark clothing. A wide opening led to another room, filled with moldy, dusty furniture.

Near the portrait rested a sagging staircase, the steps crumbling into sawdust in many locations as it rose to the second floor. Along the walls were a collection of paintings, all of men and women possessing the same severe expression and equally dark clothing.

The skitter of rats and roaches filled the air for a moment as Gouroull stepped into the nearby dust-filled room. A pair of sofas and a matching chair sat in the center of a rug, the pattern of which was invisible beneath a heavy layer of grime. The cushions of the furnishings had splits along the seams, with the filthy innards spilling out across the floor. A pair of elaborate glass lamps lay on pitted wooden tables. A portrait of the man from the hallway lay across the room, his angry eyes staring out with frank disapproval at the world. A small brass plate on the picture's frame read, "*Upjohn Warren,*" though a hand carved set of letters was barely visible, scratched into the wood.

Gouroull walked over and brushed aside the dirt with one finger. He read the hastily carved words, "*May he rot in Hell,*" next to the name and smiled. Humans were always amusing in their fury over predators of their own kind. This Upjohn Warren reminded Gouroull of the wild-eyed fanatics he had once confronted in the wilds of the American Southwest. The leader, an elderly preacher who believed the world was ending, had forced his followers into an inhospitable retreat far, far into the desert.

"Reverend! Holy Father look! A demon! A DEMON!" a woman had shrieked, pointing a withered finger at Gouroull as he stepped past their cave.

"Halleluiah! The Lord sends us a sign that our pain was not in vain, my children! Halleluiah!" croaked an elderly man dressed in a black suit and black hat, raising his hands.

He was a shrunken man with large, hateful eyes, teeth too big for his skull, and thin, disapproving lips.

"What shall we do, Father?" a large man with a sweaty, pale face and a patchy blond beard had asked.

"Kill the demon! Kill it! Kill it!" the first woman had cried, raising a fist.

The preacher had raised his hands again, silencing his little cult. He had then slowly lowered his arms, pointing a long, skeletal finger at Frankenstein's creation. He then spoke, his quivering voice raising to a near scream as he quoted:

"The God that holds you over the pit of hell, much as one holds a spider, or some loathsome insect, over the fire, abhors you, and is dreadfully provoked; his wrath towards you burns like fire; he looks upon you as worthy of nothing else, but to be cast into the fire; he is of purer eyes than to bear to have you in his sight; you are ten thousand times more abominable in his eyes, than the most hateful venomous serpent is in ours."

The cult had risen as he spoke, and their cries of, "Halleluiah!" and "Save us, O Lord!" rang out until their leader hushed them with a look.

He had gazed upon each face, his mad oversized eyes boring into each man, woman, and child. They had shrunk, terrified by the fanatical gleam in his eyes.

Gouroull had watched the spectacle, part of him amused by the insane gleam in the cult leader's eyes. Insane humans managed remarkable acts of cruelty and horror upon their own species—so much so that even monsters treated them with some degree of respect.

"Kill the demon," the preacher had whispered at last, smiling.

His skull-like countenance had made him look more like a demon than even the inhuman Gouroull.

They had charged him, running at him, waving their tiny fists, their energy vanishing with each step in his direction. Frankenstein's creation had killed everyone, snapping their necks and shattering their skulls with each movement. Possibly, by sheer numbers, they might have proved troublesome under normal circumstances, but sitting and waiting for the End Times in the barren wastes of the desert had removed what little strength they had once held in their bodies. So they had died, though each was already more dead than alive.

Within minutes, only the leader had remained. He had stood among his people, still smiling as he examined their tattered and torn bodies. Finally, he had looked up, his eyes angrier and even less sane than before.

"And the devil, who deceived them, was thrown into the lake of burning sulfur, where the beast and the false prophet had been thrown. They will be tormented day and night for ever and ever," he said, his voice rising with each word.

The false holy man had shaken and screamed, his insanity as monstrous as Gouroull's heart.

The Monster had smiled and, with but a light shove, sent the mad man sprawling to the rocky earth. He then had stepped out of the cave and smiled, knowing he resembled the demons this man so greatly feared.

The preacher had howled, his ghostly face even less human as he screamed:

"What do you plan for me, son of Perdition? I shall not cry out, for the Lord of my fathers shall give me strength! It is you who shall boil in agony in a lake of fire and darkness, tormented for all eternity! I shall rise and become the angel of death, destroying the unbelievers and mud people with the same impunity as God used upon Sodom!"

Raising a fist, Gouroull had punched the stone ceiling and stepped backwards. A low rumble filled the air and he hit the rocks again.

The preacher's eyes had widened and he had stepped forward, his hands outstretched.

"No! NO! In God's name, stop!"

A final strike from Frankenstein's monster had collapsed the cave roof, sending a shower of heavy stone across the mouth. Within seconds, the small opening had vanished from view and the cries of the insane cult leader had vanished.

Gouroull released a rumble from his chest, an amused sound. His actions had made this trip to the New World, seeking a possibly relative of Victor Frankenstein, a worthwhile trek.

The crazed man would die slowly, possibly prolonging his torture by eating his dead followers. Either way, his death was assured, and the horror the man felt was wonderful. If it was true that horrible deaths caused the rise of ghosts and spirits, this crazed holy man might transform into a terrible being indeed. Yes, this futile search had not been a complete loss…

Back to the present, Gouroull sat down beneath the painting and waited. The low skittering of tiny talons rose and fell, moving unseen through the walls, floor and ceiling. The dreadful din surrounded him on every side, a horrific scratching that sent small plumes of dust flying throughout the room. The clamor increased slowly, the unseen creatures seemingly racing madly about the hidden nooks of the abandoned room.

Then, the ghost appeared, a spectral presence emerging from the darkness. He was a short man, barely five feet-tall, with dark hair, white eyes and black clothing. He appeared ethereal for some seconds, then solid and somewhat real the next. His presence flickered and his angry countenance glowered down at the seated Gouroull.

"How dare you violate the sanctity of my home?" the ghost of Upjohn Warren bellowed. "You are not one of my blood. You have the stink of a dirty foreigner about you. Get out! Get out now!"

His voice echoed through the moldering mansion, momentarily drowning out the scritch-scratching of the unseen pests.

Gouroull looked up, his phosphorescent yellow eyes gleaming in the darkness. He watched the ghost, but did not move, unimpressed by the display.

"You ignore me? No, not allowed!" Upjohn Warren's specter screamed. "Nobody ignores me. Nobody! Nobody! Noboby!"

His face and body turned skeletal and the walls and ceiling shook from his growing rage.

The unblinking gaze of Frankenstein's creation drove the haunt to greater heights of madness. The sofas tipped over and slid several feet away. A pair of tables danced and the painting near Gouroull shook and quivered on the wall. Yet, he never rose or moved his head away from the spectacle.

"You will not leave? Then you shall never leave, you dirty foreigner!" the ghost crooned, his inhuman grin glimmering in the spare light. "Come my children, my little pets! I have dinner for you, a nice tasty treat."

Then the scratching and slither rose in volume, approaching from all sides. The source of the clattering emerged seconds later. Rats, big, small, with filthy gray coats, and tiny black button eyes. Their drooling maws revealed rows of tiny yellow brown teeth and they chittered as each emerged from their hidden homes. Hundreds of the horrific vermin appeared, a living, breathing gray wave that slowly slid closer to their seated prey.

Without a word, Gouroull rose and stared down at the rats. A malicious predatory gleam entered his gaze and his lips slowly slid back. His razor-sharp incisors gleamed and he released a low, nearly inaudible growl from his chest.

That was when the rats halted in their progress. It was almost as if they possessed a collective will, and they acted as a terrible, demonic, fur-clad hive mind. The mad chittering and squeaking rose to greater heights, with an odd, serpentine style hissing underlying the clamor. The chittering transformed seconds later into a squealing sound of naked terror from creatures rarely afraid of even the boldest predator. Then, they backed away, their unfeeling eyes still locked on the towering form of Gouroull. Gradually, they backed into their holes and secret passages, their hysterical chatter slowly diminishing with each passing second.

The spectral form of Upjohn Warren shimmered and grew mistier as he screeched:

"No! No! No! I order you, my pets! Come out, come out, and tear this dirty foreigner into pieces! Come back!"

Minutes later, the ghost stopped screaming, his empty eye sockets staring at Gouroull. He bobbed before Frankenstein's monster, his inhuman countenance frozen, his gaping maw opening and closing soundlessly.

"You," the ghost whispered, his voice barely audible despite the silence of the ancient mansion, "are not human. Leave my house, monster. Leave!"

Gouroull smiled and reached out, slowly grasping the painting on the wall. With a careless jerk, he ripped the portrait from the wall. A shower of gray plaster fell from the wall, causing a dusty cloud across the room.

"Put that picture down! Put it back!" Upton Warren screamed, his face losing all connection to humanity and becoming that of a pale, decaying corpse.

With a slow, painstakingly careful motion, Gouroull pulled the rusty nails from the back of the frame, dropping them to the ground and causing a light clattering. The ghost's shrieks rose with each act. All the while, Gouroull's expression never changed.

Pulling the painting free of the frame, Gouroull slowly crushed the rotted wood, dropping a series of splinters and sawdust onto the filthy floor. The name plate he bent in half and dropped in the detritus pile, grounding the metal and wood beneath one heavy heel.

"What? What? What? What are you doing?" the ghost screamed, nearly incoherent with rage.

The furniture nearby quivered and puffs of dust rose about the room creating miniature dust devils in the dirt.

With one huge, heavy hand, Frankenstein's Monster punched a hole through the glowering face of Upton Warren's portrait. The man's specter screamed, and the furniture shook, jumping several inches in the air and crashing to the floor with a heavy, dull thud. Several small items fell and shattered, the pieces scattering across the room.

With deliberation, Gouroull tore the painting into tiny pieces, tossing the canvas and wood randomly about the chamber. When nothing remained, he strode through the ghost, ignoring the cold chill that ran across his inhuman skin. He then pushed open the closed windows, his powerful arms breaking the frames that held nature and time locked in place. This sent a light wind blowing across the chamber, kicking up the filth, which mixed with a few leaves blown from the outside.

Gouroull then sat down, watching as the ghost's rage slowly drifted away. The ethereal form faded away, disappearing into a smoky mist. The howling voice mingled into a low whistling breeze from outside the ruined mansion.

Frankenstein's creation smiled once again, knowing the mansion would crumble at a quicker pace, torturing the specter and eventually leaving the spirit alone in a pile of dust. An amusing fate for an obnoxious being.

CHAPTER XXXI

The heavily oiled wrestlers writhed on the sand pit, their powerful bodies straining and seeking control of their opponent. They were evenly matched in size, over six feet-tall with rippling muscles, clean-shaven faces and bodies, and completely nude. One had a thick mane of dirty blond hair, the other a short mop of ebony curls, and both were astonishingly handsome.

Outside the ring where both men struggled for supremacy were rows of benches set up in the style of a Roman amphitheater. Over one hundred men and women of various ages lounged in Roman togas above the combatants, some viewing, others gaily chatting. Most held goblets in hand, though each vessel was unique and quite strange. Such as the hugely obese man who sipped red wine from the skull of what may have been a child. Or the attractive women with the complex weave of golden blond hair whose servants added portions of their blood into her beverage. Her decanter was a large upside-down crucifix made from precious metals and bright stones. These two were in no way unusual in this assembly, each of whom behaved as if their main goal was out-doing the others in showy displays of wealth and unpleasantness.

"Is this all we can expect? A pair of barbell lovers rolling about in the sand?" a tall man with a thin patrician face and a supercilious manner of talking through his clenched teeth asked.

He lounged on his bench, fanned by a young girl, probably no older than ten. She wore a loose tunic that barely lay across her narrow shoulders. Her immature triangular face appeared heavily painted with cosmetics, a garish display of Madonna and whore. Her dark eyes appeared vacant and she moved at the man's orders with the slow, languid motions of a sleepwalker.

"Yes," an elderly woman with a pear-shaped body lisped.

She wore heavy pancake makeup that failed to hide the ravages caused by riotous living across her face. A short man with thick hennaed hair dressed in a loincloth stood at her side. He fed her grapes and refilling her opium-tinged drink while gazing with hungry eyes at the many jewels and baubles bedecking her body.

"I am bored. Make them do something!"

A low murmur of assent drifted about the crowd, with eyes drifting towards a bench in the center of the amphitheater. A youth, probably about sixteen years-old, sat on large wood and gold chair, his attention upon the pretty, young children that encircled his vicinity. The young man possessed thin black hair, a weak chin, a large nose and pimples across his jaw and forehead. Yet his mass of servants, all resembling the picture of preteen beauty, stared at him with the rapturous gaze of a worshipper viewing the object of their veneration.

He glanced around, waving at a little lad with long dark hair and huge eyes. Throwing a leg across one arm of his throne, he glanced down at the struggling wrestlers and frowned.

"Who are they, Athene?" he asked in softly accented archaic Latin. "Remind me."

One girl stepped out of the crowd, her brown hair cut in a short, boyish manner. She was pretty for someone on the bloom of maturity and might possibly become even beautiful one day.

She pulled out a small scroll of paper from her tunic and read out in a voice that cracked several times with each word:

"Imperator, you named them Apollo and Ares. Their true names are Sergio and Stelios, and they are professional wrestlers from Milan and Crete."

"Tell me more," the youth said, waggling his foot in growing impatience.

"Both drank only one glass of wine before the orgies and participated enthusiastically with attractive adult women exclusively," she read from the page.

The youth smiled, causing the bursting of several whiteheads nearby his oversized nose.

"Good girl, Athene. You learn quickly what we require. You may eat a meal tonight."

The girl called Athene curtsied low and whispered, "Thank you, master," as she backed away.

The youth called Imperator stood, raising his left hand up in a slow, imperious manner. The amphitheater's inhabitants ceased speaking and stared his direction with expectant faces.

"We hear your boredom and agree. We shall make this contest more amusing for all present."

He then leaned forward and narrowed his eyes theatrically. A shimmering red light surrounded his head for an instant and a crown appeared across his wide, pale brow. It appeared made of metal and possessed radiating spikes that glowed and pulsed before vanishing. All eyes turned to the men down in the sand pit, their powerful bodies bathed in the same ominous red glow.

Then the men started dancing with each other and kissing every time they grew closer. Their faces registered their surprise and confusion as they pranced about like oversized ballerinas.

The crowd giggled and applauded, knowing this was one of the Imperator's favorite larks. If either or both men preferred the same sex, he would have them do the same with the opposite of their desires. It was his sadistic joy and they shared his amusement.

Sitting down again, the man called Imperator massaged Athene's taut rear and sighed with contentment. Even after almost fifteen hundred years of life, he found toying with humans a pleasant diversion. There was nothing better than breaking the minds and spirits of those who looked down upon him, seeing a spoiled child instead of one of Earth's oldest rulers.

His name was Flavius Romulus Augustus and he was the last true Emperor of the Roman Empire. For almost one year, the few adherents of the failing government had hailed him as the last master of the western half of the Empire. They had called him Imperator Romulus and even minted coins in his name. Then the Germans had come, led by a barbarian named Odoacer, and his moment of glory was finished.

"Sign and you live in retirement, child. Refuse and we will cut off your head and use that as a message for the Senate of Rome," Odoacer's counselor, a grey-bearded warrior named Hunulfus, had intoned as he had dropped a papyrus on the table before Romulus.

Without protest, Romulus had signed, saddened that he had not even finished a year as Emperor of the Romans. The Germans sent him to live on a pension at Castel dell'Ovo in Campania, a mansion originally built by the legendary general Lucius Licinius Lucullus after he had defeated the eastern kingdoms and looted them for everything of value. There, he was forgotten, his name a mere memory on a coin.

It was after his first year that he had taken up sorcery, having discovered an entire library of scrolls on the subject. Romulus had studied and learned; his efforts had redoubled when he discovered he was known to the Roman world as Romulus Augustulus, Romulus "the little Emperor." Worse than that, some people apparently gave him an even worse nickname, Momyllus, the "little disgrace."

The fury of that indignity had led him towards the darker magic, the ancient spells of the Etruscan witches and dark sorcerers. Those eldritch arts, already old by the time of the founding of Rome, had taught Romulus much, yet had always hinted at so much more for a bold seeker of knowledge. The deeper truth had always seemed just out-of-reach, no matter how hard he had studied and woven his spells.

Then, Romulus had found it—a simple spell that suggested so much more. Written in a language older than Egyptian, the young former Emperor somehow had understood every word. Following the preparations precisely, he had woven the spell, finally uttering the terrible, soul-shattering name and heard the sound echo for what felt like hours.

"Nyarlathotep," he had whispered, feeling something in his mind and body break.

In the distance, dogs howled, their cries both plaintive and enraged.

Romulus Augustus, the last Emperor of the western Roman Empire, had known at once that his plea had reached the dreaded power he had invoked. He had closed his eyes, wondering if this was his true end. Perhaps he should have refused abdication and accepted a fast death? Most who sat on the throne died by violent means; perhaps he should have followed that path instead of voluntary exile.

"Rise, little ruler. Rise and look upon me," a happy voice said, booming throughout the chamber.

Opening his eyes, Romulus had stared into the face of pure darkness. The man, or god, who now towered over him had been but a shadow in human form. Romulus had not been able to discern any features other than a pair of arms that looked both enormous and slender with every eye-blink.

The former Emperor had risen on shaking legs, his mouth dry, his eyes leaking tears.

"I see your desire, little Emperor," the shadowy god had said, every word biting. "You never really cared about ruling Rome. You wished the pomp and pleasures. Every sensual desire met, a life more luxurious than Caligula, Commodus, Elagabalus, without any of the bother of making laws. You planned on letting your father rule while you indulged yourself. This is the truth."

"Yes, master," Romulus had said, unsure why he called this shadowy figure by such a title.

"If that is all you wish, it is granted," the shadow man had said, his impenetrable form shifting and changing with each second. "You shall exist as you are now, young and unchanging. You will have power enough, and it shall compel the weak of mind to do your bidding. The wealthy and powerful, who require constant entertainment of the more secret variety, shall be attracted to you, driven by their own compulsions. All that I require is your continued spreading of corruption and chaos, no matter where you drift. Do you agree?"

"Yes, master," Romulus had replied, then asking, "I shall never grow old?"

A low chuckle escaped the void, followed by the same light voice.

"Yes, you shall be sixteen years-old for all time, if you plan correctly. Now, put on this crown."

A patch of the darkness moved, revealing an iron diadem with spikes radiating in every direction. This was a Radiant Crown, an honor worn by various Emperors since the time of Domitian. Romulus had worn it once, though this one was smaller and possessed a thin layer of gold over its many spikes.

"This," the shadowy creature explained, "was the Crown of Commodus. He often wore it under his lion-hide costume. Did you know that he believed he was the reincarnation of Hercules? Yes, just like Mithridates VI, he played at being the legendary warrior. To prove it, he slaughtered thousands of animals in the arena and found cheating means of doing the same to gladiators. Elagabalus wore it as well, and used its power as a means of seducing hundreds of men, women, and children into his bed. You may do both, if you so choose. Place the Crown upon your head and all your dreams and fantasies shall begin at once. It shall vanish from view to all. Only when you use its power shall it become visible."

Romulus Augustulus, last of the western Roman emperors, had not hesitated. Grabbing the crown, he had shoved it across his wide brow and felt a quick stab of pain. He had shuddered as the pain increased for a moment, but then it had vanished as if it had never appeared.

Romulus had tested his power that night by forcing his elderly maid into his bed. He had followed that with her husband, all the castle's servants, a passing musician, and a milk-maid returning home after selling her goods. All had been unwilling, which had been his secret delight, even more so when at least three killed themselves in grief afterward.

"Who needs the throne now?" he had said aloud a week later as he was resting in the hot pool of the local baths.

A pair of young beggar girls sat at his side, their scrawny, unformed bodies looking very tiny in the vast pool.

"I am the true Emperor now!"

That much was true, in his mind. No matter what occurred in the regular world, Romulus existed as a ghost. He had no home or property, other than a few togas that he wore instead of the clothing of the day. The last Emperor of Rome found followers wherever he traveled, all of whom gave him full access to their homes, fortunes, servants, and bodies.

Years later, Romulus had discovered that many of his exploits were now merged with tales of witches, Satanic ceremonies, and the history of the Roman Empire. Nearly every tale of an Emperor raping a married woman, despoiling children, enjoying vast ridiculous feasts followed by vomiting, feeding Christian to lions, or leading Bacchanalian orgies, emerged from his actions since he had received the Crown of Commodus.

This was good, and the life Romulus had dreamed of since the day his father had announced he was Imperator, and he had been hailed by a few mercenary troops.

Traveling throughout the world, his fifteen-hundred-year life was one of seeking pleasure, while sadistically choosing many unwilling for his more horrific appetites. His favorites were usually children below the age of eleven, though he usually forced a few of the lotus-eaters into his bed. Those, Romulus always ensured they indulged in cannibalism and other behavior considered abhorrent since the dawn of civilization.

Spotting a newcomer to his little court of darkness, Romulus smiled. The woman, just above a girl, was a French burglar named Irma, and she was a member of a French criminal conspiracy. Its leader had sent her as an ambassador, hoping for an alliance with the Black Imperator, ruler of the court of darkness. Romulus received these offers every few years, and even sometimes helped one conspiracy or another. Often, he simply humiliated the requestors and left them with less than they had started. All in good fun, another diversion as the decades passed. Waving over Athene, he said:

"After the revels, bring that new woman Irma to my chambers. Are my rack and whips cleaned and laid out?"

He licked his thin lips in anticipation.

"Yes, master," Athene replied after consulting a different scroll. "May I ask a question, master?"

"Yes," Romulus said, staring at the long-legged Irma and imagining her delicious wails of pain.

"Who is the grey-skinned man that just walked into the fighting pit?" Athene asked, pointing at a spot near the prancing, smooching, wrestlers.

Romulus looked confused for a moment and then leaned forward. He gazed down at the massive form, a man whose head almost reached the top of the pit. His skin was, as Athene had said, gray in tone, and his dark hair resembled the mane of a lion more than that of a human. He slowly raised his twisted face upward and stared at Romulus with terrible yellow eyes.

"You, there!" Romulus shouted down.

The Crown shimmered briefly on his head as he tapped its power once more.

"Which master or mistress do you serve? My, you are quite hideous! No matter, you need to be punished, as does your owner! Whom do you serve?"

The massive newcomer stepped closer and pulled himself into the box in one quick and inhumanly smooth motion. The pretty girls and boys backed away, leaving Romulus standing before the giant. The last ruler of ancient Rome gazed up at the twisted creature, tapping a foot on the ground with obvious annoyance.

"Answer me, damn you!" Romulus screamed, unused to defiance. "Who is your master?"

Hezekiah Whateley grinned, showing his horrific teeth and looking with amusement down at this pathetic little man.

"My master? I serve Satan, of course."

He then reached out and plucked the crown from Romulus Augustulus's head, wrenching the dark mystic item free with his considerable strength.

The last Emperor of Rome shrieked in agony and terror, stumbling backwards as the weight of ages suddenly fell upon his body. Fifteen hundred years of debauchery filled his teenage body like a terrible wave, filled with diseases and plagues. His soft skin broke out in rashes, the livid colors clashing as they tore across his body. Then boils appeared and burst in sprays of yellow and black pus, sending the pretty children he had enslaved fleeing and screaming in horror. The bones snapped as time caught up to him, and he fell over.

By the time Whateley turned away, little more than a pile of dust in a filthy toga remained of Flavius Romulus Augustus, better known to the world as Romulus Augustulus.

Hezekiah laughed, a horrific sound, and headed towards the exit. The Crown pulsed with dark, cold energy, but he felt disinterested in exploring its power. His plan was simple—get the Crown and toss it somewhere inaccessible, even to Gouroull. That would keep his master's plan intact and prevent the return of the Old Ones.

Stepping out into the dark Chicago night, he ducked as a wooden wheel crashed near where he stood. Straightening, he tucked the Crown into a pouch and looked for the source of the attack.

A massive figure stepped into view, his gray skin appearing white in the silvery moonlight.

"Gouroull," Whateley rasped, showing his fangs to the demoniac figure. "I knew we would meet again. As you can see, I am different now."

"The Crown," Gouroull replied, the words sounding odd to the ear. It sounded as if he utilized organs different from that of a human as a means of speech.

Whateley shook his massive head slowly.

"No. You shall not have it."

"Mine," Gouroull said, his voice more of a bestial growl speech.

"Try and take it, you loathsome thing," Whateley replied, quoting the words he had once heard said when he passed some women in Boston.

Then Gouroull was upon him, his powerful arms grabbing Whateley's own arms in grips of iron.

But Whateley broke free and the battle commenced!

CHAPTER XXXII

Fatimah lowered her spyglass and shook her head.

"If we try and get between those two creatures," she said, "they will tear us limb from limb and then they will get nasty. What can we do?"

"First, we can thank Allah that one evil is erased from the world," Faisal replied, leading Fatimah away from the site of the battle. "I recognize that crown from my books. It is a true object of evil. Second, their battle shall give us a chance to get ahead of them and plan our strategy. Both of those creatures must complete their fight and fulfill the next portion of the dreaded prophesy before they enter the hidden dimension."

Fatimah frowned, but waited until she boarded the airship and Faisal provided the map's coordinates. Then she turned on him, and said:

"Start at the crown and explain. You may add more details of yourself since this travel will take some time."

"The crown is known as the Crown of Commodus," Faisal explained. "He was a Roman Emperor eighteen hundred years ago. He was a fool and a lunatic, believing himself to be a modern Hercules. His favorite amusements were killing animals with arrows in his arena and fighting gladiators. Not merely one or two animals, mind you, but sometimes hundreds in a day. The Romans paid millions each year for his entertainments. He also enjoyed killing gladiators, as well as his own citizens. His favorite entertainment was tying together dozens of sick and lame people and beating them to death with a club. He pretended they were giants. A truly horrific monster of a man."

"Disgusting," Fatimah agreed.

She was a professional assassin, a killer practically since birth, but the idea of murder as entertainment offended her odd set of ethics.

"Did the blood spilled somehow curse that crown?" she inquired.

Faisal shrugged.

"Or some other creature gave him power in exchange for blood spilled. No way of knowing. Legend had it that the crown was in the possession of a repellent creature who used its power to debauch young and old. I read about it when I studied for a time under Muhammad Ahmad."

Fatimah cocked one eyebrow in surprise.

"You were a student of the Mahdi? The elders of my people believed he might actually have been the true redeemer."

"I would not know if he was, or was not," Faisal said. "Though he was devoted and disliked tribal warfare. He taught me for four months before it was time for me to move on. He possessed a wealth of knowledge about politics, an area I was unaware of before that time. This is why I navigate the lethal games of the various factions with little rancor."

"Interesting," Fatimah acknowledged. "Where did you go from there?"

"Cambridge," Faisal continued. "I was accepted as a student of mathematics. My education varied over the years, practical and theoretical. My mother planned everything, though I altered some of her plans when I grew old enough to make my own decisions. Hence my period of six months as a junior chef in a restaurant in Manhattan."

"I believe I could ask you for many stories from here until…" (She checked the coordinates and calculated briefly in her head.) "…Siberia. I think I shall do that later and simply ask one more question. *Why?* Why did your parent provide you training in so many areas? You are a doctor of medicine, an expert in mathematics, engineering, and odd skills like cooking, flower-arranging, and sword-dancing. You are skilled in battle, modern and ancient, and spend most of your time examining legends. Why?"

"A difficult question, but I can give a simple answer. My mother, along with an Englishman turned American, and possibly a French nobleman, believed in justice, and the idea that a good man could make a difference in the world. They consulted others, experts in many areas, and determined that a child with a superior mind and body could receive intensive training. This could lead to a warrior for good who would battle against the forces of evil. The Englishman's concentration was upon crime; the Frenchman's, I do not know. He left his country and moved to Russia over some political issue. My mother's concern was the supernatural. She had lost her parents and brother from monsters that reside in the ocean and walk like men. That is why I am an expert in this odd field of study. I know the ancient ways, but I also utilize the modern sciences in all studies. Does that answer your question?"

"Somewhat," Fatimah acknowledged. "However, I shall ask more later. Let us turn to the one known as Gouroull and his equally monstrous foe. Is it true that that being is a demon created by science?"

Faisal smiled and nodded while saying:

"That may be the best definition of that monster. A genius created Gouroull, and his name was Victor

Frankenstein. This madman used sciences both new and old with only one purpose—defeating death. Using the corpses of the dead and lost lore, he created a monster. The tales of Gouroull are scant, but terrible. Frankenstein's creation is a fiend, no mere mindless brute, but a wicked devil capable of evil beyond that of any mortal man. Nobody knows a method capable of destroying him. He is stronger than any man, incapable of being harmed by bullets or fire, and capable of terrible actions against any who would cross his path."

"And now, there are two such creatures," Fatimah said, adding, "Though I reject the notion that this Gouroull has no weakness. All that walk the Earth, even beings of terrible power beyond our imagining, possess some kind of weakness. The Iblis-damned monster that destroyed the Order of Assassins possessed one that may destroy his plans someday. He found my people boring and destroyed them as a joke. That was foolish and may one day cause him some small discomfort. This Gouroull is dangerous and lethal, but there must be a flaw that could lead to his destruction."

"If there is," Faisal replied, "the world has not discovered it yet. Fire, cold, bullets, knives, snakes, and other weapons, all have failed against this monster. He is stronger, faster, harder to injure and possesses the instincts of a predator and the intelligence of a human. The only area that has slowed his progress is his quest for a mate. That is his primary motivation, beside a natural instinct for evil."

Fatimah tapped her clean white teeth with one nail, an unconscious habit she had developed when thinking.

"That may be a tool or a lever for a strategic victory. However, I doubt it would allow us an opportunity to bring destruction down on this science-created demon. Let us consider the various avenues of attack…”

CHAPTER XXXIII

Hezekiah Whateley, despite his massive size since childhood, was not one who loved fighting. Oh, he had participated in many brawls in his lifetime… He had done so since he was a child playing with other Dunwich children. There were some in town, like those uppity Osborn and Sawyer children, who looked their long noses down on anyone with the last name Whateley. They bullied him and his kin, decayed, undecayed, with violence, and cruel taunts on any occasion available.

Unfortunately for them, Hezekiah had grown fast and strong. By the time he was ten, he took on the two Osborn boys, ages sixteen and fourteen, and delivered a beating that required a consultation from Dr. Houghton of Aylesbury. The locals did not consider complaining to Hezekiah's parents, knowing that the younger boy had delivered the same treatment than the Osborn brothers had planned for his face and body.

The battles that followed were from a few adults that disliked the young giant and his defense of the Whateley clan. By the time Hezekiah had reached seventeen, nobody in the region dared assault him, or any of his kin. His reputation was such that even the distant relations in Aylesbury knew that Hezekiah Whateley was not one to accept taunts with a shrug or a sheepish grin.

He never loved brawling, but he had some skill. His heavy fists punched fast and he could absorb massive amounts of punishment. One relative on the nearly decayed side of the family had even suggested that he become a boxer or a wrestler.

"You are bigger than Ruby Bob and Gentlemen Jim put together, lad. You could make more money putting down men in one day than you could in ten years working your little farm," Judah Whateley had said as Hezekiah mucked out the pigpen.

Judah was a man of medium height with a long face that lacked a chin, a stub nose and loose lips that flapped comically every time he spoke. His family resided in a small farmhouse that was slowly deteriorating thanks to a poor roof and Judah's inability to fix the structure properly.

"Not for me, cousin," was all Hezekiah had replied, that day.

He knew then that Judah had spoken the truth—his strength and self-trained skills made him more than a match for any professional fighter. Given a little training in the rules, Hezekiah knew that he could defeat any mortal man in a fair fight.

The difficulty lay with his relatives, the followers of the Outer Gods, and their insane plans. The Whateleys of the decayed branch still adhered to this oldest and most alien of religions, heading off onto Sentinel Hill and speaking to their invisible masters of air and earth. Hezekiah had watched them with a gimlet gaze, waiting for the day they sought, that of the return of the Old Ones. As of now, they merely spoke of those creatures and saw visions of lost cities beneath the poles.

No, fame using his Satan-given gifts was not possible. Not when he heard statements like the one Jonathan Whateley had whispered while reading from his tattered copy of the monstrous tome, the *Necronomicon*. The language was a debased tongue that was already old when dinosaurs had roamed the Earth; yet, Hezekiah understood every word perfectly.

"Yog-Sothoth knows the gate. Yog-Sothoth is the gate. Yog-Sothoth is the key and guardian of the gate. Past, present, future, all are one in Yog-Sothoth," Jonathan had whispered as a fire blazed in the Devil's Hop Yard. "He knows where the Old Ones broke through of old, and where They shall break through again. He knows where They have trod earth's fields, and where They still tread them, and why no one can behold Them as They tread…"

How could he abandon his mission for money when men still believed that such horrors were beneficial? Hezekiah Whateley preferred poverty to oblivion. He was a warrior, protecting humanity in the name of the King of the Earth, Lucifer Morningstar. He accepted his loss of humanity in his quest, and even embraced becoming a creature not unlike Gouroull.

With that in mind, Hezekiah Whateley threw a hard punch towards Gouroull's skull. His massive fist moved with the speed of a lightning bolt, though his blow missed the mark. Gouroull, spotting the attack, had backed away at the last moment. He then leaped forward, his massive arms encircling Whateley's body.

Raising both his arms up, Whateley broke free of Gouroull's grip in an instant. He knew all too well that such a hold could constrict his breathing and snap every bone in his body. That was his favorite form of attack when he was fighting. Grab your enemy, dangle them off the ground, break a rib or three, drop them and walk away. Under Gouroull's inhuman power, he had no doubts he would eventually burst like a squeezed tick.

Raising a leg, he kicked Frankenstein's Monster squarely in the stomach. The impact pushed the creature back several paces, but he looked otherwise unhurt. Gouroull circled to the left, his massive arms extended and protectively covering his body. His twisted countenance and amber eyes held no emotional response, no life whatsoever. Whateley may well have been facing a statue, a golem granted life through arcane sciences.

For his part, he smiled. Gouroull did not fight like a trained killer, but with the wild actions of an angry child. He relied on his massive strength and his stony skin in battles. He had never faced someone equal to his assets, but also an experienced brawler. The Frankenstein Monster would fall—in time.

With a whoop of delight, Whateley waded in, sliding closer and swinging a heavy arm towards Gouroull's side. The blow struck, sounding like the clash of boulders. Gouroull moved with the impact, avoiding a second punch from the massive, gray-skinned child of Dunwich. Frankenstein's creation continued circling, his yellow eyes glinting with a malevolence that was almost a physical force.

Seeing that Gouroull was now on the defensive, Whateley continued punching, his fists aiming exclusively at his enemy's enormous torso. Most missed, but every third or fourth hit the mark, hammering into the Monster's chest or sides. He knew he should be feeling some fatigue for such a strenuous effort, but Whateley no longer had any such weakness. He moved with the same incredible power, his motions impossibly powerful and inhumanly fast.

Seeing Gouroull's hands dip, Whateley smiled again. Victor Frankenstein's feared creation was losing heart and weakening, slowing under the unrelenting assault of his equal. This was good, and now he could conclude the battle and destroy this blight upon the Earth.

Feinting a punch, Whateley launched a hard kick towards Gouroull's face. He doubted the blow would kill his foe, for this creature was not human. It would have torn a strong man's head from his shoulders, but Whateley only hoped to stun Gouroull for a moment.

Just before his huge boot struck, Whateley caught a new look in Gouroull's eyes… amusement. Suddenly, the Monster's huge hands clamped down on Whateley's ankle, holding them in a grip that felt like bands of steel. The vice-like grasp tightened, slowly constricting the delicate, though magically reinforced, bones. Whateley groaned despite himself, also aware that he probably looked quite comical, standing on one leg in the darkness.

Hopping and hoping he could close the distance, Whateley found himself dancing about in the grass. But Gouroull kept his distance, backing away or turning left and right, all the while increasing the power of his grip with inhuman patience. After several minutes of this ridiculous activity, Whateley realized something quite horrible and frightening.

Gouroull was toying with him, tormenting him with the same amused sadism that a cat uses when teasing its terrified, cornered, prey. The many punches hitting him apparently had had no true effect. The creature moved with the same celerity as he had during their first encounter. The demoniac monster had absorbed the blows and waited, with his infamous patience, for the right moment to strike back.

A phosphorescent glimmer emerged behind Gouroull's alien eyes, a cruel delight in Hezekiah Whateley's plight. This glint grew harsher a moment later as the terrible fury of Frankenstein's Monster grew. Whateley watched this, amazed and becoming frightened by the horror as it emerged from the depths of this creature's black soul.

The stony hands gripped even tighter, snapping his ankle and grinding his bones into dust. Before Whateley could open his mouth, intent on screaming as the agony grew unbearable, he found himself in the air. His huge body crashed back to the earth a split second later. The impact knocked the wind from him and, a second later, he found himself in the air again. This time, he landed face first on the stony ground, his body and mind stunned.

Then, he was in the air again, the agony in his leg increasing exponentially as he landed on his back. That was when Hezekiah Whateley truly understood what was happening to him. Yet, he was barely capable of grasping the truth as he struck the ground twice more, and his heavy, remade, bones splintered.

Gouroull, still grasping Whateley's leg, lifted him up and slammed him to the ground, again and again. He swung the enormous servant of Satan with the ease of an experienced carpenter using a favorite hammer. Whateley now understood this, though only as a distant realization. He felt as if this bizarre, horrific scene occurred to a stranger, his mind almost incapable of comprehending his plight.

The hammering continued for what felt like hours, with a numbness slowly spreading across Hezekiah Whateley's body. Eventually, his body stopped moving and his vision became blurry in one eye, gone, incapable of seeing anything anymore. He observed the face of Gouroull hovering over his single working eye. The monster's face appeared impassive for a time, studying him with the same inhuman calm he had demonstrated earlier.

Then his massive mouth opened, revealing rows of enormous incisors. The terrible teeth glistened in the starlight as he moved ever closer to Hezekiah's prone body. Slowly the world went black and he felt himself drifting downward, away from the world, towards a distant location filled with heat…

Gouroull strode over the ridge, spotting the ocean washing up over the rocks twenty feet below. People in the area apparently called this peak Widow's Hill, though he did not know why. Nor did Gouroull care—that was a human conceit, a need for naming everything they encountered. Would it matter if local inhabitants called this cliff Widow's Hill or Happy Hill? Not in the slightest. The rocks would still lay at the edge of the ocean with the heavy surf crashing day and night, and ghosts would lay just out of sight.

The ghosts moved like light traces of mist, circling but unsure of his presence. Gouroull rumbled with amusement at the notion that the specters of the dead feared his presence. Those remnants of humanity were pure emotion—their entire being feeling only one sensation at a time. When they felt fear, that was all they experienced. Therefore, Gouroull's manifestation in their vicinity was pure torture. This he found quite amusing.

Checking his pouch again, he felt the cold, dark energies of the Shining Trapezohedron, the Skull of Sobek, and the Crown of Commodus. He had about two hundred miles to go to reach the gate, but he did have one duty that still required completion.

Lifting his other hand, Gouroull looked into the shattered face of Hezekiah Whateley. He had been dangerous, but ultimately only a pale copy of Frankenstein's creation. Not physically—they were as alike as identical twins. The difference had been in the mind behind the apex predator body. Whateley was a man; he had fought like a man; had thought like a man. Gouroull was neither man, nor beast. He was something quite unexpected, and this was his vast advantage. His alien intellect gave him the best of the humans and the animals in a compound well beyond both.

With another rasp from his throat, Gouroull flung the head out into the wide expanse of sea. He did not know if his enemy could regrow his body from only his head. Such an issue never plagued Frankenstein's monster. If Whateley proved capable of such a feat, he could do so at the bottom of the Atlantic Ocean. That is, if the crabs did not nibble his skull clean to the bone first.

Turning away, Gouroull headed northwest towards the border. The gate would take him back to Siberia and then he would see if Rasputin had lied to him. He appeared sincere, but humans were creatures of deception. Perhaps the Siberian holy man would prove as big a fool as Pastor Schlager, or as venal and grasping as Vrollo. However, Gouroull doubted Rasputin resembled either. He had appeared sincere, and believed he was behaving in a manner that could save the Earth.

Gouroull glanced back and smiled as the fog, which formed quickly where he had stood earlier, blew away. The whispering moans of the ghosts rose for a moment, then vanished. Only the sounds of the waves crashing against the rocks at Widow's Hill filled the air.

CHAPTER XXXIV

"I have another question," Fatimah said as she glanced over her shoulder.

Keeping her hands on the airship wheel, she spied Faisal as he slaved away at his workbench. The harsh acidic tang hurt her nose and she wrapped a heavy scarf over her nose and mouth. This dulled the chemical smells that emerged from the other end of the copula.

"You do?" Faisal asked with poorly mocked shock. "I am astonished! What, pray tell, brought about this odd and momentous occasion?"

"A consideration of those who are helping Gouroull. You stated that the Masked Messenger was one of their numbers, and that he is often mistaken for Shaitan. The others, like the Lurker at the Threshold, the Daemon Sultan, and the Black Goat of the Woods, are all alien beings whose very sight would drive anyone mad. Am I correct so far?"

"You are," Faisal acknowledged as he pipetted a solution. "The one you called the Masked Messenger takes as many form as he deems necessary. Other names of his include the Black Demon, the Black Pharaoh—that one I battled several times in Egypt and the Sudan—the Haunter of the Dark, Mister Jones…"

"Mister Jones? That sounds like a name of an American or an Englishman," Fatimah interrupted, glancing back to see if Faisal was joking.

"Yes," Faisal replied, never looking up from his work. "He has appeared as a European or an American businessman visiting colonies from different countries. Very friendly, though one could not remember his face afterward, only his happy smile. He caused terrible destruction and chaos in the Belgian Congo and the British South African colony."

"What type of destruction?" she asked as the fumes increased in density.

She heard Faisal turning on a ventilation system he used under such occasions and she silently sighed with relief.

"Enslavement and murder of the local population. Stripping the land of resources and leaving behind decimated, barren lands. Wholesale slaughter of the wildlife, often for fun, or some small resource like a tusk. Colonization is a great evil of our world. Under this monster's guidance, it approaches genocide. Mister Jones is one of the Haunter of the Dark's most destructive forms. Even the Black Man, another of his identities, caused fewer horrors with his spread of false Shaitan cults and creation of witch hunters."

"I see," Fatimah said. "That is, admittedly, terrible and frightening. This then returns me to my original query. How could any sane or insane human being willingly follow such creatures? Every tale you had me read, or told me, of the Lurker at the Threshold, the Daemon Sultan, and the Black Goat of the Woods were horrific. They consume their followers as willingly as would those fighting their return. Why?"

"That is the question I asked my teachers shortly after learning of such alien beings. Few possessed any answers beyond the usual cries of madness and power lust. I found both explanations simplistic and foolish. All involved are insane, that much is clear. However, few afflicted with derangements of the mind would choose a path in which they work to open locked gates between worlds." Faisal sighed. "Another failure. I must try a new direction."

"Do so," Fatimah said, "but continue with your thoughts on this subject."

"Where was I?" he asked rhetorically. "Ah, yes. My teachers and their considerations of the Outer Gods. As I said, they accepted the notion that a madman or a power-seeker, or a combination of the pair, were the only followers of these ancient beings from beyond the stars. As I found that somewhat of a circular reasoning, I delved further. The writer of *Al Azif*, which the Europeans renamed the *Necronomicon*, was a poet known as Abdul Alhazred. Tales place him in the ancient ruins of Memphis, lost sections of Babylon, and the deadly, desolate desert known as the Rub' al Khali. He reputedly discovered a lost inhuman city, and that experience provided him with knowledge about the Old Ones. That is where I came to my conclusions on the reason why humans, though miniscule in numbers, embrace these ancient god-like monsters."

"I await this revelation with bated breath. Is that the correct saying? I read it in *The Strand Magazine*," Fatimah said as she pulled off her scarf.

Faisal snorted at the tease as he turned and stripped off his heavy, rubber gloves. These he tossed in a metal container that held the chemicals and glassware he had used earlier. As he sealed the canister, he replied:

"Quite correct and well-timed. Perhaps I am slightly verbose on this subject. Most occult fighters merely seek the means of defeating their foe, not the larger implications of their battles."

He looked off in the distance for a moment and then shook his head.

"My belief was that those ancient creatures and their desire for the destruction of our race encouraged several types of humans. First, those who believed the world oppressed them and kept them from their own fantasy versions of success. Some wish they had been born kings, other desire obscene amounts of wealth, some even base their fury on being denied sexually. In most cases, these experiences result in an angry, unpleasant person. In the case of one who comprehends occult lore, it leads to the darker arts."

"Yes," Fatimah said, rolling her eyes. "I dealt with such types in the past."

"I have no doubt," Faisal said, pulling up a stool and opening a notebook.

He studied a row of formulae and shook his head. Turning the page, he continued reading and speaking.

"Second, there are those who believe their way is the true path of the world. You may consider them the same as the followers of extreme religions. They believe their way is the only truth and challenge anyone who opposes it. I think you understand this type better than most," he added.

Having been raised as an assassin by an extremist religious sect secretly in the service of the Outer Gods, Fatimah shuddered at the thought.

"All too well. Continue, please."

"Third, there are the academics and explorers of the hidden realms of science and lore. They seek answers to various questions, and the Old Ones often provide such truths—not the ones they likely wanted, but such is to be expected when you cross the borders beyond established ethics. You may consider esoteric collectors like the one whose home we visited one of that type."

Fatimah glanced back, and their eyes briefly met. She did not speak, but did raise an eyebrow in inquiry. The implication was obvious: Faisal fit many of those characteristics. Nodding, he said:

"Quite so, but I possessed a healthy respect for life by the time one of my teacher gave me a copy of *Al Azif*. I studied that soul-blasting tome, unaware that he watched me from a distance. Had I succumbed to the temptation, the doctor had planned my swift death. Happily, I passed that test. Which brings me to the final type: the insane ones. By all accounts, Alhazred was already mad when he chose to embark on his treks into the dark unknown. Did he discover a lost, inhuman race in the hidden, forgotten Irem of the Pillars? Possibly, yes; possibly, no. All that is known is that he left behind a black tome capable of destroying the universe. Does this answer your question?"

Fatimah nodded once and said:

"Sadly, yes. However, the answer provides me with no comfort"

"Comfort rarely exists when you examine the arcane aspects of our world, Fatimah. My advice is to focus only on what you can control. Once you start realizing your place in the cosmos, you will find yourself gibbering and incapable of functioning, even for the basic tasks of life. And I speak from experience," he concluded, crossing out several figures and scribbling a few lines of mathematical codes.

"You speak from knowledge," Fatimah stated, not asking. "How did you overcome your fears?"

"Exercise and work. They shipped me to a logging camp in western Canada where I labored so hard, it left me no time for thought. Then, my teachers sent me to China, where I studied Heihuquan, better known as

Black Tiger Boxing. There, my teacher taught me mind-clearing exercises as well as that unique style of fighting. There is nothing better for the troubled mind than standing in a deep horse stance for two hours, while staring at a tree. One learns simplicity and calming oneself."

"I prefer training with weapons until I cannot move. A calm mind is an unaware one," she shot back.

"There," he replied, "we are in complete disagreement. Allow me a moment of preparation at my bench and I shall explain…"

CHAPTER XXXV

The Witch of Dolwyn Moor felt Hezekiah's destruction the instant Gouroull's terrible teeth tore the Dunwich man asunder. This was not a feeling of love or any type of interpersonal connection. It was her duty for the Dark Angel. She represented him in a very minor capacity on Earth, and was his tool for certain specific duties, as she had told the now-dead Hezekiah.

However, she did have some degree of freedom. Freedom was Satan's greatest illusion and weapon when confronting humanity. The minute a human chose the path of the Devil and invoked his power, they lived like a pet dog on a long leash. Their damnation being assured, Satan allowed his followers a false sense of freedom during their time on Earth. They could kill, pillage, rape, and rob to their black heart's content, further ensuring their place in Perdition. The damned instinctively knew their duty was to spread evil and chaos throughout the world, transforming a potential paradise into a land of darkness and horror.

At least, this was the theory. The Devil was the Prince of Lies and perhaps he, as some suggested, merely took in those who had no place in Heaven and accepted them in his land of darkness and brimstone. There was no true method of comprehending Lucifer's mind; he was a being as beyond the imagination of humanity as those aliens known as the Outer Gods. The Witch of Dolwyn Moor accepted these facts and continued on her path, knowing her end would come when she met a certain smiling man with a white shirt and a face that was pure horror.

"You felt Hezekiah Whateley's death, did you not, Siani Bwt?" a man's voice asked.

The voice was smooth and spoke in the same accents as the locals, though with a honeyed undertone that possessed an obvious malevolence.

The Witch of Dolwyn Moor, also known as Siani Bwt, shivered and turned. The man behind her was of average height, with thick blond locks that fell across his shoulders and a face so handsome it made viewing it for more than a moment nearly impossible. His dark eyes were deep, enticing, and possessed equal amounts of amusement and disinterest.

"Master," she whispered, dropping to her knees, her head bowed low.

She spotted a distorted glimpse of her prostrate form in his highly polished black shoes.

"My apologies for Whateley's failure," she muttered.

"Hezekiah Whateley chose his path, Siani Bwt. Do not take responsibility for anyone other than yourself," Satan replied, leaning against the barren tree by his side. "Now, stand up and look at me. I dislike talking to the tops of heads."

"That would not be right, master. I am not worthy," the Witch replied, shaking with terror.

"Either rise up and speak to me," Satan replied, his voice hardening, "or I shall feed you your own intestines and keep you alive while you feel the agony of each bite. Your choice. All of existence is choices, Siani Bwt."

"Yes, master," She replied in a shaky voice.

Rising, the Witch looked the Dark Angel in the face, feeling terror at the very sight of the exalted ruler of the seven circles of Hell.

"Good," Satan said with a nod. "You choose wisely. Now, we shall talk. You felt Whateley's death. I shall now give you another choice. You knew his mission? Yes? Also good. Do you wish it continued?"

The Witch of Dolwyn Moor's face creased in confusion.

"Of course not, master! Do you want Gouroull's success? If he completes the final steps, all life on this world will perish!"

Satan smiled, his teeth very bright and white in the darkness.

"Why should I care about that, my slave?"

Stunned by his nonchalance, she momentarily forgot her fears and said:

"But… but… if all life is turned into dust, you will have nothing… No souls, no humans!"

Satan chuckled and shook his head.

"You are under a misapprehension, little witch. You are mistaking me for the creator of all life. He loves all life, good or evil. I do not love you, or anything."

But if all life dies," the Witch shot back, "then you will rule nothing but your dark pit."

Raising a carefully sculpted eyebrow, Satan replied:

"You think that? My, oh my, you humans are so very amusing. You see yourself as the center of all life in the cosmos, despite knowing you are naught but microscopic specks in the universe. Your entire lives are so infinitesimal and unimportant, I always feel as if every conversation with your kind is like chatting with fleas."

"If we are so unimportant?" the witch asked, "then why ask me? Why give me the choice of whether to intervene or not?"

"I will not involve myself, fool," Satan said, stepping closer.

His face was now mere inches from hers, his handsome countenance now replaced by a mask of uncontrolled rage.

"You think I care a whit whether life exists on this miserable rock? If the Outer Gods open a gate and consume all your lives, so what? I shall raise my forces and remove them a second time."

"A second time?" Siani Bwt echoed, confused.

None of this conversation made any sense to her, but she could not stop listening.

Satan stepped away, his amused, mocking smirk returning. His whole form exuded a smugness that revolted her, yet she still did not turn away.

"The Old Ones are prisoners, locked away from this world. Who do you think placed them in durance vile? The One Above All? No, he left that to me, my fallen brethren, and the demons I control."

"Then why ask me about Gouroull? If you do not care whether anyone or anything on this world exists, why ask me about that monster?"

"It is your world, after all," Satan replied, shrugging. "As one of my slaves, you have the right of limited choice. Should you wish for the power, you may send others as your tools, and protect the world from Gouroull and the Outer Gods he temporarily serves. Your choice, little witch."

"Yes," Siani Bwt answered, without hesitating. "I want this power. I will keep the Outer Gods from this world. I will summons other servants and we shall stop Gouroull and his masters."

Satan tapped the witch on the side of her head with one talon finger,

"Then, the power is yours, little Siani Bwt. Enjoy it, embrace it, and I shall see you soon enough. Farewell… for now."

The Master of Darkness vanished. Not in a puff of smoke, or in any manner written in books or other tales. One second, Satan stood by the Witch's side, the next, he was gone. No theatricality, no showy displays, which was even more frightening. Satan was a higher being who possessed no need for demonstrations of his power.

Shivering again, the Witch retrieved her walking stick and headed back along the path. She now possessed the knowledge promised and her foresight told her exactly who would and could serve her best in this duty.

"And they shall be six. Six is the number meaning man in numerology," the witch muttered aloud as she headed down her path towards the circle of stones. "Men, not monsters, shall save the Earth. This much, I see in my visions. This, I know to be the truth."

CHAPTER XXXVI

Gouroull knew that someone followed him, despite his silent passage through the deep, untouched wilderness. The ancient forest was gloomy, even in the daytime. The land held few, or no, humans, this much he knew. The animals scuttling through the trees and brush possessed no fear of men, having viewed few of them over the years. Even his odd scent, which usually engendered fear in those possessing advanced senses, elicited no response from the birds, small animals, and even a few predators.

This, in and of itself, was odd. Gouroull knew his makeup repelled those of the wild, a factor he often found amusing. The creatures of nature behaved in two ways towards the unnatural, relying on antediluvian instincts built into their very makeup: fight or flight. Upon spotting Gouroull, animals sought his destruction, or fled on mere sight of him. This was good, because he had no time for such unimportant matters.

In his delusional diary, Victor Frankenstein had written of a mythical meeting between himself and Gouroull. This confrontation was ludicrous, describing a begging monster who merely wished love and companionship after his creator's rejection. Gouroull supposed this was Victor's means of justifying his creature's actions after he himself had fled from the results of his dark genius.

The words Gouroull had allegedly stated were:

I do know that for the sympathy of one living being, I would make peace with all. I have love in me the likes of which you can scarcely imagine and rage the likes of which you would not believe. If I cannot satisfy the one, I will indulge the other.

Amusing and more words than the Monster used in a year of life. Said diary contained other long passages about good and evil, comparisons between Gouroull and fallen angels and the likes. Victor could not accept that his work had produced an apex predator whose outward shape only slightly resembled that of humankind. Though his basic shape was that of a human, possessing ten fingers, ten toes, eyes, mouth, and nose, Gouroull was not human.

But what was he then? This was a topic hotly debated by a few scholars, none of which promoted any single theory. Was he an evolutionary step forward? A scientific advancement for humanity? A demon summoned from some unfathomable dimension? An alien who had lost his memory upon landing on Earth? A Fallen Angel suffering from delusions? An Incarnation of Death itself? The theories ranged from the simplistic to the sublime, from the hysterical to the frightening.

Gouroull alone knew the answer; yet, he was not speaking on the subject. Victor Frankenstein also knew; yet, he was dead, lost but not forgotten in the frigid wastes that had become his tomb. They had debated briefly on the subject, with Frankenstein revealing the truth, and Gouroull nearly killing him for that information. His creator has later recounted this discussion in very amusing, and quite ridiculous details.

According to Frankenstein, his creation had shaken him and said:

Hateful day when I received life! Accursed creator! Why did you form a monster so hideous that even you turned from me in disgust? God, in pity, made man beautiful and alluring, after his own image; but my form is a filthy type of yours, more horrid even from the very resemblance. Satan had his companions, fellow-devils, to admire and encourage him; but I am solitary and abhorred.

Lovely language, truly magnificent use of dialogue and romantic imagery. Had Victor Frankenstein not turned his genius towards the darker arts, he could well have become a magnificent writer or poet. The man was undeniably a genius in many areas, though his greatest creation had driven him completely insane. He simply could not accept that his toil and labor had created the modern, scientific equivalent of a demon.

Gouroull considered this briefly as he traversed the small game trails. His shadow followed him, moving through hidden pathways in the dense underbrush. The figure made no sound, nor did it appear visible in any way. However, a slight spoor emerged at various times, often when this being moved within range or upwind. The smell was a sickly tang, a harsh noxious odor that smelled in equal parts of rot and fresh meat. This was the scent of a beast unlike any that walked on the planet, at least from the perspective of the widely-traveled Gouroull.

These were the normal actions of a predator stalking its prey. Examine it, classify it, and find the best location for a swift strike. Few such animals moved upwind of their victim, knowing that it could reveal their position. This suggested that this creature knew of humans and their weak senses. Despite that, the creature remained distant, possibly sensing that Gouroull was not a typical human, not even a member of that species.

This stalking and shadowing bored Frankenstein's creation. He preferred heading to the gate without thought or concerns. Therefore, he sought an immediate confrontation.

As there were no clearings visible, Gouroull stopped in a wider portion of the trail and waited. He did not move, did not blink, and, apparently, did not breathe. Frankenstein's Monster stood still, on the trail, waiting. He possessed patience beyond that of any human or animal on this planet. Should the need arise, Gouroull would stand in this place for years, a semi-living statue capable of inhuman action.

Just ahead, the stalker emerged from the tree line. Standing over ten feet-tall, it was as terrible in its own way as Frankenstein's creation. The body of the beast was vaguely man-shaped, standing upright with long arms and legs held together by a disproportionately thin torso. Each hand held five elongated, skeletal fingers with short, sharp talons that clicked when they moved.

It was with its head that all resemblance to humanity vanished. The skull was that of a stag, the skin rotting away and revealing the white bone beneath in patches. Shrunken white eyes appeared just visible in the darkness, and vast, jagged teeth peaked through its oversized mouth.

The creature smelled of corruption, blood, human waste, and rot. A nearly invisible cloud of pestilence arose from its putrefying form, wafting towards Gouroull and spreading across his inhuman form. The horrific smell intensified for a moment, before falling away as Gouroull stared at the gigantic, undead monster.

The creature's head tilted to the side, a gesture of confusion remarkably like that of a human. The dead white eyes almost bulged, and the mostly vanished nose wrinkled slightly. Small pieces of flesh fell away from its face and neck as it examined Frankenstein's creation without any visible expression.

Eventually the monster straightened and emitted an ululating cry and charged forward. Its overlong arms led the way, seeking Gouroull's massive arms. Waiting, until the creature was close, the Monster reached out and grabbed the massive, bony wrists, holding his foe at arm's length for a moment.

The flesh beneath Gouroull's fists felt spongy and pliant, squishing and emitting juices, fluids, and a thick layer of white and yellow pus. The thin bones bent slightly, but did not break, despite the overwhelming force of Gouroull's stony hands.

Frankenstein's Monster's strength matched that of his massive adversary. Instead of bending its arms, the huge, rotting creature pushed forward, forcing Gouroull back several feet. They strained against each other, their inhuman might an even contest for the moment. Gouroull pressed back, rumbling with amusement in his chest as his enemy's unshod feet dug furrows as he forced it backwards.

Then, the rotting head slashed downward, the jagged teeth snapping the air as it sought Gouroull's neck. Frankenstein's creation swung his grasping arms to the right and spoiled the attacker's lunge. Before Gouroull could attempt a biting attack himself, his enemy righted and pulled the decomposing arms closer. The undead beast's body was as horrible as its head, with exposed ribs and flaking flesh all too obvious in such close quarters. Its smell was even more noxious at this short distance and Gouroull spotted maggots slowly winding their way across the enormous form.

Suddenly, he spotted something, a crystalline substance just visible beneath the brown and white rib cage.

A second later, Gouroull saw the oval object pulse briefly; there was a shuddering motion and small chips of ice fell away and into the creature's body. Apparently, this was the undead heart of this demon—a ball made of ice.

Gouroull did not understand how this was possible, nor did he care. They resided in a world in which a science-created demon battled an undead apex predator for supremacy. Wondering how each of these monsters could exist in a sane universe was an unnecessary waste of time and thought.

Throwing both arms wide, Gouroull released his grasp and lunged forward with both hands. Grabbing the ribs with one hand, his other punched upwards through the pliant, putrefying flesh. His hand and arm sank deep into the rotted carcass, bursting through the decaying organs. A moment later, his hand grasped the icy heart.

A wave of arctic chill ran through Gouroull's arm, a sensation as terrible as a plunge beneath the depths of the North Pole. But despite this terrible feeling, he closed his fist around the frozen heart.

The monster shrieked, a horrific, nearly human scream of agony and terror as the frost-covered exterior of its heart shattered under Gouroull's iron grasp.

Seconds later, the cold feeling vanished, and Frankenstein's Monster felt the fleshy exterior of a beating heart. The organ pulsed once before Gouroull's huge hand closed, reducing its remains to a pasty pulp.

The undead monster screamed again and shuddered, falling away from Frankenstein's creation and finally collapsing to the ground with a squishy thud.

Its decomposing flesh transformed in a viscous fluid and fell away from its oversized bones. Its massive skeleton collapsed, slowly crumbling, and turning into a gray and white dust that lay across the sward in large clumps.

Within five minutes, nothing remained of the creature, but the white powder, which slowly blew away as a slight breeze shook the trees.

Sensing that he was now alone with the animals and insects of the wilderness, Gouroull continued forward. Only fifty more miles to the gate back to Siberia. Then he would test the sincerity of the man called Rasputin.

CHAPTER XXXVII

The Witch of Dolwyn Moor, better known as Siani Bwt, took her flint knife and made a pair of light cuts across her palms. The skin parted with uncanny ease, and the pain was minimal. The ancient knife was still as sharp as the day an ancient Neolithic tribal shaman had chipped the rock into existence and sacrificed one of his brethren to the unnamed darkness that ruled his heart. The blade, later known as an *athame* by practitioners of witchcraft, possessed a negative energy that ate at the mind of the holder, unless they were very well-trained in the black arts. The oceans of blood spilled over the millennia remained within the depths of the stone, creating a scarlet spirit that craved more blood and lives. This was an evil knife, the perfect tool for the Witch of Dolwyn Moor.

She had received the blade from her teacher, an ancient fey enchantress who had spread evil throughout the world for many centuries. A lovely, dark-haired woman with a regal, imperious face and manner, she had produced the blade in this very grove, laying the weapon on the center stone.

"Our master," the Witch's mistress had said, speaking in an ancient tongue long forgotten in the isles, "no longer requires me as his voice. My duties lay elsewhere, and you shall take my place."

"What if I do not wish for that place in the master's coven?" Siani Bwt had asked, frightened by the prospect of such an onerous position.

She was then young, a girl just beginning her bloom into womanhood, and knew that such a place would make her powerful, but also distant from all humanity.

The enchantress's lovely lips had curved in an ironic smile.

"I asked the same question of my teacher. I shall answer you as she did me. You shall become the master's voice because he wishes it. You have no choice in the matter; you are his, and his alone. Weep if you wish. Scream and howl until your voice cracks and your body falls to the ground in exhaustion. Then meet me here at Walpurgis Night and the ceremony shall commence."

As predicted, Siani Bwt had found herself in this very circle of stones, receiving her dark consecration and being reborn as the Witch of Dolwyn Moor.

Now, centuries later, her body older and weaker, she stood in the same center, said a dark prayer to Satan, and drew six sigils on the stones with her own blood. Then, she sat down, pulled out her pipe, and smoked for a time. Over an hour passed, then a second, and she was close to a third when the first stirrings of power touched her black heart and devious mind.

The Witch felt the gates opening in various points in the woods, the summonsed accepting the request and proceeding to the circle of stones, a short walk from their current position. Each of the summonsed individuals felt the radiating evil from the circle, the scarlet-stained stones, tainted by the blood of untold victims. This location pulled them like moths to a flame, vultures to a carcass. The blood, death and darkness called them like a beacon in the middle of a vast wasteland.

They emerged from six different directions, unconsciously approaching the circle at the same time. None of these beings possessed any outward similarities, yet all radiated a palpable air of menace that was unmistakable for even the least observant witness. These six wore their evil openly, displaying the darkness in their souls with pride and a certain amount of delight. These were not the pretend villains of penny dreadful tales or Gothic romances; nor were they merely the greedy criminals who derived pleasure and profits from the blood of their fellow men. These were creatures steeped in evil, filled with intentions so heinous that there was no mitigation.

The first one the Witch spotted was a woman, an elderly crone with a bent back and yellow and black eyes that shimmered in the darkness. She resembled every horrific, cannibalistic witch of myths and fairy tales. Her face was a ravaged roadmap of wrinkles, craters, and boils. Her hair was a mop of filthy gray tangles and she moved with the slow deliberation of one fearful of falls. If anyone were to examine this woman from a distance, they might have mistaken her for an aged prostitute from some large city, barely surviving after her "skills" were no longer useful or sought. She was a pitiable figure, at least from this viewpoint, which showed how modern man denies the truth of evil when it stands or walks before him.

This was the infamous Mater Suspiriorum, better known as the Mother of Sighs. She was one of the horrific "Three Mothers" of modern myth. According to legends, Mater Suspiriorum and her two sisters, Mater Tenebrarum and Mater Lachrymarum, had created the true art of witchcraft and spread its evil throughout the world. The Mother of Sighs was the eldest sister, the learned mistress of the macabre arts who set all three on the path of spreading evil in the name of Lucifer Morningstar.

The Witch of Dolwyn Moor considered the Three Mothers as her forbearers, her true parents. Raised by the covens in the arts of witchcraft and black magic, all her power and skills derived from the Mothers. She knew Mater Suspiriorum still spread her occult knowledge, having opened a school for dance and magic in the ancient Black Forest of Germany. It was said that a recent battle with a white witch had weakened Mater Suspiriorum, but the Witch of Dolwyn Moor doubted that was possible.

"Mother of Sighs, you honor me with your presence," the Witch said, bowing her head in respect.

Mater Suspiriorum cackled and ran a withered claw over the top of Siani Bwt's head.

"I do honor you, child. My sister, Mater Lachrymarum, will be surprised you chose me rather than her."

"I would not wish to dishonor either of your sisters, mistress, but I chose you because you are the eldest of the three," the Witch replied, horrified by the repellent caresses of this creature. She was not as cruel as her sister, Mater Tenebrarum, but she was more insidious in her actions.

"That I am, my daughter," Mater Suspiriorum said with another phlegmy cackle, before stepping away.

The second creature appearing in the clearing was a male, tall, with broad shoulders, a narrow waist and massive, hairy hands. He had a square face with a nose shaped like a raptor's beak, and heavy, thick eyebrows. The brow above the wide, dark eyes protruded from his skull, an odd deformity on an otherwise interesting face. His black velvet suit was well-tailored, and a heavy silk cape lay across his shoulders. He walked with a self-assured calm, though his eyes darted about in every direction.

There was something bestial about this man, despite his expensive clothes and quiet demeanor. He looked as if, at any time, he might tear off his coverings and run about with an axe, slaughtering, raping, and eating the corpses of anyone in his path. This image intensified when he smiled and revealed the serrated fangs of a vampire.

This was Baron Brákola, a two hundred years-old Mexican nobleman. He served as the master of a cult of vampire women, and had been transformed by their high priestess before his death. He was a brutish, lustful, lout, a dangerous killer and one of the strongest vampires in the world. The Baron pretended he was a nobleman in the old tradition, yet the barbaric monster was always present, lurking just below the surface.

"You honor me with your request, Madame," Baron Brákola lisped and bowed.

His oversized teeth transformed his speech from regal to comical. But nobody in the world seemed willing to remark upon this oddity when facing the bestial Baron.

The Witch curtsied slightly, knowing the dangerous vampire favored Old World manners from those he met. He did not understand them particularly well, but the attempt was known to appeal to his odd sensibilities.

"My lord, baron, I thank you for your acceptance of my invitation. We are honored by your presence," she said, reciting a speech that worked for centuries when confronting violent, dangerous monsters.

The Baron bowed again and stepped away, his movements slow and self-assured. The words of praise appeared to work, as the bestial side of his vampiric nature seemed suppressed for the moment. But Siani Bwt was under no illusions, this man could transform back into the sub-human leech that lay just beneath the surface in a heartbeat.

The man who approached next was also a vampire, though his presence was as different from the animalistic Baron Brákola as night is to day. He was of medium height with a slim, attractive body and an oblong face that gave the impression of ancient nobility. He had dark blond hair, a pale complexion, and a long nose that perfectly fit his face. One look at this man and you knew that he was a member of an ancient, regal lineage. His movements appeared languid and bored, and he looked down upon everything and everyone with heavily lidded eyes. His clothing was a slightly dated tuxedo, complete with opera cape.

This was Count Karol de Lavud, a European vampire who resided in Spain and Mexico, depending on his whim. He was as dangerous as Baron Brákola, though his powers possessed a subtlety that the other could not comprehend. His power over the minds of humans and his fellow vampires was reputedly only surpassed by the legendary King of Vampires, Count Dracula. Lavud was also a master of seduction, using this talent as a means of defeating even the hardiest opponents.

"My Lord Count," the Witch of Dolwyn Moor said, bowing her head.

This was the proper form of address, the lower ranked peasant introducing herself to the high-ranking Count. He could then address her or not, as was proper when dealing with those born to ancient titles.

"Witch," Count Karol de Lavud intoned.

His words sounded more like a caress than anything spoken by a man. He then smiled, never once showing his pointed teeth.

"My thanks for your acceptance of my invitation. I am honored," she replied, straightening and staring him in the eyes.

Her power acted as a barrier against his mind tricks, but she still felt some stirrings within her body and mind.

"Yes," Count Lavud replied with another small smirk. "You are honored."

The regal Count slid backwards, his movements as fluid as a ballet dancer. He almost appeared to glide rather than walk, which fit his whole demeanor. In a battle, one needed intricacy as well as brutal violence. Count Karol de Lavud was the embodiment of both. He was regal, subtle, intelligent, and as violently evil as every vampire walking the planet.

The fourth creature stepping into view was the opposite of the Count's refined behavior. This man did not even possess the thin veneer of civilization that Baron Brákola used as a mask to the outside world. One look at this man and your flesh crawled, animals hissed and fled and, reputedly, the grass and flowers died as he walked past.

He was a short man, his top hat covered head only reaching Baron Brákola's massive shoulders. He was slim, almost emaciated, with an oddly fleshy face covered by a dark beard, mustache and sideburns that joined the beard. His eyes were dark and bulged from his head, and his smile was overly wide and exuded an air of madness. He wore dusty black clothing that made him look like an undertaker and his tall top hat made his head look oversized. His tanned forehead was wide and a pair of Luciferian eyebrows lay across his brows, dancing and twitching with his every motion.

However, what set him apart, what made him obviously strange and terrible to any who viewed him, were his fingers. Specifically, his long, sharply pointed, nails. They resembled the talons of a vast, monstrous bird-of-prey, or a particularly dangerous and violent jungle cat. Every time this man moved his hands and fingers, these clicked and clacked, a sound that could drive a listener insane in a short time.

He was known as Zé do Caixão and he was a South American undertaker. His devotion to evil had started after an accidental rejection from the love of his life who had left him alone. Choosing the path of evil, Zé do Caixão had become a mass murderer, justifying his insane acts under the veneer of a search for the perfect mother for his bloodline. At first, he had rejected God and the Devil, believing himself to be the mightiest being in the universe. Upon discovering otherwise, Zé do Caixão had become Satan's servant.

Why had the Witch chosen this madman for her assault upon the monstrous and mighty Gouroull? The reason was simple: Zé do Caixão was a survivor. He had overcome terrible odds against him, somehow escaping death many times. Additionally, he was a sadist who enjoyed causing pain in others, especially rivals. Perhaps Zé's insanity was the means of destroying Gouroull.

"I am here, old woman. Why do you steal me away from my work?" Zé do Caixão spat out, smiling and waggling his talons.

"Our master shall gift you with a possible candidate for your needs, but only if we succeed," the Witch shot back.

She knew Zé do Caixão was always seeking weakness in those he confronted. She would not demonstrate any before this disgusting creature.

"Very well. I shall assist our master for the price of a perfect woman," the South American undertaker replied, smiling. "One capable of continuing my bloodline. Perhaps only the Lord of the Dark can fulfill my requirements. Humans rarely prove capable of my needs."

He stepped to his position, pointedly ignoring the others, disinterested in their existence.

The Witch of Dolwyn Moor did not reply, but turned to her fifth choice. She was about the same height and they resembled each other in many ways. Both were elderly, but still vital. Their hair were tangled masses, though the newcomer's was a deep chestnut color. Each had faces best described as "handsome," though neither was beautiful. The newcomer looked a little younger, but the angry lines running across her cheeks and near her eyes gave her an aged quality. Both women looked young and vital when compared to the frightening Mater Suspiriorum, but together, they resembled the modern interpretation of witches.

This was Elizabeth Selwyn, a witch from the American colony known as Massachusetts, and the reason for the witches scares in that location. She had sold her soul to the Devil, supposedly in the form of a talking black goat. She and her coven had faked their deaths, all the while poisoning the minds of the children of Salem. Since that time, Selwyn and her followers had existed as an ageless cult in various cities. They had survived the passing of centuries, sacrificing virgins to their dark master in return for power and living far beyond their years.

Elizabeth Selwyn herself sat at the center of her coven like a vast black spider, consuming the proverbial flies caught in her web. Like the vampires, she existed on the blood and life energies of her victims. Unlike them, she only fed twice each year, bathing in the blood of her victims, and thus maintaining her evil existence. She had power within her, not merely that of a witch, but from the oceans of blood she had swum through over the centuries. This power made her an equal to anyone present, and her fiendish, cruel mind, earned her respect from this gathering of monsters.

"Well met, my sister," Elizabeth Selwyn purred and smiled.

Her yellow teeth and harsh gaze demonstrated the hypocrisy of her words. Siani Bwt knew this daughter of the Devil classified all beings in only two areas: victims or enemies.

"I am honored you came, sister," the Witch of Selwyn Moor replied.

She did not curtsey or demonstrate any deference to her sister witch. To do so would have been to admit that Elizabeth Selwyn was her better. That could had led to a conflict, something Siani Bwt knew she must avoid at all costs.

"I imagine you are, little one," Selwyn said, her eyes narrowing. "Where did you get such power? This is a puzzle I shall enjoy solving…"

The Witch opened her mouth to snap back an answer, but closed her lips quickly. A slight figure pushed forward, a silvery gray glow in the growing murk. Elizabeth Selwyn opened her mouth, intent on snarling out a challenge or a threat, but clamped her mouth shut too as she realized the identity of the sixth person in the circle of stones.

The woman approaching Siani Bwt was tiny, barely five feet-tall. She had long, dark hair that fell past her shoulders like an ebon waterfall, and a pale, lovely face that caused men and women to stare with open fascination. Her cat-like green eyes entranced everyone she viewed, and she wore a bright crown of daisies atop her oval head. A flimsy, gauzy, white gown covered her slim figure, and she moved with the slow stride of a sleepwalker.

This was the frightening and infamous Viy, a being of dreadful power from the distant east. A graduate of one of the Devil's dark academies, she had become that rarest of horrors, a vampire witch. Only the much-feared Princess Asa Vajda and Countess Mircalla Karnstein also held this terrible distinction among the creatures of the night. To obtain such power, one had to attend—and survive –either the Deep School, or the Scholomance, and enter into a pact with the Devil for an endless youth spent in darkness. The result was a calculating, lustful, mighty witch who thirsted for power, despoiling the innocent, and sowing chaos wherever she went. Even monsters like Lavud and Mater Suspiriorum walked careful when Viy, Asa Vajda, or Mircalla Karnstein, appeared in their midst.

Viy stepped close to the Witch of Dolwyn Moor and embraced her briefly.

Her cold lips brushed across her neck for a moment before she whispered:

"Well met, my child. You surprised me with your request. My sometimes lovers, Mircalla and Asa, will be surprised you chose me first."

"Mircalla," Siani Bwt explained, "received the final death from a French fencing master. Asa Vajda is fighting for the mind of her ancestress, seeking a return to undead life."

"You chose me because I was the only available? How… disappointing…" Viy whispered.

Her words felt like a physical force, like a harsh, frigid northern wind blowing across the circle of stones. Both Zé do Caixão and Elizabeth Selwyn flinched at the sudden drop of temperature, and Count Karol de Lavud raised an eyebrow in surprise. Baron Brákola appeared oblivious to the events, looking bored. Mater Suspiriorum shot the Witch an angry look, the meaning of which was quite obvious. Fix this situation before Viy's feelings of hurt pride triggered the frightening vampire witch's fury.

"I would have chosen you first no matter what, my lady Viy," the Witch rushed to say, bowing her head with respect. "Your power and wisdom are the envy of all."

Viy's lips twitched up and she tilted her head in thought.

"I think I shall believe you, daughter. But I may discuss this matter with you again soon."

"You are always welcome in my home, my lady," Siani Bwt replied.

She knew that if Viy wished entry, nothing short of a holy crusader would keep her from crossing her threshold. The normal limitations vampires suffered rarely applied to ones such as Asa Vajda, Mircalla Karnstein, and, of course, Viy.

Viy licked her pale lips with a tiny pink tongue, resembling a kitten viewing a pot of cream for a moment.

"Very well. I accept your offer," she stated.

"Can we get on with the reason for this summonsing?" Mater Suspiriorum snarled. "Though this was not a rude request, I demand to know, immediately."

"Before we get to the why," Lavud said, looking down at the Witch of Dolwyn Moor with hooded eyes, "I should like to know the how. You are not merely speaking for the Lord of Darkness this day, Siani Bwt. This is beyond your skill and power… And yet, here we stand…"

"Yes," Elizabeth Selwyn hissed, her face a mask of fury. "You are the Devil's tool, not an agent in his service. You are powerful and deadly, sister, but limited. Now, you radiate darkness like one born to the pit. How is this possible?"

The Witch of Dolwyn Moor realized that her fellow witch was jealous. Selwyn was one who valued her power and place in the hierarchy of Satan's servants. Finding that Siani Bwt was now her greater than her rankled the evil one's dark heart. She replied:

"Our master, Lucifer Morningstar, brightest and most beautiful of the angels, Lord of the Fallen, He who is called by a thousand names, offered me a pact. I could hold the power required to save this world from the Outer Gods. I agreed and chose each of you as His warriors."

"The Outer Gods' powers are virtually limitless," Mater Suspiriorum spat out, her face twisting into a mask of even greater horror. "All of our power combined could not so much as interest them. We would be like ants screaming curses at the stars, daughter."

"We face not the alien deities themselves, my lords and ladies," the Witch explained, "but their instruments. Our Lord's followers have sought an ancient tome capable of opening a permanent gate between Earth and Hell.

Now, the agents of the Old Ones have learned of this book, and plan to wrest its ownership from Satan's own servants. If they succeed, the once-banished deities will return and reduce the Earth to a lifeless lump of rock. I selected you six as the ones who may succeed in our quest to stop them."

"Six?" Zé do Caixão asked. He sounded outraged and he slashed the air with his wicked talons. "I could destroy any servant of those degenerate, forgotten, monsters alone."

"I tore a worshipper of Him Who Is Not To Be Named in twain last month. I then fed on his wife and the rest of their silly little cult, leaving the children for my wives. None were of any threat, or importance," Baron Brákola said, throwing his cape across his chest in a gesture meant to look noble. Sadly for the nobleman, he merely looked as if a bit of wind had caught his cape.

"Who is this agent?" Count Karol de Lavud asked, ignoring the other two monsters.

"The creation of an insane scientist named Victor Frankenstein. The monster calls himself, Gouroull," the Witch said, keeping her tone intentionally neutral.

"Ah! That one!" Elizabeth Selwyn said, frowning. "I believed him to be a myth, a tale told as a means of frightening light and dark alike."

"Oh, no," Lavud intoned, "Gouroull is quite real. I enslaved an Irish woman whom he had once imprisoned. She held more fear for that creature than she did for myself."

"Gouroull is an abomination," Mater Suspiriorum growled. "A dark force of nature. He destroys everything in its path without regard. He is a disaster in the shape of a man."

"No matter, old woman, I shall break this Gouroull over my knee and he shall be no more," Baron Brákola declared, extending his chin as he spoke.

"No!" Zé do Caixão roared, "I shall slice him to ribbons, and then we shall take him back to my parlor. There, I shall teach him the torments of the damned. This Gouroull shall beg for death after I show him the true meaning of pain. His death shall be glorious, and I shall make shoes of his hide!"

Count Lavud smiled, once again hiding his teeth as he said:

"Then you may attack first, my friends. I shall find it most instructive to see who emerges as the victor in this battle."

Baron Brákola and Zé do Caixão eyed each other without favor. They reminded the Witch of a pair of stags squaring off for a battle for breeding rights. This posturing might have continued for some time, but Viy spoke up and all attention turned in her direction.

"I am growing bored. Send us away or amuse us, daughter. I shall tarry in these woods no longer. What is your decision?" she whispered, once again causing flinches and fearful responses.

"I will go," Count Lavud intoned, stepping into his station in the circle.

"As will I, child," Mater Suspiriorum replied, hobbling to her place.

"The Devil repays those who favor his plans," Elizabeth Selwyn intoned as she moved to her place.

Baron Brákola straightened and walked in a manner he thought looked stately, but which resembled a child's poor imitation of a nobleman's stride.

"I, Baron Brákola, do not flee battles!" he intoned, raising both his caped arms.

“Zé do Caixão,” the taloned undertaker added, “has already stated his intention. Let us depart, witch!”

“In the name of Satan,” the Witch of Dolwyn Moor chanted, “Prince of the Air, Lord of the Darkness, Wicked One, King of the Earth, Tempter and Serpent, I open the way for you, his servants. Depart in the name of the Morning Star!”

Each of the Six slowly merged with the darkness, looking as if the murk had swallowed them up one at a time. The effect was unsettling, especially for the caster of this spell, Siani Bwt.

“Where are we going?” Elizabeth Selwyn asked as her body faded from sight.

“Siberia,” the Witch of Dolwyn Moor said.

She smiled at the unhappy look on her sister witch’s face.

CHAPTER XXXVIII

The long dark tunnel stretched into infinity. At least, that was how Gouroull viewed this walk through the dimensions. Time felt frozen, as if he strode though a land where such concepts did not exist. The ground beneath his feet felt pliable and nearly liquid, as if he walked across a vast unseen marsh. In the distance, a white light glimmered, sometimes appearing closer, other times further away than at the start.

Gouroull did not mind the oddity of this realm; his mind accepted the strangeness as a product of the travel. Had he been human, he might have gone mad from the unsettling properties of this other world. But since he was a unique life form, the strangeness of this universe passed over him without any effect. The distance would settle itself and he would arrive near his destination in Siberia.

He did recognize that eyes, or something approaching such appendages, were watching him from the abyssal depths of this world. Gouroull smiled as one of the hidden beings moved closer, remaining just outside the field of his vision. He knew they tested him, studied him. and asked themselves if he was predator or prey. Frankenstein's Monster sent them a simple response, a non-verbal message that he was just as capable of hunting them as they did him.

A few steps later and the gate opened before him, depositing him in the middle of the vast Siberian steppe. Somehow, whether by instinct or some information transmitted by the gate, Gouroull knew that he was only fifty miles from the cabin inhabited by the monk Rasputin. It was not far, despite the thick, ancient trees and steep rolling hills. Only the heavy snow laying like a blanket across the sward would slow him down, turning this trek to a four-hour journey.

Gouroull ran across the wilderness, moving far slower than his normal rate, but still faster than any human could have managed on foot. The few animals in the vicinity hid in the nests and unseen dwellings, recognizing the danger he represented.

He was halfway to his goal when a scent wafted his way and slowed his travel. The odor was familiar, human in origin, and completely unmistakable. Burning leaves in a clay vessel... Someone was smoking a pipe in the midst of these gargantuan, uninhabited wasteland. The odder part was that the temperature was at least twenty below zero, a frigid level that would kill humans with ease.

Continuing forward, Gouroull eventually spotted the man seated on a fallen tree. He was at least as tall as him, with broad shoulders that looked even larger under his heavy fur coat. A fur hat lay upon his dark, wooly head, and his thick black beard spread across his chest like the pelt of a titanic animal. A long sword lay across his back and a well-worn axe rested across his oversized legs.

"You would be Gouroull, no?" the stranger asked in oddly accented Russian.

"Yes," Gouroull rasped back, stopping a few feet away. "How?"

"How what? How did I know your name? The Baba Yaga told me you may pass this way. I confessed I found myself intrigued. You are something of a legend. Then again, so am I. I am Koschei, also called the Deathless One. Have you heard of me?"

Gouroull shook his head slightly and growled:

"No."

Koschei threw back his head and laughed.

"Ah, such is the way of the world. In Russia and Siberia, I am a legend. They believe I am a skeleton of a man, who is very ugly and old. I am neither, as you can see. The tales do call me a monster, a bad man who steals brides and kills enemies. This is true. I heard you are much like me, though I see that is only a little correct. You seek a mate?"

"Yes," Gouroull said, surprised that this giant conversed with him in such an easy manner.

"I did too, for many centuries. The unwilling ones slipped through my fingers, and the ones who sought me were unworthy. This is one area where humans are our superiors. Though they live short lives and are easily killed, they find companionship with ease. A puzzlement, no?" Koschei asked.

He laughed again and puffed on his pipe, blowing large blue and white clouds of smoke into the air.

Gouroull waited, confused by this large Russian man. He smelled like a normal human, yet he sat in the frozen tundra, unmoved by the cold, discussing living for centuries. Was he mad, or a different type of immortal?

"Do you wish to test your strength against mine? I cannot die, a spell prevents any from killing me. By reputation, you, too, may be deathless. A test of strength might be a pleasurable challenge. This is the difficulty of immortality. Time robs one of worthy opponents. Powers such as ours further destroys a chance of experiencing defeat. Without the possibility of loss, is life worth living? I wonder. No matter, shall we fight? Two immortals seeking superiority. It would be a glorious respite from the doldrums of eternal existence."

His wide eyes looked hopeful as he stood, the heavy years falling away from him with each pleading word.

Gouroull stared at the immortal, and possibly insane, Russian man. His black lips peeled back, revealing his razor-sharp incisors. Battling this man would be a kindness, and that was not in his interest. If this immortal human was so miserable with life, leaving him suffering was a delight.

"No," Gouroull rasped.

And he ran onward in the wilderness.

He glanced back, watching as the legendary Koschei the Deathless collapsed back on the tree, slumping over like a man who has just received the worst news in his life.

This was a very good day.

CHAPTER XXXIX

Faisal looked at Fatimah over his shoulder, watching as she gamely strode through the snow without complaint. The snowshoes he had supplied made movement slightly easier, but only by a little. The harsh, frigid air and biting winds slowed them both, despite their hardy demeanors.

The airship lay hidden a mile back, locked away and awaiting their return. The ship itself was safe, the systems running the advanced craft held locks and puzzles that could keep any intruder busy. Just turning on the gas required knowledge of a derivation of Sanskrit as well as the teachings of the Zoroastrianism scholar Shayast-na-Shayast.

"Two miles remaining," Faisal called back.

He heard a grunt in reply. Fatimah never looked up, her head lowered against the wind, her walking poles moving with each step. Faisal reflected that her training must have been impressive since she confronted every environment without difficulty. His training in such weather had cost him two toes from frostbite

The heavy, thick trees surrounded them, though each appeared skeletal and dormant as the breeze shook their empty branches. The gusts threw up billowing clouds of snow; ice, like microscopic darts, peppered the scarves that covered their faces, and the goggle which protected their eyes. Despite their heavy protection of furs and woolen clothing, both felt chilled to their bones. This land was virtually uninhabitable, a frozen waste close to the arctic, capable of killing humans in mere minutes. Walking through this tundra caused one to feel weak and unimportant in the face of nature's frightening fury. Humans, who viewed themselves as kings of this planet, were little better than insects in a Siberian winter.

"We are being watched," Fatimah said in a soft whisper.

Faisal kept walking, but realized a moment later that she was correct. He now felt the palpable energy that humans unconsciously experience when someone is staring their direction with intent. This innate experience derived from our ancient ancestors, a protective instinct meant to protect humankind from the many carnivores it had battled in its infancy. With the coming of civilization, this predisposition became somewhat muted, but trained hunters and killers like Fatimah, daughter of the legendary lost Order of Assassins, still had it.

Ten more minutes passed before Fatimah called out:

"Stop!"

Faisal obeyed. He felt her fur-clad back pressed against his.

"Whoever it is," she added, "knows we are prepared for them. Draw your weapon."

Faisal removed a two-foot dagger with a leaf-shaped blade and a well-worn rawhide handle. This was a *seme*, a weapon used by the Maasai, a tribe whose skill in hunting was legendary throughout the world. He had learned tracking and cattle-herding after a member of the tribe had rescued him from dying at the hands of a dangerous sorcerer. He carried this *seme* with pride, trusting the weapon as he would a long-standing comrade.

"Oh, how delightful," a mocking voice called out.

The voice echoed throughout the forest, seemingly emerging from every direction.

"A pair of children skipping through the forest. I am sorry, my little ones, we are fresh out of daisies this day. Perhaps when the weather grows a little warmer?"

"Perhaps," Faisal echoed, hearing the spiteful laughter ringing through the trees.

"Oh, you are brave. I like that… I do like that very much," the voice continued. "It always feels better when the brave die. They do not beg for lives, but accept the end with a forward thrusting chin. Obviously, this is after I tear out their eyes and tongue, but the theory is quite sound. Now, drop the weapons and come to my side," it added with an almost lascivious growl.

"That seems unlikely," Faisal replied, gazing about every direction.

He saw nothing but the trees and the muted sun reflecting on the heavy blanket of virginal snow.

"Now, that was rude," the voice snapped back.

The pitch was that of a woman, not young, yet not elderly in his opinion.

"No," Fatimah replied. "That was just a statement. This is rude. Come out and fight, you hideous creature. Your shrieking from the shadows might impress fools, but we've faced your kind in the past."

Faisal nodded once, still scanning the vicinity while saying:

"Yes, that truly qualifies as rude."

"So be it!"

The voice spat out and a slight form appeared several steps away. She was an older woman, her head covered in a hooded robe that was speckled with snow. Her lined face was not unattractive, though she stared at them with open fury.

"I am here, mortals! Look upon me with fear."

"Ah," Faisal said, "yes, you are there, madam. My apologies, but who are you?"

"I am Elizabeth Selwyn," she replied, raising her plump hands up and pushing back her hood. "I am a witch in the service of Satan. You two made a mistake when you chose this location for an excursion. Unless you are foolish cultists, come to support your alien masters."

"We are neither," Fatimah said. "You may leave us."

"No," Elizabeth said, smiling a vicious smile. "I do not believe you. Nobody comes to this misbegotten frozen hell unless there is a reason. There are only two. Either you came to support those multi-angled monsters and bring them to our world; or you are explorers or scientists on a mission. Neither of you are Siberian or Russian, so you are not from here."

"There is a third reason for traversing this steppe," Faisal replied. "We fight for the other side—Allah, called God in the West, who sent your master into the dust and fire, where he lives in agony and terror to this day."

As expected. Elizabeth Selwyn's face split into a frown of surprise, followed by naked rage. She curled her heavy hands into claws, spat upon the frozen ground and said:

"In the name of the Lord of Darkness, I call upon you, Lucifer, for…"

Her words cut off as a thin sharp blade entered her waddled neck and sliced deep into her throat. She coughed, and a small wave of blood exited her mouth. She fell back and yanked out the knife, dropping the weapon to the ground and spitting out more blood. Her eyes glittered with malice and she lifted her hands up again. The air suddenly became charged with electricity and a darkness spread across the sky above.

"You… will… die… slowly… bitc—," she whispered.

Her almost inaudible words were cut off as a loud whooshing sound cut across the clearing. The source was a large brass gun whose barrel was only a few inches long, but very wide. A long trail of smoke extended from it to Elizabeth Selwyn, who fell back from the impact. A second later, she burst into flames.

Shrieking so loud that the trees shook and the darkness vanished, the American witch was engulfed in a yellow and red fire that spread across her whole body. She ran into the woods, screaming as she vanished into the distance. The glow lasted a long time, as well as her screams of agony.

"What did you do?" Fatimah asked, staring at the odd weapon in Faisal's hand. "And what is that in your hand?"

"This is a French Navy flare gun," Faisal explained, breaking open the device and ejecting a huge metal shell. "I adapted the flare by adding a touch of phosphorus. The perfect weapon for confronting talkative witches."

"A vicious weapon, young one. Perhaps you would like to use that device on me?"

Viy stepped into a patch of sunlight, her face looking sad and mournful. "Do you wish to light us on fire, little human?"

"Allah protect us," Faisal breathed, taking a step backward.

Fatimah stepped back as well, though only because he was close to bowling her over.

"What is wrong?" she asked.

"How shall I put this?" Faisal said, thrusting his flare gun in a pocket and reaching into another. "Do you remember when I said that the vampires we met in Athens were lesser creatures? Even though they nearly tore us into pieces with relative ease?"

"Yes, the memory comes back to me nearly nightly as I often wake in a cold sweat," Fatimah replied, now moving backwards on her own.

"That," Faisal said, nodding towards Viy, "is what I referred to when I hinted at greater dangers."

"Are you positive?" Fatimah asked.

She felt confused by the pretty, oddly dressed woman with the daisy chain in her hair, who watched them with wide eyes and a head tilted in confusion.

Faisal nodded and stopped.

"I have a way of recognizing graduates of the dark schools of the occult. Our friend here graduated from the Deep School."

Viy nodded slowly and studied Faisal.

"How very wise of you, child. You shall tell me how you can detect one that attended such an elite academy."

Before Faisal could reply, Viy smiled and showed her oversized incisors. Her dark eyes glittered red and she licked her pink lips with a long, red, forked tongue.

"Allah protect us," Fatimah whispered, echoing Faisal's earlier sentiment.

CHAPTER XL

Gouroull stepped down from the snow mound, knowing he was only a short distance from the cabin. This small frozen lake was the last obstacle before it. The first time, he had circled around it—a long trek in the thick snow and ice. Its pale blue white surface appeared slick, and could save him hours of travel.

Stepping onto the lake, Frankenstein's creation felt, through his inhuman senses, that he was not alone. He felt presences, more than one, possibly from the lake, or the woods beyond. But the sensation was not precise, which was odd. His unique view of the world was a factor known only to himself, which was not surprising. Having christened himself shortly after waking from the dead, his words were rare, and he almost never expressed any details in those rare moments of talk.

This detail had disturbed Victor, possibly causing his break from sanity. In his journal, he had written long passages of speeches by Gouroull, none of which the Monster had ever uttered or contemplated uttering. One of the more verbose was so patently out-of-character that he recalled it regularly:

Shall each man find a wife for his bosom, and each beast have his mate, and I be alone? I had feelings of affection, and they were requited by detestation and scorn. Man! You may hate, but beware! Your hours will pass in dread and misery, and soon the bolt will fall which must ravish from you your happiness forever. Are you to be happy while I grovel in the intensity of my wretchedness? You can blast my other passions, but revenge remains—revenge, henceforth dearer than light or food! I may die, but first you, my tyrant and tormentor, shall curse the sun that gazes on your misery. Beware, for I am fearless and therefore powerful. I will watch with the wiliness of a snake, that I may sting with its venom. Man, you shall repent of the injuries you inflict.

What Gouroull said was simple and direct, using as few words as possible. Holding Victor up by his shoulders, he had in reality growled at his creator:

"A mate—or I kill you. Choose."

Though Gouroull had read human works in his early days, art, poetry, music, and prose held no place in his dark, cold breast. Those were transitory human creations, unimportant when compared with survival and the continuation of one's bloodline. The Monster knew he was alone in the universe, a factor he would remedy in time. Other immortals possessed the same drive—Dracula and Koschei had said as much in recent days. The difference was, neither possessed Gouroull's inhuman determination.

When he reached the center of the lake, the elderly woman hobbled into view. She was tiny, twisted, wrinkled, and smelled of death. Her rheumy eyes brightened at the sight of Gouroull, his massive frame easily supported by the two-feet thick ice below his feet.

"You are taller than I imagined," she said in a warbling whisper.

There was something repulsive about this aged creature, as if she stood rotting before his inhuman eyes.

Gouroull continued walking, disinterested in her and her statements. He was too close to his goal and dismissive of the ravings of witches—for she was a witch, this much was clear and apparent from scent alone. They all smelled of brimstone, rot, blood, and suffering. The older they were, the more their inner evil rose to the surface and revealed their true selves. This one, with her arthritic limbs, cracked lips, and ravaged countenance was both ancient and immersed in darkness.

"Yes," the aged hag said. Her voice was thoughtful and considered as she continued. "The few surviving witnesses said you spoke very little. One called you a bear in human shape. That is not right. I think you are like the shark, or the giant black and white whales of the north. A relentless predator in the shape of a man. It matters not… I am Mater Suspiriorum, also called Helena Markos in my youth. Have you heard of me?"

"No," Gouroull said, never slowing.

"Truly an animal. As I said, no matter. *Vodyanoy ego oriri et occidere eum iubes*," Mater Suspiriorum said, sounding closer to a crow cawing than a human.

Gouroull knew that "*ego oriri et occidere eum iubes*" freely translated from Latin meant, "rise and kill I command it." The word *vodyanoy* sounded Russian, or at least a language like it. However, the meaning of the curse was lost upon him.

He received his answer a heartbeat later when the ice around his feet crack and split open. A pair of oversized webbed hands grabbed his ankles in a grip of steel. With a quick yank, the powerful clutches pulled Gouroull downward, dropping him into the murky black waters of the lake. Just before he went under, Frankenstein's Monster caught sight of a bizarrely shaped green head with massive, bulging, black eyes and a long, whip-shaped tongue that wrapped around his neck like a slime-covered serpent.

The last sound he heard was the shrieks of spiteful laughter from the elderly witch...

CHAPTER XLI

"Invoking your deity for protection?" Viy asked. "How very… quaint. Humans are so very odd. Has your God ever protected you from harm?"

In the literal blink of an eye, she moved at least twenty yards closer, to behind their position. Her lovely, ethereal looks returned with this change of position, her massive teeth and reptilian tongue no longer visible.

"Yes," Faisal replied, no longer retreating. "Many times."

Turning her huge eyes toward Fatimah, Viy asked:

"You have doubts, pretty, pretty. I can smell that you do not believe as your master."

Fatimah glanced in Faisal's direction, while keeping her eyes on the frightening undead woman.

"Master? Is she serious?"

"Vampires view the world as dominance games," Faisal replied. "Do not feel insulted. However, answer the question before she believes you are ignoring her."

Fatimah stared at the daisy chain on Viy's head, having learned of the mesmeric power of vampires.

"Of course, I hold doubts," she said. "Though I do not reject the words of the Koran, nor the Jewish Bible, or the Christian Testaments."

Viy smiled, not hiding her pointed teeth this time.

"Then you accept there is a Satan. Good. I choose you, pretty, pretty. You will be my handmaiden and together, we shall live forever."

"Why does this always happen to me?" Fatimah asked throwing a blade at Viy's chest.

The tiny, young vampire caught the weapon in one hand and then yelped in pain. Her hand and fingers smoked and withered, turning black in every place where she had touched the weapon.

"What did you do to me, you *suka*?" Viy hissed, her pale face losing what little color remained in it.

Her bleached skull resembled that of a desiccated corpse devoid of any fluids. This hideous image heightened as her dark hair drained of color and soon resembled a tangle of snowy cobwebs atop of her head.

"Blessed weapons, corpse-eater," Fatimah replied, removing a pair of blades from her coat. "My weapons received blessings from five holy men before I took them into battle."

"*Suka!*" Viy screamed, her pale, pointed incisors nearly invisible in her current condition.

"Die, monster!" Fatimah screamed, throwing another dagger at the vampire's chest.

With a rush of air, Viy vanished, appearing a few feet to Fatimah's left. Her arm moved like a blur and the former assassin flew off her feet, feeling a rib, possibly two, crack under the inhuman impact.

Faisal fired his flare gun at the vampire's back. Viy whirled and slapped the missile aside. The white-hot shot struck a heavy snow bank, which melted, turned to steam, which then froze in the air. The vampire witch then appeared before Faisal and snatched the gun from his hand. With a quick twist, she bent its barrel and dropped the destroyed weapon to the ground. She then reached for Faisal, only to scream in pain again. Her blackened hand reached behind her and pulled another of Fatimah's blessed blades from her back.

Viy dropped the knife, still shrieking, and spinned in Fatimah's direction. Her hand flaked away, falling into charred dust as she turned towards the fallen assassin. All that remained were blackened bones, which fell into the snowy sward and vanished. The screaming vampire appeared at Fatimah's side, and lifted the lovely assassin up by her neck.

"I shall feed on your soul, *suka*!" Viy snarled, her teeth lengthening as she hissed.

But suddenly, Faisal touched her head with his old, battered, leather-bound Koran. In Arabic he called out, his voice ringing with power and majesty:

"In the Name of Allah the Merciful, I perform *Ruqyah* for you, from everything that is harming you, from the evil of every soul or envious eye, may Allah heal you. In the Name of Allah, I perform *Ruqyah* for you!"

Ruqyah, the ancient Islamic exorcism, meant to heal a body of the horrors caused by demons, djinns, and other monsters inhabiting the Earth. When used upon one of those creatures, the prayer from a holy man or woman was a potent weapon. The difficulty always lay in closing upon such creatures, but Fatimah's daring assault had provided Faisal with this much-needed opening.

The vampire witch called Viy moaned as her body glowed with a white light from within. She crumpled to her knees; her eyes, transformed from brown to a feverish red. Fatimah fell to her knees, rubbing her throat in obvious agony.

"Cut off her head, quickly!" Faisal said before resuming his prayer: "In the name of Allah, The Most Compassionate, the Most Merciful. All praise belongs to Allah, the Lord of all the worlds. The Most Compassionate, the Most Merciful, Sovereign of the Day of Judgment…"

Fatimah grasped her fallen knife and swung hard. The blade bit through the pliant, undead flesh, slicing through the vampire's neck with impressive ease.

Viy's enormous maw flapped open and closed before the head fell off the emaciated body. The skin on the undead woman's head and body turned gray and fell away, leaving a shattered skeleton lying across the frozen tundra.

"How," Fatimah asked in a soft, weak voice, "did we defeat that Allah-cursed creature?"

Faisal helped Fatimah up.

"Your attacks surprised her and she, like many vampires, acted with too much bravado. She caught your thrown knife as a way of showing her superiority. The act was meant to dishearten you… especially after she snapped the metal in half, as was her intention. The burns confused her, and she lost all self-control. We then took advantage of her lack of forethought."

"Translation," Fatimah replied, pulling out her canteen, "we got lucky."

"Astonishingly so," Faisal said with a nod. "However, you can count yourself as one of the few humans on Earth who has destroyed a vampire witch. Count Karnstein has two relatives who claim that act. You are the third I know of in history."

"I shall include that in my memoirs," Fatimah replied.

She did not hide the acid in her tone as she stomped on the skull of the dead vampire and kicked the fragments aside.

Faisal turned away and continued towards the gateway between worlds.

"You are writing your memoirs?"

“No,” Fatimah shot back. “Why did you want that Iblis-cursed thing’s head removed? Beyond that it would hasten her death.”

“Vampire witches have one final power that makes them a danger to their last and beyond. They can utter a death curse. Once spoken, the oath often destroys its chosen victims. Had that one spoke, we might both become vampires—or worse. Princess Asa Vajda cursed the witch-hunters who sent her into the arms of her black master. Would you like to hear it?”

“Oh, more than anything in this life,” Fatimah said, her voice dripping with sarcasm.

“I will tell this to you regardless, because it is of interest for our future. The Princess intoned: *You will never escape my vengeance, or Satan’s! My revenge will seek you out, and with the blood of your sons, and of their sons, and their sons, I will continue to live forever! They will restore me to the life you now rob from me!* She almost rose once, and there is a fear she may attempt to return to our world again. In fact, she may have done so already...”

“Is this your subtle way of preparing me for another vampire-fighting adventure?” Fatimah asked, her voice still husky from the attack. “If so, I am coming down with a headache, a cold, the plague, and frostbite in all my extremities/”

“We will talk about this if we survive the current mission,” Faisal replied with a chuckle.

CHAPTER XLII

The frog-headed creature dragged Gouroull down, pulling him for a full minute before releasing his ankles. The monster's powerful, inhuman hands closed around his throat. Powerful, clawed, web hands dug into his neck, pressing hard against his unyielding flesh.

At last, Gouroull succeeded in ripping the hands from his neck and now reached for the frog monster. But his huge hands moved in slow motion and missed it completely. The creature had vanished from sight. Even Gouroull's keen eyes did not penetrate more than a foot or so from his face. Untrained in swimming, Frankenstein's creation was nevertheless undaunted by the terrible cold and ice beneath the water. As a being not quite alive, but not dead either, breathing was unnecessary for his existence. That, like the need for warmth, were unimportant to Gouroull, thanks to his creator's genius.

With a few hard pushes of his enormous arms, Gouroull sunk to the bottom of the lake. His booted feet struck the rock and mud bottom and he turned to the left. Then he began to walk along the floor, feeling a slow incline with every few steps.

A blur of motion to his left, caught his eyes and he tried to turn again, but the water slowed his usually inhumanly fast movements, preventing him from seeing the frog-man as the creature bowled him over. The monster's claws shredded the front of Gouroull's clothing, but bounced off his gray skin. The creature then turned around and swam off, disappearing into the depths.

Righting himself again, Frankenstein's Monster corrected his direction and continued onward. He sensed that the frog-man was nearby and strode forward with a relentless step. The bottom of the lake rose slightly faster now, the incline heading toward the thick ice pack that covered the surface. Just as Gouroull reached the heavy layer of ice, the frog monster attacked again, from behind. The webbed hands reached for Frankenstein's Monster's shaggy head, its wicked talons aiming for Gouroull's amber eyes.

This was the first mistake the aquatic monster had made in this battle which it had, so far, controlled through its mastery of his environment. By placing its hands before Gouroull's face, they were now in range of his terrible teeth. Lunging forward before the claws could reach his eyes, Frankenstein's creation's wicked incisors sliced through the alien fingers. The frog-man released a bubbling cry as five fingers popped off his hands, red blood suddenly flooding out from its wounds.

Gouroull grabbed his enemy's wrists and pulled him over his head and against the ice pack. Moving one hand from the frog-man's wrists to the slick, rubbery neck, he dug his fingers in tight and swung the monster upward. Its head and body struck the ice, provoking another burbling cry from the creature. Gouroull slammed the monster over and over against the ice, cracking the thick, heavy layer. By the tenth swing, the frog-man was little more than a twisted sack of meat and blood. Its oval head's eyes were missing, and its oversized mouth hung open at a bizarre angle.

Releasing the corpse, Gouroull swung his heavy fists upward, punching through the ice layer seconds later. He broke a large hole and pulled himself from the frozen lake, straightening as he stepped onto the snowy sward.

Mater Suspiriorum stood in the same location, her hideous countenance twisting with shock and fury.

"What did you do to the vodyanoy, you misbegotten beast? That was an ancient spirit of the land and water, a being whose ancient lore could fill volumes of books. What did you do?"

Gouroull smiled and opened his mouth, removing an object from his teeth. Tossing the item at the feet of the hideous, elderly witch, he rumbled with amusement as her face drained of all blood. The partially webbed green fingertip and black talon protruded from the snow bank, a bit of color in the pale environment.

"Animal," Mater Suspiriorum hissed, spitting on the ground. "You are mankind's greatest mistake since Creation. Victor Frankenstein was insane, and his experiment was as wrong as those alien gods you serve. I curse you, monster! I curse you in the name of my master, Satan Morningstar. May you live forever, alone and despised by darkness and light. May you never rest, never sleep, and never forget that you are forever the most despised creature upon this world!"

Gouroull studied the elderly witch for a moment, a vicious, sadistic gleam causing a phosphorescent shimmer in his alien eyes. He then took two swift steps forward and lifted her up by her shoulders, pulling her from her feet. She struggled for a moment, before laying limply in his huge hands. His titanic frame blocked all sight from where he was heading.

"Where are you taking me, you stupid, ugly, oaf!" she hissed as he strode onward. "Kindness will not save you from the curse of Mater Suspiriorum, the Mother of Sighs! Put me down, I say!"

A few minutes later, Gouroull stopped walking and turned the hideous witch around so that their destination now lay before her unbelieving eyes. They stood in the very center of the lake, next to the vast hole made when the vodyanoy had pulled him into its frozen depths. The ancient witch's eyes widened, and her mouth dropped open, just as Gouroull's powerful clutches shoved her into the water.

"No!" she screamed as her body fell into the black, icy waters of the unnamed Siberian lake.

With a hard push, Gouroull propelled Mater Suspiriorum beneath the ice, away from the hole. He brushed aside some snow as he stared down at her through the ice, following her progress. Mater Suspiriorum's face was wild with terror as her bony, hands clawed at the ice in a futile hope of escape.

Slowly, though longer than most mortals, her scrabbling slowed, and eventually her panic motions ceased. The terrible mistress of witchcraft, eldest and wisest of the infamous Three Mothers, stared up at her executioner as she died, possibly for the final time. Her emaciated corpse floated beneath the thick ice for a few seconds, before falling away into the ancient depths of this lake—now the tombs of herself and the eldritch water spirit known as the vodyanoy.

Gouroull turned away and strode towards the cabin. This would only be a short walk now.

CHAPTER XLIII

"I can smell the monster," Baron Brákola intoned. "He is but a short distance away. However, I do not sense Lady Viy, Mater Suspiriorum, or Elizabeth Selwyn. Surely he did not destroy all three so easily?"

"I believe that is precisely what our monstrous friend has done this day," Count Karol de Lavud replied.

He did not hide his amusement at their plight. The division had been his idea. Upon arriving in Siberia, they had held a brief council of war and determined the best strategy for their attack.

Why had Lavud separated the team, leaving him with the sadistic, psychotic Zé do Caixão and the foolish, bestial Baron Brákola? Simply put, Count Karol de Lavud preferred using others as chess pieces.

Using this analogy, he had sacrificed his queen in Viy, a bishop in Mater Suspiriorum, and a knight in Elizabeth Selwyn. Now, he had two pawns that could assist him in the completion of his aims. Count Lavud did not wish for the Outer Gods to return to this world, but neither did he wish for a gate between Earth and Hell. That would make the world a fiefdom of the Devil, a being whose power and skill at manipulation dwarfed all other creatures. Count Karol de Lavud was a plotter and a schemer at heart. One could not live in that manner if the First of the Fallen ruled the Earth.

He had his own plans…

CHAPTER XLIV

Grigori Yefimovich Rasputin paced the small cabin, checking the clock on the wall. Only five minutes had passed since he had last gazed upon its dial, though in his mind, it felt like hours. He was feeling quite impatient, knowing the chance of transforming the world was slipping away. Only three hours were left before the opening the gate and the ceremony. For today, the day of the Chinese Ghost Festival, the paths between worlds weakened and allowed travel from and to impossible places.

Five more minutes passed, and he glanced at the bottle of kvass on the table. He must resist its lure, in case Gouroull succeeded. The *charodeyka* would otherwise tax his mind and body. Entering battle with a primeval witch was a risk few could undertake. However, Rasputin's dream guides had informed him that he could succeed, if he obeyed their orders.

He was preparing to look at the clock again, when the door slowly opened and the bedraggled figure of Gouroull stepped into the small room. His wet clothes appeared shredded and ragged, hanging across his grey skin in strips and patches. Only his boots, though worn with hard use, resembled actual human clothing.

Gouroull stopped before the table and unslung a heavy, soaked sack, placing it on the table with a dull thud. Rasputin practically leaped across the room and threw open the well tied cord that held the bag shut.

"You have succeeded? Holy Madonna in Heaven, I had my doubts anyone could overcome such guardians. Let me see…"

Rasputin reached in with a shaking hand and removed the largest object.

The gold covered, jeweled skull glistened in his hands as he lay it down on the wooden table.

"The Skull of Sobek," he pronounced, studying the oddly shaped cranium and jagged, jeweled fangs. "It smells of darkness and blood. An ugly object, my friend, but potent. I am impressed it did not affect you. I feel the tentative tendrils of power seeking my mind even now."

Gouroull did not reply; he simply watched the holy man with close attention. He did not appear deceptive, simply fascinated by the contents of the sack.

Pulling out the second object, Rasputin placed the metal, spiked diadem on the table, his face wrinkling with disgust.

"The Crown of Commodus. A repulsive object that is filled with blood and death. Much power, too, but dark and diseased. I feel filthy just touching that terrible diadem."

For a third time, the monk reached into the sack and removed the odd stone known as the Shining Trapezohedron. This, he studied briefly, before shaking his head and laying it next to the skull.

"This one interests me more than the other two. I suspect that, if I studied this long enough, I would learn secrets not meant for the minds of man."

Rasputin turned and looked at Gouroull, his face splitting into a wide, strange grin.

"You are another miracle in many ways, my friend. Now, we shall enter the other world and, after I defeat the *charodeyka*, you shall have your mate. The guides of my dreams told me you must receive payment first. Follow me and we shall open the gate."

Scooping up the objects, Rasputin headed out the door, stopping two short steps later. He waved at Gouroull behind him and stooped down near the snowy sward. For a moment, he brushed away at the ice covering the ground, revealing a flat gray stone. A slight indentation in the rocky surface appeared when Rasputin pushed aside more snow.

"I have been shoveling and clearing the land around the cabin in hopes of your success," he explained as he placed the Shining Trapezohedron upon the indentation. "We place the artifacts here, in three points, and stand on a fourth. Then, according to my dreams, the cabin shall disappear, and the gate shall open..."

The tall, hairy monk repeated this procedure on the west and south sides of the cabin, before leading Gouroull to the north side. There, he cleared a larger area, revealing another gray stone with a surprisingly flat surface. The space was just wide enough for both of their large frames, with no room to spare.

"Now, we begin," Rasputin said, covering his face and whispering: "Great Haunter of the Dark, open your three-lobed burning eye and show us the path to the forgotten tower of Eibon."

For a moment, everything around them seemed to freeze, as if every creature on Earth held its collective breath. Then, a light emerged from the three points surrounding the cabin, a glow that rose higher and brighter until the cabin vanished from view.

In the place of the small wooden structure now was a shimmering red energy circle, about ten feet high and wide, with small dots of black energy chasing across the surface, sometimes in masses, occasionally individually. Within this gateway was a dark tunnel, a void so dense it resembled an ebony wall. Nothing stirred in this abyssal gloom and no sound escaped from it.

"Here is our path, Gouroull. Are you ready?" Rasputin asked.

His voice shook with a obvious excitement and possibly, a trace of fear.

In answer, Gouroull stepped forward, entering the murk without pause or delay. He vanished from view, followed a few seconds later by Rasputin.

CHAPTER XLV

Gouroull and Rasputin found themselves on a stone walkway under a gray, sunless and starless sky. The stones beneath their feet were massive, cut in a rectangular pattern, and at least twenty feet wide and fifty feet long. The surface material was of the same odd, smooth rock that had surrounded the cabin in the Siberian woods.

Looking around, they soon realized the rock covered the entire surface of this world in a precise pattern. It resembled the hide of some great reptilian beast of legend, giving the land an inhuman, alien texture. The air was warm, though infused with a musty odor like that of an unused, locked room freshly opened after decades of being sealed.

"No grass or trees," Rasputin mused, glancing about with nervous eyes. "No form of life at all."

Lifting an arm, Gouroull pointed over Rasputin's shoulder and slightly to the left. The tall monk turned, spotting a tower about five or six stories high and made from the same gray rock. It was a perfectly round cylinder, with a shattered stone door at the base and an unmarked surface rising to a rounded top. The structure resembled an oversized extended finger thrusting upwards towards a featureless sky.

It took a minute, but Rasputin realized that Frankenstein's Monster was not merely pointing at the structure, but to the zenith of the tower. He spotted a large oval window near the rounded roof. A yellow light flickered briefly in it, before vanishing a moment later.

"Come along," Rasputin said, grinning again. "The spell the *charodeyka* is invoking requires two or more days of weaving. Still, we should not tarry."

Gouroull took the lead, his long stride covering more ground than the tall Rasputin. They arrived at the tower ten minutes later and headed for the jagged rip in the surface of the building. The opening was a triangular tear in the stone, as if a massive hand had pulled the stones in one quick yank. Tumbled down rocks lay strewn about the area, and a thin layer of gray dust lay across every surface.

Steeping inside, they immediately adjusted to the low light that radiated within. A long, spiraling ramp wound up through the inner surface, leading to a vast platform that glowered with a bright, dancing, yellow illumination. Standing on the surface of the stone ramp stood a host of men and women, their bodies, torn, tattered, and bloody. Their unseeing eyes, many white, others with gaping, bloody, black holes in their battered skulls, stared at Gouroull and Rasputin.

A collective moan escaped their ripped mouths and they stepped forward, their arms extended. Rasputin stepped back slightly, his eyes wide with shock and disgust.

"Blasphemy," he breathed. "Keep them from me, my friend. I shall remove the curse that keeps these poor creatures clinging to a false life."

Closing his eyes, Rasputin raised his hands and began whispering in an odd language that sounded closer to the clicks and chitter of insects than human speech. The walking dead moaned again, moving with impressive speed for revenants with damaged, and sometimes badly mangled, limbs.

Gouroull waded in, his massive hands tossing the creatures and further damaging their ruined bodies. He had faced such monsters in the past on an island in Scotland, led by a Haitian mystic who had destroyed his chances of getting a mate that day. Frankenstein's creation found the raised undead a difficult foe, relentless and devastatingly dangerous since they felt no pain and possessed no fear.

These monsters possessed the same power. For every one Gouroull pummeled, ripped, and shattered, two more stepped forward and attacked. Steadily, Frankenstein's creation found himself pushed backwards towards Rasputin. He knew he could survive this attack, but Rasputin did not possess his inhuman physique. One strike from the bloody hands of the walking dead would snap the hairy Siberian monk's neck like a matchstick. Fighting with the fury of a cornered beast, Gouroull denied the dead access to the mad monk.

A minute, or perhaps an hour, later, one of the risen dead, a female, finally reached Rasputin's side. Gouroull could not move and rescue the praying man because four of the revenants pressed him back, attacking with growing intensity. The dead woman, her eyes torn from her head, her scalp half-ripped away, cast her bloody hand towards Rasputin's throat. She was mere inches away, when the bearded Siberian's eyes flew open and he smiled and spoke:

"*Amen!*" he cried, waving his hands in a circle.

The attacking dead ceased their moans and motions, their bodies suddenly frozen. Then, they all toppled over, falling to the stone floor and landing with soft, squishy sounds. Gouroull and Rasputin were ankle deep in corpses, but no other creatures emerged from the top of the tower.

"You struggled against such weak enemies? They were just useless *muertos*, not even good enough to till a field," Baron Brákola said with a laugh.

He stepped into the tower, his stance impressive despite his ill-fitting outfit. He smiled, showing his oversized fangs and hissed at Gouroull.

Rasputin backed away, seeing that the huge vampire had no eyes for him. Gouroull looked at the newcomer, his yellow orbs shimmering in the low light.

"Yes, yes," Baron Brákola said, flicking a hand towards the fleeing Rasputin. "Run and hide, little man. Baron Brákola shall destroy you later. For now, I have a pathetic dog I wish to destroy."

A low bestial growl escaped the massive vampire's throat and he pulled his head back towards his shoulders. Baring his teeth, he curled his hands like claws, narrowed his eyes into slits, and pounced.

CHAPTER XLVI

Faisal and Fatimah waited a full minute before following Gouroull and his hairy friend into the gate between worlds.

They arrived on the same stony plain, disoriented and instinctively standing close. Faisal held his *seme* in one hand while keeping the other thrust inside his jacket.

"Where are we?" Fatimah asked, slowing studying the horizon. "It is warmer than Siberia, but not so hot as Jahannam is said to be in all the teachings. Also, I see no sinners and children of Iblis attacking them for their crimes."

"This is not Hell," Faisal replied. "Though I would hazard to guess that we're closer to that proverbial neighborhood than our world. This is a small pocket universe created by the wizard Eibon before recorded history. His legends are many, and some say he had mastered the magic of demons from beyond the stars. He built that tower over there in the distance."

Fatimah studied the tower as she threw off her heavy coat and fur hat.

"I see the one called Gouroull in the distance and his strange friend. Let us run and meet them before they advance too far."

Faisal shook his head and headed in that direction at a leisurely pace.

"No. We must remain calm and strong if we are to fight Victor Frankenstein's horrific mistake. If we are winded or weak, he will kill us both… Then all life across the Earth…"

"Very well," Fatimah agreed.

She fell into step by his side.

"Oh, oh," Zé do Caixão moaned, staring at Fatimah.

His breathing grew heavier as he studied her face and figure with open lust.

"That is a woman fully capable of successfully ensuring the continuity of my blood line."

"Yes, I imagine," Count Lavud said, amused by the man's antics.

They were only a short distance from the Arabs, hidden by Lavud's mind powers for the moment. But this would not last, for both of the two they were studying possessed strong wills.

Why are a pair of Easterners chasing the Frankenstein Monster and a smelly priest? the Count thought. *They are not what one would expect in the middle of the Siberian wastes.*

"Do not forget! I am a living breathing man. You two are but dead!" Zé do Caixão spat out.

"I am proud to be one of the nobles of the night," Baron Brákola intoned, straightening his back and composing his features to what he believed was a superior expression. He resembled a large child who had sniffed out a terrible odor.

"Very well," Count Lavud said, barely containing his derisive laughter at these two fools. "Senhor Zé, the woman is yours to do as you will. The noble baron shall demonstrate why he is considered the Maciste of the dark lords. I shall enslave the male Arab, and then, we all shall murder the hairy holy man."

"That is acceptable," Zé do Caixão stated, before smiling again. "The woman shall serve me and produce many children!"

"I shall eat Frankenstein's Monster's heart before his dying eyes," Baron Brákola said, flashing his fangs. "Then I shall take his skull and place it on my throne as a symbol of my power. Perhaps I shall make a cane of his bones."

"I wish you both good fortune," Count Karol de Lavud said as they ran off.

The huge vampire outpaced the mad undertaker, his undead celerity propelling him across the stony plain.

Rolling his eyes, Count Lavud spread his arms wide and transformed into a bat. With a screech, he took to the air, flying past his pathetic pawns and slipping into the cylindrical tower.

Brákola and Gouroull would soon lock horns, providing the perfect opportunity for his mental assault on the Arab male.

Transforming back into human form, but staying in the shadows, Lavud smiled as he first touched Faisal's mind. Reaching his hand up, he then slipped his consciousness into his victim's unconscious mind. It was far too long since he had fed upon the terrors of another's spirit.

Dear me, Count Lavud thought as he practically shook with delight, *this one has quite a mind. This will be a pleasure*.

CHAPTER XLVII

When Faisal froze in place, Fatimah knew at once that their mission had gone very wrong.

He turned his head her way, a puzzled look on his face, before stopping and staring past her, a glassy look in his eyes. Waving a hand before his eyes, she frowned and tapped his face with her hard, calloused fingers.

"Faisal?" she asked, tapping a little harder. "Can you hear me? Sheikh Faisal Hashim Haji Sabbah, speak to me!"

"He cannot," Zé do Caixão said, laughing. "My new friend, Count Lavud—such a silly name, no?—has taken his mind and is putting him through the torments of the damned. Soon, he shall find himself reduced to a mewling infant, begging for slavery or death from his new vampire master."

Fatimah raised her blade, smiled and replied:

"You think he shall fall to silly mind tricks and games? I am sorry, but I cannot watch as your accomplice discovers the horrors that exist within that terrible brain."

"Forget him, my beauty,". Zé do Caixão whispered sliding closer and smiling. "What is your name? You possess the child-bearing hips and succulent skin I require for the mother of my child."

Fatimah stepped to the side and kept her blade pointed directly towards the caped man.

"Mother of your child? What nonsense are you speaking?"

Zé do Caixão stopped moving, straightened and looked furious as he spat out:

"I asked you a question, *puta*. What is your name? Answer me!"

Raising an eyebrow, Fatimah realized this man was insane. She had no interest in placating him, nor in furthering this conversation. However, there were better methods of dealing with dangerous lunatics. As in fighting, redirection was a better defense than outright assault.

"Should not a gentleman introduce himself first?" Fatimah asked, stopping in her place.

"Do forgive me, my beloved," Zé do Caixão said, bowing deeply at the waist.

Somehow his top hat remained in place, not moving as he bobbed up and down.

"Beloved?" Fatimah asked, finding this madman very confusing.

"I am Zé do Caixão, an important man in my home country," he replied, bowing and smiling again. "Now, please to tell me your name before we begin planning the continuation of my bloodline."

His grin was too wide, showed far too many teeth, and added to the psychotic expression in his eyes.

"Zé do Caixão?" Fatimah asked, tilting her head. "They call you Coffin Joe? Truly? Why are you not insulted? Or are you an undertaker who lives only for his morbid duties?"

"You dare insult me?" Zé do Caixão whispered, raising his oversized, sharp fingernails. "Me? The man who will breed you and allow you the chance to raise my children! You dare?"

"Children?" Fatimah replied. "Coffin Joe… Forgive me, but that name is ridiculous… May I tell you something?"

"Speak," he whispered, "but quickly, for we have much to plan."

"Then I shall tell you this, Coffin Joe," Fatimah replied, snorting. "If you and I were the last two humans on Earth, I would sooner try and mate with a camel. You are unquestionably the most repellent insect in human form I have ever met in my life. And the last man I executed ate babies on bread for snacks."

Glowering, Zé do Caixão raised his hands, revealing his wicked talons. Clicking them together, he snarled, spat on the stone ground and whispered:

"Then I shall take your body and break your mind. After a few months in my care, you shall beg me to accept you as my mate."

Fatimah opened her mouth to snap back a harsh rejoinder, when the caped man closed the distance in a blur of motion. He slapped aside the hand holding the knife, sending the weapon spiraling across the rocky surface of this odd world. His vicious claws sliced open her arm and across her chest, drawing blood and sending lancets of pain throughout her body.

Pushing her back, the evil undertaker cackled and licked some of the blood from his claws.

"No screams... Good, very good. Breaking your body shall be my first task. Then, I shall destroy your mind, and finally, your spirit. You shall kneel before my feet and beg to serve as Lilith to my Adam. If you beg long enough, I shall..."

His next sound was a strangled gasp as Fatimah kicked him in the chest.

He stumbled backwards, throwing out an arm and preventing himself from falling. Straightening, Zé do Caixão tapped his top hat, threw back his cape and screamed. There were no words in his howl, just naked fury and animalistic lust. He bounded forward, moving like some monstrous insect, his talons clicking madly with each movement.

Fatimah stepped aside from the evil undertaker, only avoiding the slashing claws by mere inches. Her booted foot kicked out again, catching Zé do Caixão in the side and giving her a chance to step out of his attack radius. A thick strand of her hair broke free from her scalp, this being the only part of hers that his talons reached.

Zé do Caixão stopped, stooped, and picked up the lock of hair. He sniffed it deeply, smiled, and tucked it inside his belt.

"Mine," he said, giggling.

"You are truly pathetic," Fatimah replied, picking up her fallen knife.

In one motion, she threw the blade straight at the evil undertaker's eyes. But with a bored motion, Zé do Caixão slapped it aside. He threw back his head and laughed a high-pitched yowl of triumph.

The laughter was cut off a second later when Fatimah snapped his neck. While he had gloated over avoiding her knife attack, Fatimah, who was almost as quick as him, had closed the distance between them and struck. Her hard fingertips had slashed forward as fast as a striking adder, and shattered his neck!

Not content to trust in one attack, she also brought her other hand up, knuckles extended, and punched the under part of Zé do Caixão's long nose. His head snapped back as the cartilage, driven upward by the blow, penetrated his brain, slicing through the delicate tissues.

Zé do Caixão dropped to his knees and collapsed on the stony ground. His last sight was that of the booted feet of the object of his lust as she walked back towards the tower.

I will return, he thought as the blackness enveloped his mind and body. *I shall be back and she will be mine... she will be... mine... I...*

CHAPTER XLVIII

Faisal stepped through the dust-covered door, confused by his sudden translocation. No longer did he stand in a warm, alien world with a stuffy atmosphere. Now he stood inside a dark wooden structure, probably a house, filled with dust, cobwebs, and absolutely no scents.

Faisal touched the door and felt the wood and grit across the frame. He listened as the hinges creaked with a soft groan.

The room before him was wide, murky, and furnished with dark wooden furniture. The layers of dust and webs covered every inch of the room, though nothing lingered in the air. Faisal spotted only one clean surface—a painting hanging above the filthy fireplace.

Striding across the room, raising a small cloud of dust, he stopped before it. For some reason, a soft glow covered this vicinity, revealing the painting of a man in black. He was regal-looking, with pale hair, an imperious face, and dark clothes that gave him a sinister aspect. A black signet ring sat on a long, thin hand that rested on a round object that appeared slightly out-of-focus.

Studying the round item in the painting, Faisal sighed with annoyance. The item in question was his own face, eyes rolled back in his head, mouth open in a silent scream. He now understood the situation and felt vaguely disappointed with the result.

"An attack of the mind," he said aloud. "Meant to invoke a fear response that empowers the assaulter. How very... disappointing..."

Faisal's own head on the painting slowly transformed into a skull and the head of the seated figure turned his way and smiled broadly, showing sharp fangs in a wide mouth.

"Good evening, Sheikh Faisal Hashim Haji Sabbah. Welcome to your nightmares," the man in the painting, said.

"And good evening to you, Count Karol de Lavud," Faisal replied, glancing around. "Fortunately for you, this does not represent a nightmare to me."

Lavud looked surprised and confused as he gazed down from the painting.

"How do you know my name?"

"It's right there, beneath your torso," Faisal replied, pointing at the painting's frame. "I am guessing that you are a vampire. Only vampires possess enough conceit for such a silly, wasteful addition to the planned nightmare."

"I was already ancient when the Romans nailed Christ on the cross," Lavud intoned. "I was there that day, watching and laughing, for Pontius Pilate was my servant."

His words echoed about the room, coming to Faisal apparently from every direction at once.

"You are the twenty-fourth vampire who has claimed as much to me. Based on your kind's collective boasts, Pilate had a dozen masters, and vampires secretly milled around, dressed as Romans on the day of the crucifixion. Forgive me if I have my doubts. Based on your accent, I surmise that you are a nobleman from Spain, probably with estates in the New World, though your pronunciation indicates some age. You enjoyed your pleasures until a vampire taught you some witchcraft. As a present for selling your soul to Satan, she made you into a vampire, too. I will make an educated guess that your undead mentor was Countess Luisa Karnstein."

Count Lavud appeared behind Faisal, his imperious look in place.

"You know of my dear, beloved mistress? She is a most remarkable woman."

"You are misusing your pronouns, señor," Faisal said, turning his head and looking at the vampire. "You said she *is* a remarkable woman. The correct term should be *was*—she was indeed a remarkable woman, until Count and Countess Karnstein executed her in 1820 and disposed of her remains in the ocean."

"You lie!" Count Lavud snarled.

He grabbed Faisal and held him off the ground as a child might lift a small toy.

"I think you will find that I do not," Faisal said, sounding unconcerned and almost bored. "Besides having no reason to prevaricate, I think you might be perceptive enough to detect falsehoods."

"Bah!" Lavud snarled, dropping him to the floor, "We waste time. See your true fear!"

The vampiric count waved his hands about, but nothing happened. They stood in the same filthy room illuminated by the soft glow near the empty painting of the nobleman and Faisal's painted skull.

"I am still waiting," Faisal said, leaning against the fireplace. "Unless you believe boredom is my greatest terror."

Count Lavud compressed his lips and his eyes took on a distant quality. Some time passed, but still no change occurred. He closed his eyes and his shoulders shook as he concentrated. More time passed and Faisal stood there, watching and waiting, studying the nobleman as he vibrated in place.

Finally, the vampire opened his eyes, his head swiveling left and right.

"I do not understand. What is happening? Why are we still in my nightmare world?"

"Again, you must learn the proper use of pronouns, my good Count," Faisal replied, crossing his arms again. "You said, this is *my* nightmare world. The proper use for you would be to look at me and say, *your* nightmare world."

Count Lavud frowned and slowly shook his head.

"No, I brought you here. This is *my* world."

"...That you created in my mind, yes. But I took control of it seconds after I determined this was the work of an untrained amateur. Count, I was battling for my mind in my childhood. That was the first art I mastered in my training. You possess power, but use it with the subtleness of a charging rhino. You snuck inside a small portion of my unconscious and created a false world that could not frighten anyone with a modicum of self-knowledge."

"If you die in your mind, little man," Count Lavud spat, flashing his fangs, "you die in life. I shall kill you here and now!"

The vampire lunged forward, hands outstretched... and smashed into the fireplace. Turning and swiveling his head, Lavud searched for his enemy, finally spotting him a minute later. Faisal was across the room, seated on a small wooden stool.

"I projected myself there while you were still hiding in the painting," he said as he rose. "Do not bother attacking me, Count. I can be in as many places as I wish. This is my mind, not yours. The only rules are those I create."

"Then I shall kill you when I return to my body. I am far stronger than you, little human dreamer," Count Lavud said, straightening and resembling the regal figure in his painting.

Faisal raised his hand and held up three fingers.

"For the third time, you make a mistake of pronouns, señor. It is not *when* you return. The proper word is, *if* you return."

Faisal's expression now turned to anger—the killing rage of a warrior pushed to his limit. He suddenly appeared at the vampire's side, lifted him off the ground with the same ease the Count had used moments earlier.

"You wished to see my nightmares, Count Karol de Lavud? I think I shall grant you a glimpse."

Faisal's words shook the very walls of the room.

The floor fell away beneath their feet, yet neither fell. The entire room had vanished, replaced by a gaping pit, a void of abyssal darkness whose shadows shifted around as if they were alive. Unseen eyes stared up at the hovering figures, and Count Lavud shrieked with fear and horror.

"Take a look, vampire. See my true fears!" Faisal roared

And he threw the Spanish nobleman into the murky depths.

In the outside world, Count Karol de Lavud convulsed for a moment, his eyes fluttering madly, before falling to the floor. His face turned ashen, then dark gray, before collapsing in on itself.

By the time Rasputin passed by, all that remained was a black cape, a suit of clothing, and a small pile of dust…

CHAPTER XLIX

Rasputin felt the growing energy as he strode up the stone ramp, a viscous, oily, corrupting power that wrapped around him and sought entry into his mind and body. The invocations held both a feverish newness and an ancient quality at the same time. A scent of blood, rot, and fear filled the air, smells Rasputin associated with slaughterhouses, sick wards, and battlefields.

Despite a thin sheen of sweat covering his cheeks and brow, he pressed forward. He began praying to himself as he strode up, in words from that ancient language he had learned from the guardians of his prophetic dreams. The words sounded odd to his ears, as if created for inhuman mouths. Still, onward Rasputin walked, knowing that he, a Siberian *strannik*, held the fate of Russia, and possibly the world, across his broad shoulders.

"N'gai, n'gha'ghaa, bugg-shoggog, y'hah, Yog-Sothoth, Yog-Sothoth... Y'AI 'NG'NGAH, YOG-SOTHOTH, H'EE--L'GEB. F'AI THRODOG, UAAAH," he chanted as he rose upward.

He soon reached the summit, a large platform that covered the entire top floor of the odd tower. The space was one large long room, devoid of furniture or wall coverings. An unadorned circular brazier lay in the center, with a dancing yellow flame flickering and illuminating the chamber. At the far end of the room, near the oversized window, rested a dais with a massive opened book in its center.

The woman leaning over the huge tome was attractive, mid-to-late forties, with pageboy length curly brown hair and a triangular shaped face. Her eyes were almond shaped and piercing, bewitching green eyes that gazed at Rasputin with unhidden interest.

The corner of her lips twitched with a slight smile and she carefully straightened her dark tunic with hard, stubby, calloused fingers. She closed the book with a quiet thud, her hands reluctantly leaving the pages.

"You would be the *strannik*, Grigori Yefimovich Rasputin," she said in a husky voice.

Rasputin frowned, but realized he recognized those hands and eyes. The revelation gave him a start, far more than this woman's knowledge of his identity.

"Mater Tenebrarum, the Mother of Darkness, I presume? Your portrait still sits in the secret annex of an old Constantinople chapel beneath the Byzantine execution grounds."

Mater Tenebrarum's lips twitched again and she nodded slowly.

"That was a lovely painting of myself and my sisters. The painter went mad by the end. He pulled out his own eyes and the authorities discovered him in a closet, chewing his own fingers to the bone. Such a delightful little man and such a talent for seeing the true soul of his subject. Does it still hang there?"

"No," Rasputin replied, showing his square, stained teeth to the ancient witch. "I burned the chapel and the contents as a blasphemy under God."

"Under God?" Mater Tenebrarum asked, rolling her eyes. "But you do not serve the King of Heaven, but monstrosities who believe they are gods. To Above and Below, the only true blasphemy in this room is you, Grigori Yefimovich Rasputin. Lecture me not on your heroic behavior, slave of the many-angled ones."

Shrugging, Rasputin stepped closer as he said:

"You are a servant of Satan, and you lie in all things. I know my god speaks to me at night through my dreams. I am *His* prophet."

"That explains so much! Before I destroy your mind, I shall send you a true seeing of the faces of your true masters."

"You will find me no easy victim," Rasputin said.

He raised his hands up and ready. This time he imagined himself chanting the words, an exercise as difficult as speaking the odd sounds aloud.

Mater Tenebrarum languidly raised one hand and pointed her palm towards the praying monk. Her eyes narrowed and she exhaled slowly. The room subtly darkened, with shadows and murk appearing on the edge of the chamber. The brazier's light seemed to mute as the power of the Mother of Darkness rose up, seeking the destruction of her enemy.

Rasputin invoked more power, calling upon another patron of his dreams and nightmares:

"*Ph'nglui mglw'nafh Cthulhu R'lyeh wgah'nagl fhtagn Ph'nglui mglw'nafh Cthulhu R'lyeh wgah'nagl fhtagn...*" he shouted.

CHAPTER L

Gouroull launched his massive body at Baron Brákola, meeting the huge vampire in the air. They rolled across the tower floor until they crashed into a wall. The impact forced them apart and both monsters stood and circled each other with greater caution. Brákola's ill-fitting suit was now torn and dirty, and much of Gouroull's tatters lay strewn across the floor.

"Is this the vaunted strength of Frankenstein's Monster? You are nothing compared to the great Baron Brákola," the vampire stated, his words slurring as his teeth lengthen and his face grew bestial. "Surrender now, beast. Otherwise I shall tear you apart, limb by limb!"

Gouroull's amber eyes blazed with a malicious fury as he bared his massive, razor-sharp teeth. A subsonic growl of demoniac rage rippled through his gargantuan frame as he dashed forward and locked arms with the powerful vampire.

Brákola remained crouching low as a lupine hunting howl escaped his pale lips. Fur emerged in patches across his face and hands, and slowly his eyes shifted from black to an icy blue. With each passing second, the vampire's humanity fell away, revealing the beast within.

With a growl, he bit down on Gouroull's shoulder, his pointed fangs ripping a fleshy chunk from the meaty shoulder of Frankenstein's Monster. Gouroull tensed and pulled the vampire away from his body, feeling the flesh tear with an audible, wet, ripping noise. Brákola reared back and spat away the gray, inhuman meat that was Gouroull's flesh.

The Baron pushed the Monster back against the stony wall. He snarled and barked again, rearing his head back for another strike. Lunging forward, his motion ceased inches from Gouroull's other shoulder as the iron sinews of Frankenstein's Monster tensed. Brákola growled and struggled, spittle and blood flying from his rubbery red lips. The vampire was now berserk, incapable of anything other than following his brutish fury.

Then Gouroull bit off the Baron's nose, his elongated incisors slicing through the vampire's rubbery flesh with ease. Brákola shrieked and pulled back as blood sprayed from his terrible wound, covering the Monster's face and torso.

Gouroull did not fight Brákola's backward motion, relaxing his powerful arms and body. With a hard push off from his legs, he bounded forward, launching himself at the shrieking undead creature. His terrible teeth locked in on the vampire's throat, cutting off the wails of agony as its larynx was shredded into meaty pieces seconds later.

Releasing his enemy's arms, Gouroull grabbed the vampire's head and pulled, ripping the skull free of the body. Baron Brákola's massive frame spouted blood and other fluids for a moment, before slowly drying and crumbling into gray black ash.

By the time Frankenstein's creation looked down at his foe, all that remained was a rapidly diminishing pile of dust and bits of bone. Even the outdated clothing had vanished by the time Gouroull straightened and glanced upwards. Sensing that the events taking place above his head were vital to his quest, the Monster pressed a hard palm against his badly injured shoulder, then, strode up the winding ramp, his movements a little slower than usual…

CHAPTER LI

The battle between Mater Tenebrarum and Grigori Yefimovich Rasputin was nearly even. The Mother of Darkness was the youngest of the frightening Three Mothers, but her knowledge and power made her a foe of nightmarish danger. Tales of Mater Tenebrarum's cruelty were the stuff of nightmares, whispered in the dark as a warning against those who sought dark power.

The power Rasputin invoked flooded into his body, using him as a channel more than a mere agent. They did not care what happened to him in this battle, the Siberian strannik was but a vessel for their needs, and nothing else. This realization shocked Rasputin as he discovered the witch was entirely correct. His dream guides were not angels from Heaven or agents of the Lord. They were, as the Mother of Darkness had said, creatures of unimaginable might who sought entry into this world. He, Grigori Yefimovich Rasputin, had been their puppet, a human they had manipulated for their own aims.

"Now you see the truth at last, little monk," Mater Tenebrarum gasped.

Her skin retracted with each passing second, her hair burning away and leaving behind her true self. She was the very image of death, a skeleton held together by tiny flaps of flesh. Her eyes were empty sockets filled with a cavernous, bottomless black emptiness.

Rasputin found he could not respond or even control his own body. The puppet masters that manipulated his life held him in their grasp, and he stood as a mere witness to their struggle for supremacy.

Moments passed and the world receded for Rasputin. His body stood locked on the precipice of a terrible void, with only the skeletal Mother of Shadows as his witness. The Siberian strannik felt pains and weakness emerge in his body as the battle continued. He knew in his heart the truth, even before the witch hissed:

"Your body is failing. You are human. Exceptional in some ways for a mortal, but still only a man. I am Mater Tenebrarum of the Three Mothers. My sisters and I abandoned our humanity centuries ago."

Even if he could speak, Rasputin could not deny the truth of her statement. His body dropped to one knee as the strength in his limbs slowly leaked away. This, he viewed from a distance, almost clinically, since all control was now in the hands of the other powers. Rasputin felt like a thin channel in which a vast river of unearthly energies rushed and flowed. His mortal body could only receive and release so much power before he found himself overwhelmed and, ultimately, destroyed. That sad end was close and then, he knew, Mater Tenebrarum's victory would be assured.

That was when the ancient witch started in surprise. The growing murk parted and, without warning, the brazier blazed brighter. It looked to Rasputin as if some powerful wind had blown asunder the deepening shadows. The assault upon his body ceased. Straightening, the Siberian *strannik*'s eyes locked on a massive gray hand as it lifted the skeletal witch off her feet, shaking her body. A low series of clicks joined Mater Tenebrarum's screams of shock, surprise, and finally, agony as her bones rattled like some madman's massive maracas.

Gouroull shook the witch again as his other arm lay limply against his side. His black lips peeled back as he lifted Mater Tenebrarum higher and locked eyes with the ancient witch. This was no smile of triumph, but the snarl of a furious, wounded animal with a raging blood-lust. The phosphorescent glow in his eyes held no intelligence, only an overwhelming, inhuman thirst for pain and death.

"No!" Mater Tenebrarum screamed, her hands scrabbling madly for release.

But her strength, though inhuman, was no match for that of Frankenstein's creation.

"Let me go! You know nothing of what they plan!"

Gouroull, still staring at the ancient witch, stepped across the room. He shook her with each step, snapping some of the delicate bones with each long stride.

"You must know what they plan! The Russian's masters lied! They shall never give you what you want! NEVER!"

That last word boomed out, a powerful, ear-splitting explosion that shook the tower, causing a shower of stone chips and dust.

Stopping before the last open window, Frankenstein's Monster reached out, slowly extending Mater Tenebrarum out and into the open air. She dangled in space, only Gouroull's vast inhuman strength keeping her from plummeting to the stony ground of this unusual world.

"Wait!" she said, holding onto his wrist with both bony hands. "Listen to me for just a moment. The Russian's masters only seek entry onto the Earth. If the way is open, they will consume all life... Nothing will remain! Earth will be a lifeless cinder, a vast rock with nothing living on it!"

Gouroull looked at Mater Tenebrarum for a moment and pulled her close. His yellow eyes glinted with malicious glee and he breathed one single word:

"Good."

Then, he opened his hand and flicked the skeletal witch aside, tossing her ten feet away. She shrieked and scrabbled uselessly in the air as she fell to the rocky ground that covered this world. Her bones shattered into an untold number of pieces, the remains spreading across a surprisingly wide area.

"She was correct, my friend," Rasputin said, righting himself and finding his body partially under his own control again. "When I read the words of this, the legendary Book of Eibon, I shall doom the Earth. The Lurker at the Threshold is the gate, and the key to the gate. Once the gate opens, the Outer Gods and the Great Old Ones shall rise and consume all life. It is possible that the Haunter of the Dark shall give you your mate for a time. Then, again, he might not. The God of a Thousand Names is capricious, and he enjoys the pain of lesser creatures."

Gouroull pointed at the book and said:

"Read."

Rasputin walked over to the book.

"It shall happen," he said, "for I am under the domination of those entities. They will make me read it, whether I wish or not..."

The book was two feet long and wide, and made of a metal substance that felt warm to the touch. Its cover was thick and heavy, with old green and yellow runes etched into its gray metal surface.

Rasputin pushed the book open and slowly leafed through the pages. They appeared made from the same substance as the cover, though far thinner. The same strange runes appeared on every page, some of which pulsed with a yellow and green energy.

"Ah," Rasputin said, tapping a row of characters. "Here is the spell the masters said would grant you your mate. Let us begin… *Y'AI'NG'NGAHYOG-SOTHOTHH'EE…*"

Suddenly, the table exploded, tossing Rasputin and Gouroull back several feet…

CHAPTER LII

"Good throw," Faisal called as he ran ahead of Fatimah.

He pulled his scarf over his head as she tossed a second ball into the room. He tapped his goggles, making sure the tight seal was in place as he scanned the chamber.

The glass ball she had thrown had struck the ground near the brazier and exploded into dozens of shards. A heavy gray gas now filled the room, obscuring everyone's vision.

A heavy cough emerged from the fallen Rasputin, but Gouroull made no sound as he slowly rose.

Locating the book, Faisal reached into his jacket and removed a stone cylinder. Opening the stopper, he dumped its liquid contents over the open pages of the Book of Eibon. The liquid was yellow and pink in color and exuded a noxious odor that activated Faisal's gag reflex. The substance was thicker than water, a gelatinous fluid-like paste. It flowed slowly over the book, encompassing the pages and cover with irritating slowness.

Holding his breath, Faisal watched the pages, hoping his calculations were correct. Guesswork in science was never clever, yet he had no choice. The Book of Eibon was an artifact of pure evil. Allowing its existence any longer endangered all life in the universe.

Just when he was about to cry out in despair from failure, a large bubble rose on the book's surface. The rune beneath the bubble dissolved. More bubbles slowly appeared as the acid ate away at the metal pages.

Without a word, Faisal turned and ran, grabbing Fatimah and leading her quickly down the ramp. Within a few steps, she moved under her own power, though slower than normal thanks to her injuries.

"Why are we fleeing?" Fatimah asked as they dashed out the shattered door and headed back towards the gate.

"Two reasons," Faisal panted back as they paused and snatched up their winter clothing. "First, I believe this world will be no more once that book dissolves. I think only the magic of the book kept it from collapsing upon itself."

"And the second?" Fatimah asked, pulling on her coat and hat and wincing in pain from her broken ribs.

"Second, the monster known as Gouroull just had his plans thwarted by our actions. Though injured, I do not believe we can destroy him even if we were healthy and fully empowered. I will not be capable of relaxing until we are back in Cairo, sipping fruit drinks by the pool."

"What of the artifacts Gouroull seized?" Fatimah asked as they found the gate.

The black energies appeared greater in number as they crossed over to the frigid Siberian wastes.

"Let them remain lost in this terrible tundra. Once the gate collapses, they shall be buried beneath the snow. When the thaw arrives, those cursed artifacts shall sink beneath the mud and remain hidden, possibly forever."

Faisal checked his compass. They had a five-mile walk in the arctic temperatures before they reached the airship. There was no time to waste!

Five minutes later, Gouroull emerged from the gate, gazing left and right, searching for the pair that had destroyed the book. Neither were in sight and the cold winds hid any scent. They had escaped, but he would remember them, and make both pay for their actions.

Rasputin groaned, still barely conscious as he dangled over Gouroull's uninjured shoulder. Frankenstein's Monster possessed no sentimentality, yet he did recognize debts. The Siberian holy man had proved true to his word and was not to blame for the failure. So he had rescued him from the dying world, which meant his debt was now discharged.

The gate vanished minutes later, replaced by the small wooden cabin. Gouroull walked inside the unlocked door, seeing nothing out-of-place. Even the jug of *kvass* sat upon the rude wooden table, and the clock slowly ticked away. Crossing to the small cot, Gouroull deposited Rasputin on it, and closed the door behind him as he left.

He then turned towards the west and walked, wondering if it was true that Ingrid Schleger still lived… Perhaps she had a baby too…?

CHAPTER LIII

The Witch of Dolwyn Moor lifted her lantern up and studied the moss on the side of the rock. In a few more days, the substance would ripen enough for harvesting. Then, after crushing the plant into a thin paste, and mixing the remains with some henbane, rat's blood and other roots, being preserved two years in a sealed jar, a love philter would emerge that always destroyed both user and victim. A delightful substance that she gave away freely for the asking.

She turned and headed towards her mandrake patch, when the crackle of feet across the wooded path caught her attention. A visitor or a customer? She wondered, waiting as the crunching grew closer.

A man appeared from around the bend. A tall figure with narrow shoulders and long arms. He walked in her direction, tunelessly whistling an odd tune that sent strange shivers up her spine. His clothing confused her, looking quite out of place for this sharp winter evening. He wore a loose white linen shirt, khaki jodhpurs, knee-length black boots, and, of all things, a pith helmet, the rim of which hid his face. He walked with his head low and his hands behind his back.

"What are you doing out at night in Dolwyn Moor, young man?" she called out, leaning on her cane and speaking in her sharpest tone of voice. "Do you not know that if you take one wrong step, you may fall into a mud pit and drown?"

"Young? I do not remember the last time someone called me youthful," the man said, his malicious mirth apparent in every spoken word. "Good evening Siani

Bwt. I traveled all this way, just to look at your wrinkled face."

"How do you know my name?" she hissed, reaching into her pouch for her iron ring.

This was her favorite weapon for tossing curses at her enemies. Yet it was not there… Nor were any of her vials, wands, or other magical equipment. This made no sense. The bag was empty and yet, she never went anywhere unprepared.

"Your witchcraft toys are on the bottom of a cesspit in the middle of Congo," the man said, stopping a few feet away, his helmet and bowed head still hiding his face. "That was where I spent some time before deciding to grant you some of my special attention."

"That is not possible," the witch spat.

She stepped backwards—or at least, she tried. For some reason, her body did not comply with her mental commands.

"I think you will find that it is, and that, in fact, it occurred seconds before I arrived. Forgive me, in my pleasure I am telling this story from the middle, not the start. Do you remember when you contracted with the being you call Satan for more power? Yes? Excellent. In doing so, you caught my attention. When you sent your little army against my agents, I was impressed, and also annoyed. Now that this game is over, I am still annoyed. You irritated me, Siani Bwt, formerly known as Lucifer's speaker, and the Witch of Dolwyn Moor. I do not like feeling annoyed; I prefer laughter… at other life forms' expense of course. Therefore, your slow, torturous end shall return my good mood."

Siani Bwt felt her mouth go dry and her body began quaking in terror. Somehow, she managed to mumble:

"Who are you? What are you?"

“I have many names, little human. The learned ones call me Nyarlathotep…but you may call me, Mister Jones…”

His head tilted back, revealing the inhuman countenance.

Siani Bwt shrieked in horror as a universe of nightmares appeared before her eyes…

CHAPTER LIV

Old Boris knew she was coming. He felt the power of the witch as she entered his woods. He sat where he always did and waited, knowing his end was near, smoking his pipe. He reflected on the last pair of boots he had made, for the one known as Gouroull. They were his last masterpiece, a legacy that would outlive his short lifespan.

Then she appeared, a shapely woman who towered over him. She wore a simple red hooded robe and appeared naked beneath the thin cloth. Throwing back the hood, she revealed herself, an overwhelmingly lovely woman with thick black hair, a heart-shaped face, soft, silky pale skin and plump red lips.

"They call you Old Boris," she said. "I think I shall call you that too. Your other names are unimportant."

"That is correct," Old Boris replied with a nod. "I do not know your name, but I did dream of your coming. May I know your name before I die?"

"Why not?" she asked. "You meet your end with dignity. That shall not spare you the pain I plan to visit upon you, but I shall grant you this one boon. I am Mater Lachrymarum, the Mother of Tears, last of the Three Mothers. Your and your master's schemes have destroyed my two sisters. For that alone, I shall visit upon you tortures that even the damned never experienced. Then I shall track down your agent, and the one known as Gouroull shall discover the true power of the Three Mothers!"

Despite himself, Old Boris screamed as Mater Lachrymarum enfolded him in her rotting arms…

CHAPTER LV

"Your Excellencies," the German soldier said, clicking his heels and bowing his head in salute to the two men in the temporary shelter. "We found the site. It is three miles east. There is a single body frozen beneath the ice."

"Estimated height?" Masud Asim Gamil asked, sipping his tea and looking across at his English colleague.

"We estimate between five feet eight inches and six feet tall, sir," the German soldier stated.

"That fits our information," the Englishman replied after checking his notebook again.

All present knew he read the book more for effect than actual need. His memory was famous and he rarely made any mistakes in that regard.

"Proceed with rescue operations," Gamil stated after he and the Englishman had exchanged a nod.

The German saluted again and left, leaving both members of the Holy Conclave alone.

They sat silently for several moments before the Englishman asked:

"Do you think this could work?"

"I have no means of knowing," Gamil replied, with a shrug. "I simply believe this is the best means of defeating the creature known as Gouroull. That unholy monster imperiled the entire planet. He must be destroyed."

"Agreed," the Englishman said with a sigh. "I confess, I still have misgivings. Our choice feels… unholy…"

“I share that feeling, my friend. However, we have failed in every other attempt. Perhaps this man holds the answer,” Gamil replied.

“Resurrecting Gouroull’s creator, the late Victor Frankenstein, may be our only chance at ending this plague upon mankind. But I fear we risk bringing a greater evil back to the world,” the Englishman stated, staring into his cold tea.

Afterword

Now we come to the end of a third Gouroull tale, a different direction for this series. The H. P. Lovecraft flavor to this book comes from a lifetime of reading that very unusual writer. I shall refrain from discussing him in detail here—the history of his life and his writings are well-known to the reading public. I will simply add that his cosmic horror changed the way I view fiction.

Gouroull is still my favorite force of nature, a dark, horrific monster whose alien mind terrifies all who realize his intentions. Jean-Claude Carrière's version of the monster is, in my opinion, the most frightening ever crafted. The sheer inhumanity of the creature makes him a pleasure for the writer and, I hope, the reader.

The current book is located between Carrière's *La Nuit de Frankenstein* (*The Night of Frankenstein*), which takes place in 1895, and my own *The Quest of Frankenstein,* which I set in 1914. The series will probably not go past 1940, which was the setting for *The Triumph of Frankenstein*, since Gouroull and Nazis are a poor mix in my opinion. Fortunately, there are many years between the Monster's revival in 1875 in Carrière's *La Tour de Frankenstein* (*The Tower of Frankenstein*) and the probable conclusion to the series in 1940. I say "probable conclusion" because anything is possible in my demented imagination...

Craig Jones was my tribute to the dilettante characters Lovecraft used in many of his stories. His horrible end played perfectly with the ethos of such individuals.

Happy endings never occur, and are rarely deserved by these fictional "heroes."

Grigori Rasputin is one of the few real people that have appeared in my novels. An odd holy man, from a mostly forgotten sect of Christianity, he has been the subject if much fiction since his unusual death. It was a pleasure writing a character whose actual photographic images resemble that of a fictional supervillain. For a man whose role in world events was arguably negligible, he is still better known than most of his contemporaries. That I made him a stooge of cosmic powers was pure fun.

Hezekiah Whateley came from an odd thought I had after a rereading of Lovecraft's *The Dunwich Horror*. The writer in me wondered what if there was someone in that terrible town who subtly fought men like Wizard Whateley and his dangerous plans. The result was Hezekiah Whateley, a character that lived in my head for decades. His death under the hands and fangs of Gouroull is a writer's dream come true.

One thought on Hezekiah and his history… Was he really working for Satan and the likes, or was that simply another game by Nyarlathotep? Questions like these are the reasons people consider writers odd.

Old Boris and the characters from the Conclave came to me as I wrote this book. My writing style is known as being a "pantser"—i.e. I write by the "seat of my pants." What this means is I have the characters, some idea of the direction they are going, and I just write. The work itself is almost a subconscious act, and I perpetually find myself surprised by what happens. The idea of writing with an outline is alien to me, though many writers I know prefer that style. Like one of my writing heroes, Stephen King, this is the only way that works for me.

Sheikh Faisal Hashim Haji Sabbah came from an idea I had while considering a pulp series about a team of heroes led by Philip Wylie's proto-superman, Hugo Danner. Faisal was an occult version of pulp legend, Doc Savage, though, sadly, the concept never got past the discussion phase. I think my notion was a blend of Doc Savage, horror writer Dennis Wheatley, with a touch of James Bond. I enjoyed writing him and I hope he paid tribute to one of my favorite forms of fiction.

Fatimah and her history were part of that same original idea. The Order of Assassins was a real group, supposedly formed around 1090 A.D. and destroyed by the Mongols in 1275 A.D. According to historical records, its members were religious fanatics who fought their enemies through murder and threats. Supposedly, they executed some of the European crusaders who fought for control of the Holy Land. Legends have it that they continued to exist many years past the destruction of their group in the 13th century and that is the basis for Fatimah and her story. Making them slaves of Nyarlathotep was a fun by-product of the current backstory.

The Witch of Dolwyn Moor came from a life spent reading folklore, horror fiction, and watching similar-styled films and television shows. Many tales of ancient witches exist, though few had stories beyond the sale of their soul for power. I had not planned on her appearing in this book, but she popped in suddenly and spoke to Hezekiah Whateley. Happily, her story emerged easily, and I enjoyed seeing her rise and fall through the tale.

Percy Queely came from a memory I had when I was sick many years ago, and watching television. I ended up watching *Lifestyles of the Rich and Famous*, a show I found completely stupid and vapid. Being too sick to search for an alternative, I watched the horrible excesses of the wealthy, which included a group of men who buy dozens of cars and stack them on their lawns. Percy Queely came from that style of spending, though his behavior is worse than any characters I viewed on that silly program. Still, his death was quite justified, even if it was executed by monsters.

The Tcho-Tcho are another of Lovecraft's great ideas, expanded by many writers over the years. For more information on this inhuman tribe, I would suggest you read August Derleth's short story, *Lair of the Star-Spawn* and T. E. D. Klein's short story, *Black Man with a Horn*.

The Count Dracula that appears before Gouroull is one of the many which have appeared over the years in various forms. His musing on the name and identity of Dracula echoes some of my thoughts on the subject. The character of the Vampire King has grown beyond Bram Stoker's incredible novel and has taken a life all its own.

Upton Warren the ghost is a result of being raised by parents who loved films. I watched many ghost movies, and then read even more over the years. I think that was the first time I ever wrote a haunted house, which was fun. That Gouroull defeated the spirit with relative ease was amusing, to say the least.

Flavius Romulus Augustus was the last listed Emperor of Rome, a teenager who was deposed after a short period and vanished from history. This version came from the anger I imagined a frustrated teenager might feel after briefly being crowned ruler, then losing his throne. In this case, he chose badly and that resulted in a sad end.

The six servants of Satan all emerged from the tradition of fictional and film horror. Here are where I found them for this novel:

* Mater Suspiriorum is one of the infamous Three Mothers of the film trilogy by Dario Argento. She is a horrific creature who gave me chills of disgust and fear when I first viewed her in *Suspiria* in a Manhattan cinema in the 80s.

* Baron Brákola is the villain of the Mexican *luchador* horror film, *Santo vs Barón Brákola,* a terrifying, brutish vampire that was one of Santo's most dangerous enemies. I love this style of low-budget films, where Mexican wrestlers battle supernatural menaces. Baron Brákola, was played by wrestler/writer/actor Fernando Osés.

* Count Karol de Lavud is also a Mexican horror villain, played with debonair style by actor German Robles. He is totally opposite to Barón Brákola in character, which made him quite enjoyable to write.

* Zé do Caixão, a.k.a. Coffin Joe, is a character created by Brazilian filmmaker, José Mojica Marins. He first appeared in three decidedly odd horror films that were among my favorites during the early days of videotape rentals.

* Elizabeth Selwyn is the evil witch from the low-budget horror film, *City of the Dead.* I liked her character, played with an amusing, mocking style by character actress, Patricia Jessel. The film, written by screenwriter and novelist George Baxt, is an effective, spooky, tale that has some truly excellent moments.

* Finally, Viy is a legendary monster created in an 1835 short story by the famed Russian novelist, Nikolai Gogol. He is a truly terrifying creature and the story is

one of Gogol's best. There are many adaptations of this tale, most recently in a 2014 Russian film.

Mister Jones is a new version of Nyarlathotep, created after I spotted a grinning man with a hidden face. He stood among the dead bodies in the Belgian Congo, and I was terrified by the sight. The horrors of that period of history, combined with a smiling man, made me wonder if the man in the picture was even human. Hence, Mister Jones became an avatar of the Crawling Chaos, Lovecraft's second-best known god after Cthulhu. He is the cosmic trickster, possibly the true Satan himself, possibly not…

There you have it, a smattering of where I got some of my odd ideas. It seems possible that Gouroull will return, especially with a group of determined men who plan to resurrect his crazed creator, Victor Frankenstein. I hope you will tune in for that future tale.

Special thanks to Mary Shelley, Jean-Claude Carrière, Jean Marc Lofficier, Gail Schildiner, Shihan James Amorosi, Ruth Schildiner, H. P. Lovecraft, Howard Hopkins, Win Scott Eckert, Peter Rawlik, and my many supporters on Facebook. Thank you one and all for your help and guidance.

Frank Schildiner

FRENCH HORROR COLLECTION

Cyprien Bérard. *The Vampire Lord Ruthwen*
Aloysius Bertrand. *Gaspard de la Nuit*
André Caroff:
1. *The Terror of Madame Atomos*
2. *Miss Atomos*
3. *The Return of Madame Atomos*
4. *The Mistake of Madame Atomos*
5. *The Monsters of Madame Atomos*
6. *The Revenge of Madame Atomos*
7. *The Resurrection of Madame Atomos*
8. *The Mark of Madame Atomos*
9. André Caroff. *The Spheres of Madame Atomos*

André Caroff, Michel & Sylvie Stéphan. *The Wrath of Madame Atomos*
André Caroff, Michel & Sylvie Stéphan. *The Sins of Madame Atomos*
Jules Claretie. *Obsession*
Harry Dickson. *The Heir of Dracula*
Harry Dickson. *Harry Dickson vs The Spider*
Jules Dornay. *Lord Ruthven Begins*
Alexandre Dumas. *The Return of Lord Ruthven*
Renée Dunan. *Baal*
Paul Feval. *Anne of the Isles*
Paul Feval. *Knightshade*
Paul Feval. *Revenants*
Paul Feval. *Vampire City*
Paul Feval. *The Vampire Countess*
Paul Feval. *The Wandering Jew's Daughter*
Paul Féval, *fils. Felifax, the Tiger-Man*
Charles-Marie Flor O'Squarr. *Phantoms*
G.L. Gick. *Harry Dickson and the Werewolf of Rutherford Grange*

Raoul Gineste. *The Second Life of Dr. Albin*
Léon Gozlan. *The Vampire of the Val-de-Grâce*
Jules Janin. *The Magnetized Corpse*
Paul Lacroix. *Danse Macabre*
Etienne-Léon de Lamothe-Langon. *The Virgin Vampire*
Gabriel de Lautrec. *Vengeance of the Oval Portrait*
Maurice Level. *The Gates of Hell*
Maurice Limat. *Mephista*
Jean-Marc & Randy Lofficier. *The Katrina Protocol*
Jean-Marc & Randy Lofficier. *The Vampire Almanac* (2 Volumes)
Catulle Mendes. *The Exigent Shadow*
Marie Nizet. *Captain Vampire*
C. Nodier, A. Beraud & Toussaint-Merle, V. Hugo, P. Foucher & P. Meurice. *Frankenstein & The Hunchback of Notre-Dame*
J. Polidori, C. Nodier, E. Scribe. *Lord Ruthven the Vampire*
P.-A. Ponson du Terrail. *The Vampire and the Devil's Son*
P.-A. Ponson du Terrail. *The Immortal Woman*
Jean Richepin. *The Crazy Corner*
Henri de Saint-Georges. *The Green Eyes*
X.B. Saintine. *The Second Life*
Frank Schildiner: *The Quest of Frankenstein*
Frank Schildiner: *The Triumph of Frankenstein*
Frank Schildiner: *Napoléon's Vampire Hunters*
Frank Schildiner. *The Devil Plague of Naples*
Norbert Sevestre. *Sâr Dubnotal vs. Jack the Ripper*
Norbert Sevestre. *Sâr Dubnotal 2: The Astral Trail*
Angelo de Sorr. *The Vampires of London*
Brian Stableford. *The Empire of the Necromancers 1: The Shadow of Frankenstein*
Brian Stableford. *The Empire of the Necromancers 2: Frankenstein and the Vampire Countess*
Brian Stableford. *The Empire of the Necromancers 3: Frankenstein in London*
Brian Stableford. *Sherlock Holmes & The Vampires of Eternity*

Villiers de l'Isle-Adam. *The Scaffold*
Villiers de l'Isle-Adam. *The Vampire Soul*
Philippe Ward. *Artahe*
Philippe Ward & Sylvie Miller. *The Song of Montségur*

Lightning Source UK Ltd.
Milton Keynes UK
UKHW040607271119
354298UK00001B/4/P